SAVAGE BEAST

Sinfully Savage: Book Three

KRISTEN LUCIANI

Savage Beast © 2021 by Kristen Luciani

This book is a work of fiction. Names, characters, places and incidents are the product of the author's imagination or are used fictitiously. Any resemblance to actual events, locales or persons, living or dead is purely coincidental.

Except for the original material written by the author, all songs, song titles, and lyrics mentioned in this novel are the property of the respective songwriters and copyright holders.

All rights reserved. The unauthorized reproduction or distribution of this copyrighted work is illegal. This book or any portion thereof may not be reproduced, scanned, distributed, or used in any manner whatsoever, via the Internet, electronic, or print, without the express written permission of the author, except for the use of brief quotations in a book review.

For more information, or information regarding subsidiary rights, please contact Kristen Luciani at kluciani@gmail.com.

Cover Design: Book Cover Kingdom

Editing: Allusion Graphics

Photo Credit: Rafa Catala

❦ Created with Vellum

PROLOGUE

MARCHELLA: TEN YEARS EARLIER

I peer at my reflection in the full-length mirror, doing a half-twirl in my new dress. I swipe the pink lip gloss wand across my lips and pucker them, puffing out my chest. Then I flip my long, dark curls so that they snake down one of my bare shoulders.

The corners of my lips lift.

Perfect.

Tonight is the night that Roman Villani will see me as a woman, not as Frankie Amante's little sister.

I've caught him staring on more than one occasion. I know it. But he's never made a move.

And I'm about to give him a reason.

My heart thumps in my chest as I pull open the door to the ladies' lounge and walk back into the wedding reception. The music pulsates and the lights flash in the darkened space.

Dinner has been served, and now all of the guests have migrated onto the dance floor to work off the scrumptious meal.

I smile and nod at whomever I pass, not really paying much attention to anyone except my target.

When I spot him standing casually against a wall a few feet away from the deejay, my breath hitches.

Good Lord, he is a delicious specimen of a man. Short, dark hair, olive skin, piercing blue eyes. Just staring at him from across the room has my panties smoking under my dress.

But I'm tired of staring and wondering and hoping.

I want action.

And since he's not going to make a move, I'm prepared to do it myself.

I don't care that our fathers are business partners.

I don't care that he's my brother's best friend.

And I definitely don't care that he's way too old for me.

For once, I just want to see him look at me the way I always dreamed he would.

I take a deep breath and smooth down the front of my dress, and just as I take a step toward him, he turns in my direction. His bitable lips lift into a knowing smile as his gaze sears my skin, making it tingle from the tips of my toes to the ends of my hair.

Chills dance across my skin and I smile back, slowly walking toward him.

My pulse throbs against my neck, my hands cold and clammy against my sides.

What am I even going to say?

We've barely exchanged ten words since he and Frankie have been friends.

I've spent most of that time admiring and lusting from afar.

But the way he's staring at me now tells me I haven't imagined anything.

He wants something.

And my God, I hope it's me.

I swallow hard as I cross the dance floor, perspiration pebbling on the back of my neck when a tall figure in a black tux steps in front of me, blocking my path. I look up with a scowl.

"Frankie, what do you want?"

His eyes narrow, his jaw twitching as he grabs my arm. "Something's happened with Papa and the Villanis. It's bad, Chella. The kind of bad where someone ends up dead." He tosses a look over his shoulder in Roman's direction. "And right now, I don't know who it's gonna be."

Chapter One
ROMAN

PRESENT DAY

"I swear I didn't touch her!"

My fist tightens around the collar of the guy whose head I currently have held over an open flame. His name is Salvatore Giaconne, a guy my brother Matteo fired right before he took off for Vegas with his wife, Heaven, a few months ago. I don't know how the hell Salvatore even got into our nightclub, Risk, tonight, but it looks like I need to have a chat with the door guys after I dispose of this piece of garbage.

Without warning, I shove his face closer to the burning wick as he yelps like a little bitch. I grit my teeth and pull him away from the lit candle, throwing him against the wall. It shakes from the impact, the framed photos hanging next to him fall to the floor, glass shattering around his feet.

"Don't lie to me," I creep toward him, my shoulders squared and my lips twisted into a sneer. "Do you understand the rules, fucko? Or do I need to translate them into another language for you?"

The guy shudders against the wall, all six feet and two-hundred-and-fifty pounds of him.

He could crush me with that mass.

But he doesn't, because he knows I don't need mass in order to do the same…or worse…to him.

"N-no," he whimpers. "Please, Mr. Villani. I didn't mean to—"

I roll my eyes. Fucking pussy. He got caught with his hands in the cookie jar and now he thinks he can cry and beg and walk out of here with his cock still intact?

With a quirk of my brow, I fold my arms over my chest. "So now you're admitting that you did something."

The whimpering stops. Idiot. If you're gonna be a pussy, at least own it. Don't play a game that you know is gonna get you maimed. That's just fucking stupidity right there.

Salvatore blinks fast, obviously realizing a little too late that he is a complete moron for contradicting himself like that. "It was an accident," he says gruffly.

"Oh, so you didn't mean to tear off Zoe's G-string with your teeth while you held her down with your knee? It just got caught in your mouth, and when you pulled away, you took it with you?"

And that's when I see it.

The flicker of annoyance in his deep-set eyes. He grimaces, reverting to his tough-guy routine. "She had it coming," he hisses.

I narrow my eyes. "Oh yeah? And what exactly did she do to deserve your face between her thighs?"

"I don't answer to you anymore," he says coldly.

"When you're in my club and you've just been caught harassing my employee, then yeah. You fucking answer to me!"

Adrenaline floods my veins as I launch myself at him, grabbing the sides of his jacket and slamming him against the wall as hard as I can. Christ, it's so forceful, I think I scrambled my own brain for a second.

He makes a loud *woof!* sound when his body collides with the sheetrock, and a loud crash next to us makes my back stiffen. The glass jar candle I'd almost plunged Salvatore's face into tumbles onto the floor and cracks against the marble floor tiles. The flame shoots out, dangerously close to igniting the woven area rug in the center of the room. I stomp it out just as it catches the edge of the carpet, gritting my teeth at the damage I've almost certainly done to the soles of my Ferragamo loafers.

Salvatore lets out a loud grunt as he lunges for me. I sidestep the still-lit candle as he charges, swinging one of his fists at my temple. I'm just about his height, but since I don't weigh the same as a baby elephant, I dance around him, narrowly avoiding his next punch.

A loud pounding at the door reminds me that one of my security guys, Ray, is waiting outside, ready to jump in if I need him.

But that's not how I operate. I put up with security, a necessary evil, but I prefer to handle things on my own.

My way.

That's what happens when you're the youngest in a family of gangsters driven by bloodlust. Everyone already has their own calling card, and they've established their own reputations. Nobody has anything left to prove to the rest of the underworld.

Except me.

Matteo left me in charge here in Manhattan to run shit while he's in Vegas. He gave me his trusted security team as backup, but I can't delegate this kind of thing to just anyone.

Security, my ass.

If I can't handle scumbags like Salvatore on my own, nobody will take me seriously, including my own brothers. They won't see me as a leader. And they sure as hell won't give me my own territory when the time comes.

People who delegate the hard shit don't command respect. And if you're trying to claw your way to the top of the food chain, delegating equates to weakness.

Weakness will get you eaten alive.

So I ignore Ray's furious knocking and duck down and around Salvatore's next punch. His fist pummels the sheetrock wall instead, leaving my nose and jaw still intact. He lets out a sharp groan, clutching his bloody fist. Spittle flies out of the corners of his mouth, his breaths morphing into angry pants.

I could kill him.

But I don't.

I know there's only one reason why he's here tonight.

Revenge.

He figured I'd be an easy target since Matteo is away.

That I wouldn't have enough backup to take him and his thug crew on.

He didn't count on the fact that I am my own muscle and that my sole priority right now is making sure the kingdom we've built is strong enough to withstand assholes like Sallyboy and his gang of fucknuts.

I thought about putting a bullet between his eyes, but then I'd never find out why he's really here.

It's not because of Zoe's pussy, that's for damn sure.

Matteo has his fair share of enemies, and they're always lurking, angling to find a crack in the foundation of our empire.

They will search tirelessly, but they'll never find one.

And just to make sure Salvatore's guys get the message, too, I think I need to show them that their searches will come up empty. That while this empire is in my hands, it won't ever fucking crumble.

Salvatore fists his hand, wincing as he clenches his scratched knuckles.

"Looks like it hurts," I say in a mocking voice. "Maybe you shoulda sent someone else in here, someone who can actually make contact with something other than the wall."

That pisses him off and he launches a fist out at me again.

But when that big body of his loses balance, I yank the back of his collar, pulling him back toward me. I want to make sure he hears this next part before his ears go up in flames.

Literally.

I grab the jagged piece of the candle holder and fist his hair, singeing the bottom of his ear with the flickering wick. "You cross me again and I'll make sure you're incinerated, not just a little seared, do you understand me?"

He roars as he leaps toward me, shoving me into an end table. It tips over with me on top of it, hitting the nearby wall. A lamp crashes against the floor along with a tube of lube, a pair of handcuffs, and a flogger.

"Looks like you thought you were gonna have some fucking night before I showed up and blew up your plans, huh?" I smirk as I regain my footing, jumping off the table and inching toward him. I drop the candle, stepping on the wick with the heel of my shoe. "Haven't had enough yet, have ya? You still want more, Sallyboy? Come and fucking get it!"

Another guttural yell pierces the air, and this time when he swings his fist out, I grab it, twisting it backward. Now he's really crying like the bitch I always knew he was. "You feel that?" I hiss at him. "That's how your wrist feels when it's about to break." I twist harder, my grip tight on his hand. "So unless you want me to take the next step and snap the goddamn thing off, why don't you tell me why you're here and who you're working with?"

"Fuck you!" he yells.

"Oh, yeah?" I scream back.

Good God, I want to crack it so badly. I want to prove to him that he can't screw me over, that I'm just as strong, if not stronger, as the rest of my family, and if he doesn't give me what I want, that I'll cut out his tongue, too.

"You owe me!" he screams. "And you're gonna pay!"

"You didn't deliver," I seethe against his ear. "So, no, I'm not paying you a fucking cent!" I press his wrist farther back against his forearm so that the top of his fingers are practically kissing it.

"Then Zoe ain't the only one who's gonna be violated tonight," he growls.

My eyes widen, my teeth clenched tight as I snap his wrist, shoving him face-first into the cold floor tiles before I open the door to the room.

The screaming isn't a big deal.

There are plenty of other, way more disturbing sounds floating into the hallway from other closed doors in the vicinity. I'm sure nobody gave Salvatore's screeches a second thought. Risk is an exclusive sex den, so nothing really raises eyebrows, especially sounds of pain.

Ray comes into the room and glares at Salvatore writhing on the floor. He then looks up at me, his forehead pinched. He lets out a deep breath, shaking his head. "You should have let me in sooner."

"I had to handle things with Salvatore," I say, sweeping a hand through my hair.

"That's the thing. Salvatore isn't the problem. He's the distraction."

"What the hell are you talking about, Ray?"

"You know the shipment of blow that was delivered this afternoon and locked up in the storage room below the club?" Ray's lips press together into a tight line. "I just got confirmation from Johnny. The lock was sliced off. The blow is gone." His eyes narrow as they fall upon Salvatore. "And so is Zoe."

Chapter Two
MARCHELLA

"Why are you so fidgety?" I ask my older brother Frankie as I smooth my hair back into a ponytail. "You're going to wear out the rug from all of your pacing. And since I just vacuumed, it would have been nice for you to take off your damn shoes first!"

"Sorry," he grumbles, raking a hand through his wavy, dark hair. With a nod toward the rug, he shrugs his shoulders. "Not like the vacuuming helps anyway."

I purse my lips. "That's hardly my fault. And just so we're clear, I'm working endless hours at the restaurant to make sure there's still carpet under our feet." With a raised eyebrow, I glower at Frankie. "What about you, hmm? Did you collect any money this week?"

Frankie's nostrils flare. "You know, Chella, I'm doing the best I can!"

"Really?" I fold my arms over my chest. "Because I haven't seen a freaking penny from you in the past two weeks! You do know that rent is due at the end of the month, right? Or are you just counting on me to save us? *Again!*" Anger bubbles deep in my chest, threatening to boil over for about the tenth time today.

"Stop being such a fucking nag!" he thunders. "Do you realize how much stress I'm under right now? No! You don't! And you want to know why? Because you're too busy being a goddamn martyr!"

I gasp, my eyes widening. "Did you seriously just…call me… holy shit, Frankie," I mutter, shaking my head. "Do you realize if it wasn't for me that we'd be on the street? Hungry? Homeless? Possibly dead?" I clench my fists, my voice rising. "I had plans, too! Did you know that? Did you even care? Do you think I wanted to give up my dreams to move into this shit-ass apartment in one of the worst areas in the city? Do you think I have any desire to live in this fucking hell?" I stomp toward him, stopping directly in front of him. "No!" I scream at the top of my lungs. "I didn't! But here I am!"

He flashes me a sheepish look, then averts his gaze. "I'm sorry."

"Sorry for what, exactly?"

"Being an insensitive ass."

"And?" I say in a sharp voice.

"And for taking advantage of your good nature," he mumbles, sneaking a look at me. His lips curl into a grin.

"*And?*"

"And for wearing my shoes on the shitty rug."

I flop onto the worn sofa that we were lucky enough to score from a nearby Salvation Army store. Although, it's more apropos to say we were probably luckier that it wasn't infested with anything that could eat us alive or spread a communicable disease. "What the hell are we going to do?" I murmur, dropping my head into my hands.

Frankie sinks down next to me. "Chell, we're gonna be okay. I promise."

I roll my eyes, collapsing against the back of the couch. "Oh yeah?"

"Yeah. I've, ah, got some things in motion." He scrubs a hand down the front of his face and I see his spine stiffen.

I jerk upward. "Frankie," I say slowly. "What the hell is that supposed to mean?"

He shrugs, still not meeting my suddenly panicked gaze. He's almost thirty and hasn't had a legitimate job in his freaking life. He worked with Papa as an enforcer and made plenty of cash over the years, but he's been struggling to find work for the past six months now that Papa is behind bars. I'd hoped it would light a fire under him to get a real job, but that hasn't happened. I love my brother to pieces, but he's not at all the hard-working type. He's more the avoid-hard-working type. And by avoiding hard work, I mean doing shady things that can get him hurt, arrested, or killed.

It's how we got into this mess in the first place.

"Why aren't you answering me?" I say. "Do you want to end up like Papa? Rotting in some minimum-security jail cell because he chose the life over his family? Because he was always after the money and never cared about consequences, which, by the way, is why we were chased out of Sicily years ago? He lives in that prison hell just waiting for someone to pop him! I mean, it's only a matter of time!"

His eyes blaze as he stares me down. "Don't say that shit about Papa," Frankie grunts darkly.

"How can I not?" I yell. "I mean, look at us! Mama is gone and we have collection agents camped outside our door, breathing down our necks for hundreds of thousands of dollars we owe in medical care, legal fees, and an assortment of other bills that got pushed aside while we were trying to make ends meet?"

"Papa did the best he could," he retorts.

"Well, I don't really see things the way you do," I mutter. "He could have gotten out. But he made a choice! A lot of choices. Really bad ones!"

"He did what he felt was right for our family!"

I let out a disbelieving laugh, waving my hands around me at the small, cluttered space we now call home. It's a far cry from the penthouse apartment where we lived in Central Park East. Now we have an Inwood address, so far uptown, we're practically in the Bronx. It's clean-ish, and that's probably the best it'll ever be, regardless of how much I scrub and sanitize and disinfect. But it's still in the city, the only home we've ever known other than Sicily. And even though it takes me almost an hour by subway to get to my job downtown, I can feel that connection to Mama just by being here. She always loved living in Manhattan and I inherited that same love. Living in Sicily was great, but the action and the energy here is something we both adored.

So Frankie and I scrimp and pinch to get by until things get better. And good God, I hope they get better soon because I'm quickly running out of patience, almost as fast we're running out of money.

"Yes, well, that's exactly what *I'm* trying to do right now and why I need to go to work at an actual job, to make real, legitimate money to pay our painfully real, legitimate bills." I give my head a quick shake. "What the hell are *you* doing, Frankie?"

We've had this argument so many times in the past six months. It gets super-heated when it comes time to sign away all of the hard-earned cash I've made for the monthly payments we're now responsible for handling.

Mama's long battle with cancer came to a devastating end, but the bills keep coming. I didn't realize how much financial trouble Papa was having when she was sick. But he's not the kind of guy to ever admit defeat, so he stole from Peter to pay Paul and it finally caught up with him. I rub the back of my neck.

Christ, did it ever.

I keep waiting for the call from the prison that someone iced him in his sleep the night before. Whenever my phone rings with an unknown number, my chest tightens and I can't squeeze out a breath until I hear that it isn't the warden bearing horrible news.

"Fucking-A, Chella!" Frankie jumps off the couch. "You think you know everything, but you don't! You have no idea—" He stops, mid-shout, and I furrow my brow.

"I have no idea about what?" I ask, my eyes narrowed. "I may have been young, but I know why we had to leave Sicily. I remember…" I suck in a quick breath. I remember the events so clearly. Another family. A business deal gone seriously bad. A falling out. A lot of threats made against us. The humiliation of having to leave our home because Papa had screwed over so many people to climb the proverbial ladder.

I've never forgotten any of it, especially my brother's best friend.

Roman Villani.

The guy I'd dream about, night after night, while I waited for the day when he'd see me as a woman and not only as Frankie's little sister. Unfortunately, that day never came because Papa screwed over Roman's father, Paolo, his own business partner. Papa didn't like that Paolo was making moves with other families, and he wanted to take him out.

Instead, we were the ones who suffered.

"Papa never learned," I say softly. "He made enemies everywhere, and if you're not careful, you're going to fall into the same trap."

"He isn't some deadbeat, Chell. He saved…" Frankie's voice trails off and once again, his gaze drops.

"He saved what, Frankie? Who?" I say. "Because as far as I can see, there isn't one single person in this family who isn't struggling to put the pieces of their life back together right now after his latest mistake. Not one."

Frankie stomps into the kitchen, which is about five steps away, and pulls open the refrigerator door. He peers inside and grabs a can of Miller Lite, popping off the top and guzzling the beer before answering.

I let out a deep sigh. I really didn't want to get into this with him tonight but the pile of bills staring at me on the kitchen counter got my mind and mood in a serious twist. I walk over to him and place a hand on his tensed shoulder. "Look," I say in a quiet voice. "I don't want to fight. We're all we have, and I love you, okay?"

He slams the empty can on the counter and turns to look at me. "I love you, too, sis."

"We'll figure things out," I say. "Hey, maybe we can go for a run in the park tomorrow if you're around? Get some fresh air, maybe scrounge some money together for a dirty water dog or five." I grin, nudging his shoulder. "It would be fun."

He pauses, then gives a stiff nod. "Yeah, it would be."

I force a smile. There's a strange look in his dark eyes that I don't like, but I decide not to press him on it. I know he's sensitive about Papa, and I don't have the energy to argue about it right now. I have a long night ahead of me and I can't be worried about what glimmers in the depths of my brother's gaze. "I'll see you in the morning," I say, squeezing his arm. "Please be careful."

"You say that to me every time you leave," he grumbles.

"It's because I worry."

He rolls his eyes. "I'll be fine."

"I'm going to hold you to that," I say, picking up my handbag and jacket. "'Night."

"'Night," he replies, and there it is again. That damn look.

It makes my stomach twist because it always—without fail—means trouble.

And we really can't afford any more of that.

Literally.

We can't afford *anything*.

I carefully pull the apartment door closed since the landlord who goes by the name Mr. Raynor lives on our floor, and I don't want to alert him since I won't be able to cover the rent for this month and last month for another week. Yes, I'm behind. Yes, I want to choke my brother for putting me in this position because he insists that he's going to be making good money soon with his new-ish job. And I use the word 'job' lightly. I know he's gotten himself tangled up with some mafia thugs here in Manhattan, not that he's admitted as much. He's probably beating the shit out of people for his bosses and collecting money owed, not that *he's* the one doing any of the actual collecting, as far as I can tell.

Jesus, who knew the mafia offered unpaid internships and that my stupid brother was qualified?

A chill slithers through me as I take the stairs as lightly as possible so as not to make any unnecessary sounds. Mr. Raynor has ears like an elephant, and the only way I know to keep him off our backs is to flash him a glimpse of boob every now and again when he confronts me.

I really don't feel like watching the lecherous look on his face tonight as his eyes drop down the front of my shirt.

Blech.

But hey, it is what it is. I have to work with what I've got.

Who knew that six months ago our entire world would come crumbling down around us the way it has? I mean, I thought being forced out of Sicily ten years ago was bad, but this? This is complete decimation.

Regardless of the reason, Papa killed someone. I'm not naïve enough to believe he's never done that before, but at least he'd never been caught red-handed. I could have convinced myself that he was innocent if it wasn't for the fact that he quite literally had the man's blood on his hands when the cops arrived at the scene.

Second-degree murder. That verdict just about blew my whole life out of the water.

He claimed it was self-defense, but if you saw my dad and the guy he popped, it doesn't really add up. Luckily for my father, the jury bought it and that's the only reason he wasn't sentenced to death.

Unluckily for me and Frankie, all of the money we had that wasn't already seized by collections for my mother's medical bills was sucked up by exorbitant court fees and defense lawyers who couldn't seem to get out of their own way enough to win a 'not guilty' verdict.

But the reality is, Papa killed a member of the Volkov Bratva, a vicious organization out of Brooklyn, and his own lawyers didn't have death wishes.

The bank took our house and our cars, and we had to sell any possessions with value just to cover necessary living expenses.

Talk about seeing your future get swallowed up by a black hole.

And at twenty-four, I'd just barely began my career in bilingual childhood education before my job was yanked away from me halfway through the year. Seems as though New York State wasn't a fan of hiring teachers whose parents are convicted murderers.

Some people can be so prickly.

Insert eye roll.

I was fortunate enough to have kept up a good relationship with the owner of the bar I'd worked at through my years at New York University, and even more fortunate that he re-hired me after being dishonorably discharged by the New York State Board of Education.

The pay is shit, but hey, it's still pay, and I normally work about eighty hours a week just to make ends meet.

I tell myself that someday we're not going to have to live paycheck to paycheck anymore.

Someday we'll catch a break.

That is, if nobody breaks Frankie first.

I really don't think my reputation can handle another mob crime blackmark.

Those will sink you faster than an anchor chained to your ankle.

I walk outside of the apartment building, hoisting my bag over my shoulder as I head toward the subway station. By the time I get down to the platform, a crowd of people has gathered. Tiny beads of sweat slide down my back as the minutes pass. It's always so oppressively hot down here, even in the winter, and I say a silent prayer that the next train flashing its lights is the A train.

I check my phone for the time.

Ugh! Forget the heat. If it's *not* the A train, I'm going to be late.

And my boss Jimmy is only so forgiving.

I let out a sigh of relief when I see the train screech to a stop at the platform. The doors slide open with a loud double ding and I practically leap into the car. I lean against the pole since I refuse to ever touch it. If I can't get a seat, I find a place to rest my ass or my arm, preferably not on a fellow passenger, although it has happened in the past.

Regrettably.

That guy still gives me the creeps when I think about him.

As if I meant to rub myself against his crotch. For Pete's sake, the train was crowded! And touching the pole — good God, the germs! Just thinking about it makes bile rise in the back of my throat.

Twenty minutes later, the train arrives at my stop. West 4th Street in Washington Square Park. The Grammercy Tap Room is only a few blocks away, and the weather is unseasonably warm for March, so the walk is actually refreshing.

I try not to focus on Frankie and whatever scheme he's running because he is definitely up to something. I just hope that whoever the target is doesn't know he's involved, otherwise, who the hell knows how I'll find him in the morning?

Or, *if* I'll find him.

People that Frankie associates with—hell, mobsters, in general—are magician-types, and their best trick is making others disappear.

I just hope Frankie doesn't do something stupid to prove himself to those thugs.

I know from experience what they'll do in retaliation.

I let out a deep sigh as I walk past my old dorm. NYU doesn't have a traditional campus, so the buildings are spread out in Greenwich Village. I remember long, raucous nights of bar crawls with friends, treks to Bleecker Street Pizza at two in the morning when pulling all-nighters, and parties with cute fraternity guys. I loved those times. I had no cares in the world other than getting good grades and having a freaking amazing time.

Graduation came much too fast.

And then Mama got sick.

I trudge the remaining block to the bar, the heaviness in my gut weighing me down like there is a pile of bricks sitting on my shoulders.

It's hard to accept that she's really gone.

Walking these streets brings back such bittersweet memories of us embracing the little time we had left and basking in the sunshine of Washington Square Park. She always loved the Village and would often come for a visit when I was living here to take me shopping or to dinner.

A pang assaults my chest.

God, I miss her so much.

I'd give anything to hold her hand again and to traipse through the foliage and brick pathways in the iconic landmarks of lower Manhattan.

Tears sting my eyes and I blink them away before they have a chance to fall.

She wouldn't want me to cry. Lord knows, I've done enough of that over the past year. She'd want me to be strong, to find some sliver of light in the murky existence that's become my life. And dammit, I've been searching for a while, coming up empty every time.

There has to be a way out of this ominous maze that's become my dismal life. There has to be a way to finally regain control over my future.

The one bright spot that I look forward to each week is the two hours when I volunteer at the local community center and read to the young neighborhood children. I help them learn English, and they give me a little shred of happiness to cling to in return. I miss my students so much and this at least keeps me on top of my game.

I swear to myself that one day I will get back to teaching. My father's recent conviction won't hang over my head like a toxic black cloud forever.

I won't let this break me.

I can't let the past rule me forever.

I pull open the door to the bar and flash a smile at Michael, the big, broad bouncer. He gives me a wink and steps aside so I can pass. I run my eyes over the tables in the main dining room as I scurry toward the back room. I give Jimmy, the owner, a little wave as I hurry past the bar, stopping to scoop up a wrap on the floor behind a woman sitting on one of the stools.

"Thank you so much," she gushes when I hand it to her.

I grin. "No problem." I'm about to turn around when a hard force collides with my back. A cool drizzle slips down the back of my black shirt, soaking the fabric, and I gasp, jumping at the unwelcome, wet and sticky sensation now assaulting my skin.

When I turn around, I find myself staring into the bluest eyes I've ever seen. So deep, so penetrating…oh, crap. Why did I have to think of that word? *Penetrating.* It's been a long time since that word had any applicability to my life.

Chiseled jaw, rich olive skin, full lips curling into a sinfully seductive grin. A heavy fringe of thick, dark hair falls over his one quirked eyebrow. And when this man-god speaks, holy shit. The vibrations ripple through me like I'm a body of water, and he's a smooth stone skipping over the surface.

"Consider yourself lucky I didn't order a double," he murmurs. "I think you owe me one now, though."

Chapter Three
ROMAN

Dark lashes frame wide eyes that I can stare into for a lifetime and still not know exactly what color they are. Flecks of gold fire ignite in the depths of blue, green, and caramel swirls. In the dim lighting of the bar, the green is fighting for center stage, flashing with intensity as I lose myself in her shocked and slightly appalled gaze.

Holy fuck, I didn't think I'd ever get a chance to look into those eyes again.

I remember them…the heat, the emotion, the desire flickering in the aquamarine pools.

Yeah, I saw it. And I hated myself for ignoring it, but what the hell was I supposed to do?

She was my best friend's little sister.

I could look, but I couldn't touch, or Frankie would have cut off my balls.

Besides, it's not like our families parted ways as friends. My father and his associates chased them from their home, forcing them out of Sicily.

The Amantes became our enemies and I never saw her again.

I was actually surprised that Pop let her father live after he fucked us over. But I guess karma came back to bite him in the ass since he's rotting in prison now, and my family has built a billion-dollar empire here in the States.

But fuck me, Marchella Amante is standing right in front of me now after all of these years, and she clearly has no idea who I am.

I mean, yeah, I look different. It's been ten years, so I've put on about fifty pounds of muscle and my dark hair is longer. But the biggest change is that I'm no longer that clean-cut pretty boy she once knew. This older version of me gets dirty…gritty…and bloody.

I was able to escape all of that back in Sicily but here? Now?

It's my way of life.

No wonder she can't see through all of the darkness.

Her pale pink lips are slightly parted, enough that if I grabbed her by the back of her head and pulled her close, my tongue could slip right through them, just like I'd always fantasized about doing.

She might punch me if I did that right now.

She may try to scream.

But she'd definitely enjoy it and everything that would follow.

I'm a lot of things, and confident about my sexual prowess is one of them.

For a second, I get lost in my daydream, watching her lips form words, but not hearing a single one.

Then the arms start swinging around, the forehead becomes pinched, and the eyes take on a kind of murderous glow.

I decide it's time to perk up my ears.

"Are you just going to stand there, staring at me?"

She still doesn't recognize me…

But I sure as hell recognize her. Damn, the years have been very fucking generous.

And while I want to look a little longer, now is the time for me to speak. So I have fun with it, keeping my cover for the time being.

"That depends. Do I need to order food?"

She makes a face. "What's that supposed to mean?"

"Well, that's the rule at the bar, isn't it? If you're gonna hang here, you need to order food." I wink at her. "I was just making a joke."

"Oh. So smooth. Just like your lame pick-up line!"

I furrow my brow. "Lame? I actually thought it was kinda clever, you know, since you banged into me and made me spill my drink all over you. I figured it was a good opening." I let out a chuckle. "Guess I figured wrong."

"You figured *very* wrong!" she says, her fists clenched at her sides. "And I don't appreciate the harassment!"

"How is it harassment if I just want to talk to you?" Her face is bright pink now and she's angry. So I play along because it's just too much fun watching her get all hot and bothered.

She pushes her chest against me, and fuck me if my cock doesn't tingle a bit despite the world of shit I've recently been plunged into. "It's harassment if I don't feel the same way!"

"Chella, do we have a problem here?" A guy behind the bar wanders over, his eyebrows furrowed as he looks from me to the girl.

Chella.

I'd always loved her name. it always sounded sensual. Sexy. *Savage.*

And I just ignited a spark inside of her.

Let the flames roar.

She jerks around, stumbling over her words of assurance that there is no problem, that we just had a minor collision.

I'd like to make it a major one next time.

The guy lifts an eyebrow at me, nodding at my empty glass. "You need another?"

I smirk. "You read my mind."

"What'll you have?"

"Macallan, neat." I give the girl a sidelong glance, feeling her glare sear my skin.

He hands me a full glass. "I'll check on your table, Mr...?"

"Just Joe," I reply, holding up the glass. Average Joe. I never give my real name. It's too recognizable, and I'm the guy who likes to blend into the shadows. Makes me more menacing. More of a ghost.

I turn toward Chella, but she's already storming off toward the back room, her long brown ponytail swishing behind her, the scotch-soaked ends slapping against her back.

Mmm.

Booze and pheromones.

Fucking magic combination. Lethal in their complexity.

I look around the crowded room. None of my guys have shown up yet, and even though I'm anxious to get answers and figure out how to handle the scumbags who snatched Zoe and my blow, something about Marchella makes me forget what's at stake.

Luckily, it's no longer Zoe's life.

Whoever pulled the job the other night stuck her in a nearby hotel room, half-naked and a hundred-percent panicked. They tied her up just enough to give themselves time to escape, but not so tight that she couldn't free her wrists from the restraints.

They wanted me to know what they did.

They wanted to show me that I could easily be duped.

And I fucking was, something Matteo will not let go of if he finds out about it.

I'm supposed to be his right hand, his eyes and ears while he's away!

How the hell do I tell him I that took my eyes off the ball and let piece-of-shit Salvatore manipulate me?

Salvatore.

Fucking guy is lucky I didn't choke him with a chained cinderblock and sink him to the bottom of the Hudson River.

Although, I still may do that.

I should have just set him on fire and let his ass burn when I had the chance!

I loiter at the bar, waiting for Marchella to reappear after she stormed into a back room. Another glance at my watch confirms that my guys are officially late.

I toss back the amber-colored liquor, enjoying the heat snaking through my insides when a finger taps me on the shoulder. A pretty blonde smiles at me when I turn around.

I came here tonight because I wanted to keep a low profile in the wake of the supposed heist. I didn't want any of my enemies watching me strategize…and sweat. There are plenty of other places down here in the West Village where I'm considered a regular but tonight, I wanted…no, needed…anonymity.

"Joe, right? Your table is ready."

Yes. Exactly what I ordered.

The hostess shows me to the table and places a stack of menus in the center. "There's a girl working here tonight. Chella is her name?"

The hostess smiles. "Yes. She's one of our best servers."

"I'd like her to handle my business tonight," I say, sitting down in the corner with the entire room in my view. I don't speak another word to the hostess. I just nod. She flashes a quick smile and hurries toward the back room.

I'm not a guy who likes to hear the word 'no'. I'm glad she got the memo.

And I'm damn curious to see how well-received it is by my waitress for the evening, *Marchella.*

My phone buzzes and I pull it out of my pocket. My brother Dante's name flashes across the screen.

Huh.

It's not like Dante to just pick up the phone and shoot the shit with any of us. He's usually on assignment…*paid* assignment. He's basically a problem solver. Whenever there is someone causing a problem, he makes them disappear.

And voila! Problem solved.

He is truly the best at what he does, but he always keeps a low profile as a result.

He has to pretty much be invisible at all times in order to do his job as swiftly as possible.

If you so much as see him coming, it's already too late.

You're dead.

Dante thrives on the element of surprise in his kills.

He'll get you either way, but he favors the sneak attack.

I stab the Accept button. "What's the good word, bro? I thought you were holed up somewhere in South America."

"Yeah, well, now I'm in your living room," he says with a loud yawn. "And I need some pizza. Who do I order from?"

"Bleecker Street Pizza," I say. "Best around and they'll deliver fast."

"Good, I'm starving. What time will you be home?"

"A couple of hours," I say. "Hey, you'll never guess who I just ran into. Marchella Amante."

"Get the hell outta here. She still hot as fuck?"

"You have no idea." I crane my neck to see if she's returned to the seating area, but there's no sign of her yet.

"Too bad her father fucked shit up. I'd have loved a chance to get her on her back."

"Shut up," I grumble.

"Still so sensitive about that, huh?" Dante chuckles. "You never could close the deal."

"Like I ever had the option."

"Yeah, Frankie was a sick bastard. He'd have castrated you."

"Or worse," I quip. "I wonder what she's been up to. Her father caused a real shit show when he killed that Russian. I hear he's in gen pop on Rikers Island. His days are numbered, that's for sure."

"Oh yeah? You gonna make a play to comfort her?"

"Nah, she didn't recognize me," I say, seeing Ray and Bobby finally walking into the restaurant. "Listen, I've gotta go. The guys are here. Don't drink all my booze. I'm gonna need some when I get home."

"I'll try to save some of the booze. But don't count on any pizza."

"Don't worry, I won't." I smirk, clicking to end the call.

Ray and Bobby shuffle over to the table. I watch the patrons peer curiously at them as they walk over to meet me. They stick out like sore thumbs with their slicked-back hair, wearing expensive suits and shoes.

Definitely not the uniform for this type of place.

The guys pull out their chairs and sit down. Their eyebrows are knitted, their jaws tight, and I'm damn anxious to find out what they know.

And ready to take action against the pricks who tried to pull one over on me.

I lean forward, my hands folded. My eyes dart between their faces for a minute or two. "Are we speaking tonight? Or are we doing the whole mental telepathy thing for privacy's sake?"

Ray takes a deep breath, raising his eyes toward mine. "Sorry, Roman. We, ah, have some information for you, but you're not gonna like it."

My back stiffens. "Tell me why."

"Well, first, Dario was the one who was shielding the coke."

I rub the back of my neck. "And why did he leave his post?" I hiss through clenched teeth.

"He was banging one of the cocktail waitresses from the club. She went looking for him, flashed her pussy, and bing, bang, boom. The blow disappeared while he was getting a blow."

I drop my head into my hand. First Salvatore, then Dario. The guy thinks with the head of his dick, so luring him away from his domain isn't much of a challenge. I slam my fist on the table, vaguely aware that people are beginning to whisper and point.

All I care about is getting this situation under control and fast. If I have guys playing both sides of the fence, it means that one of our enemies has already burrowed into our organization like a fucking infection that will just keep getting worse and worse until I douse it with gasoline and fire. "Where is Dario now?" I ask, trying to keep my voice steady.

"I figured you'd want to handle things with him directly. Somewhere other than here," Ray says in a hushed voice. "Gio will take you to him."

"Smart move. Do we have any leads? And in case you were wondering, that was a rhetorical question because we'd better have some fucking leads!"

The guys exchange a look.

Bobby clears his throat. "Yeah, um, when I found Zoe—"

"And she's fine, yeah?" I interject. I'd been told she was unharmed when he got to her, but I want to hear it straight from Bobby that those fuckers didn't hurt her before he blows me away with any more betrayals from my crew.

"Yes. Just scared shitless." Bobby rubs the back of his neck. "I took her home and had Berto stay the night with her until we found the guys who snatched her."

I nod. "Okay. So it was an inside job. Was it the Dominguez Cartel? Those bastards have been waiting for a chance to get us back for fucking up their whole trafficking ring months ago."

A deadly hit led by my sister-in-law, Heaven.

She has the look of an angel…but the fire of the devil rages deep inside of her.

And damn, she lets that flame roar like wildfire when she needs to.

She's seriously one of my favorite badasses.

We didn't always have bad blood with the Dominguez Cartel, though. It wasn't until Matteo violated an agreement with Dominguez himself that we were put at the top of their hit list.

Heaven initiated the ambush on his sex-trafficking ring after his guys tried to pop Matteo.

The day after their wedding.

Those motherfuckers don't play around.

Ever since Heaven killed Dominguez, I've heard that his sons have been working hard to put the pieces of their shattered organization back together.

I always knew it was only a matter of time before they came back to finish what their father started, even if I'm the only one in my family who believes they're looking for revenge. Matteo always blows it off when I mention that they're still a threat, but I know it's real. And the robbery could be just the beginning.

Bobby shakes his head. "It wasn't the cartel."

"Well, don't keep me in suspense," I mutter. "Who the fuck is responsible?"

"That's the thing," Ray interjects. "You're not gonna like it."

I rake a hand through my hair. This conversation should have been cut and dry. An exchange of names, torture plans, and body part disposal methods. Period! "Let me ask you this — have I given you any indication that I like a single bit of this? No matter who is responsible? And why do I feel like you guys are dicking me around by dragging things out? This meeting was to deliver information, okay? And you two dipshits were late. So tell me what the fuck I need to hear so I can take action!"

"Ooh. You sound a little tense." A sugary-sweet voice drawls, jolting me from my next sentence. "You also look pretty heated, so I figured you could use another one of these."

I stop short, mid-tirade, staring up into Marchella's captivating eyes. My mind immediately snoozes on the threat I was about to unleash at my guys if they didn't come up with a name. I momentarily forget that I'm planning to bring holy hell to Dario in a matter of minutes. And the fact that our organization has been infiltrated by Christ only knows who has shifted to the back burner.

All because Marchella just entered my fucking orbit.

Something about this girl makes my brain cells fizzle out. It's been that way since we were teenagers. It's dangerous. Very fucking dangerous. She has me completely off my game right now. For all I know, this whole Dario meeting might be a setup. I mean, I could get into the car with my 'trusted' driver Tony, and all of a sudden, I become Joe Pesci in *Goodfellas*, driven out to the middle of the cornfields and beaten with a baseball bat before I'm thrown into a goddamn ditch and buried alive.

Not ideal for a guy who's the interim ruler of this savage kingdom.

I should be focused, for fuck's sake!

Anyone could be plotting my death in this very second.

But all my mind allows are looping, X-rated thoughts of this sexy vixen.

Chella lifts an eyebrow and holds up a glass, clinking the ice cubes around. "Was I right? Are you…thirsty? I pride myself on reading my customers and tending to their needs."

Ray and Bobby just stare at her, their jaws practically hitting the table.

But they don't hit the floor until she jerks forward and tips the glass so that the liquor pours right into my lap, joined by one single ice cube.

Fuck me.

That cooled me off.

And made me even hotter for her, if that's possible.

"I'd say the drink's on me, but…" She shrugs her shoulders with a challenging smile on her face. "Oops. I guess it's really on you." She grabs a linen napkin from a nearby table and dabs at the liquid in my lap. It takes me a second to rebound from the sudden shock of cold in my crotch, and when I do, I close my fingers around her wrist to stop her from tending to my groin. When the daggers shoot from her eyes, she hisses into my ear, "I hear you requested me, but they really should have told you how clumsy I am. And how I'm always spilling drinks and plates on my customers."

"Is that how you think this works? You dump a drink on me, thinking I'll ask for someone else? You think I'm gonna let you get away that easily?" A mischievous smirk lifts my lips because she has no fucking idea how patient I can be when it comes to her.

"I think that looks like a really expensive outfit, and I'd hate to see it ruined," she whispers.

"Is that supposed to be a threat?"

"I don't have time for threats. I'm here to work. This job is important to me. So if this is your way of getting me back for yelling at you before, let's just say we're even and I'll get you someone else—"

"No," I say. "There won't be anyone else."

She furrows her brow. "You're serious?"

"Deadly," I reply. "It's you and only you."

Her nostrils flare and she folds her arms over her chest. I can tell she has plenty more to say, but like she told me, this job is important to her. She won't risk it. "Are you a glutton for punishment?"

"We both know you're not gonna rock the boat with this job. You just told me so yourself. Never show all your cards, babe."

A flash of annoyance shadows her face when she realizes her bluff is total bullshit.

"If you even try to proposition me, I'll have the bouncer kick you and your friends out on your asses," she snips.

"My friends are just enjoying the show. They didn't do anything," I reply, goading her. "Don't project your anger at me on them."

"Oh, so now you're a shrink?"

"Trust me, sweetheart, there's nothing small about me," I say with a chuckle.

Chella rolls her eyes, and even though she tries hard not to, her lips turn upward in the slightest hint of a smile.

"See? You do like me. Don't fight it. Just accept that we're friends." And I want to say to her that it would be so much better if there were benefits involved.

"I don't know. The jury's still out on you," she quips with a quirked brow, folding her arms over her chest.

I sneak a glance at the guys. They don't know what to do right now. I can see them fighting against the smirks that threaten to tug at their lips. They think if they laugh I might kill them.

They may be right. I've certainly killed for less.

But right now, I'm feeling generous, so I keep the banter going.

"The jury says I can be your best friend or your worst nightmare," I say, leaning back against the wooden chair.

"Mm. Tempting, but no," she replies. "I've got enough friends, thank you." She forces a smile and looks at Ray and Bobby for the first time. "Why don't you spend a few minutes looking at your menus, and I'll be back in a bit to take your orders?"

The guys nod their heads, still silent.

She walks away and my eyes fall on her shapely ass as it gently swings from left to right, accentuated by her tight black pants. It isn't until Ray clears his throat that I drag my gaze away from her bent over the bar, whispering into the bartender's ear.

Hairs on the back of my neck prickle, and I can feel my mouth twist into a grimace.

"Boss?" Ray asks.

I turn my head away from her backside and look at him. "You were saying that there's something I need to hear while I wait for Dario to show up?" I say in a curt voice. "Well, let's fucking have it."

"The thing is," Bobby starts. "Zoe caught a name when they were wrestling to get her into a van. The guys were all wearing ski masks."

I furrow my brow. "Did she catch a name?"

"No," Bobby says. "But she saw something, a tattoo of a black viper that wound around the guy's wrist."

"Fuck," I hiss, balling my hands into fists under the table. "So all we have is ink. And how much blow did they escape with?"

Ray sighs. "At least four kilos."

"That's like five-hundred fucking grand." I shake my head. "I want to talk to Salvatore," I seethe, leaning in close. "As soon as possible, do you understand?"

"Yeah, boss. We'll find him and make the arrangements." Ray looks down at his phone. His eye meet mine, his jaw tight. "And, uh, Dario is outside. Black Range Rover. Tony is driving."

Tony. I always liked Tony. He was hired by Matteo before he and Heaven left for Vegas and he's reliable, respectful, and grateful for every penny he earns, for any bone thrown at him. He's old school, which is why Matteo liked him so much and decided to take him on. He's become a confidante by default because he has this annoying habit of seeing right through me. It's like he can sense what I'm thinking. He's kind of become a weird type of father-figure over the past months, and he's the guy I trust most.

But everyone has a price. And I'm a big bone.

It'd be nice to not have to shoot him in the head if he's stupid enough to make a move against me. I shove back the chair, standing up abruptly, adjusting my jacket over the gun stuffed in the waistband of my jeans. I back away from the table, thanking God I wore black ones so that the spill is camouflaged by the dark fabric. "Eat. Drink. And then get me Salvatore on a fucking spit," I seethe. "I want him alive." I pull five hundred-dollar bills out of my pocket and toss them onto the table. "For the waitress." Then I stalk away from the table, not bothering to say another word.

A chill slips down my spine as the gravity of the situation hits me. I've been in charge for a grand total of six months, and I've lost five-hundred grand worth of blow that I know about. We fired Salvatore, but who knows how long he and his guys have been stealing from us? A little here, a little there, just to see if they can get away with it, to see if anyone notices.

Nobody did.

Until they went after the big payout.

And that's one-hundred percent on me.

I storm toward the front of the restaurant, not seeing anything but flashes of red.

A chill settles deep in my bones, the feeling of being watched…hunted…grabbing hold.

This could be a bigger ambush than I ever imagined. They were able to get access to the club, they snatched one of our girls, they got away with the drugs…

And they weren't even careful.

Could it be because they had a bigger objective, one I wouldn't be able to prevent?

Like a fucking coup to take over our empire while Matty is away?

Or like my death?

Thoughts pop between my ears like bullets, and I almost miss Chella as she brushes past me.

"You still look pretty hot," she says with a teasing smile, jolting me from the mind fuck they've assaulted me with. "Can I get you another drink?"

I force a tight smile. "Thanks, but I think I'm done for the night."

She nods her head toward the table where Ray and Bobby have their heads bent together, whispering. "Yeah, I couldn't help but notice your quick exit. Lemme guess, it's a case of worst enemies?"

I let out a dry chuckle. "You have no idea. But please take good care of them anyway."

"Always," she says, a smile tugging at her lips.

Full. Glossy. Pouty.

God, I want to take a bite out of them so badly, and she has no idea.

"Have a good night," she adds. "*Joe.*"

I wink at her, letting my eyes drink her in for one more long minute before turning away and grasping the brass door handle. "You too, *Chella.*"

For a second, I feel strange. Different. *Normal.*

Sharing snarky banter with a beautiful girl who doesn't know who I am, what I do, or for that matter, what I'm about to do. It was easy, flirty, and…fun.

Shit. I can't remember the last time I considered an encounter with a woman any of those things.

And I liked it. A lot, not that I can ever have it for longer than that fleeting moment.

Let's face it, there's nothing about my life that's easy, flirty, or fun.

I can think of a lot of adjectives to describe it, but none of those come into play. Ever.

Much as I might want them to.

A whoosh of air blows against my face as I push open the door of the pub, and instead of walking over to the Range Rover waiting for me at the curb, I do an about-face and head back inside. I sweep a hand through my hair as my eyes scan the restaurant, not really thinking clearly with the head sitting on my shoulders. I'm being led exclusively by the one between my legs right now. I see Ray and Bobby huddled together at the corner table I just left, but Chella is nowhere to be seen.

I let out a defeated sigh and turn back to the door. It was stupid to come back in here when I have so much shit to deal with on the outside. Who knows? I might have my gun stuck down Salvatore's throat in a couple of hours. My life isn't exactly conducive to romance. Besides, what did I expect to happen between us anyway? I tell her who I am and then what? Our families are enemies. I'm sure she must hate me because it was my family who sent hers packing. Sure, I fantasized about getting her naked every chance I got, but it was a long time ago.

A fucking lifetime ago. A lot of water under a very long bridge.

And we just weren't meant to be anything more than—

"Hey, you forget something?"

My breath hitches as I find myself staring into her twinkling, blue-green eyes. They're smiling just as big as she is and fuck, as much as I want to convince myself otherwise, I'm hooked.

Still, after all of these years.

"Maybe," I say. "Depends on how you answer."

She tilts her head to the side, dots of bright pink appearing in her cheeks. "Okay, so then there's an actual question."

I nod. "Yeah."

"Well, ask away." She nods over her shoulder toward the crowded dining room. "I've got a lot of tables."

A quick look confirms that Ray and Bobby haven't looked up once since I strolled back in here, which is a good thing...for a lot of reasons.

"What would happen if I came back here tonight after your shift was over?" I take a step closer to her just so I can breathe in her sweet citrusy scent as she considers her answer. "And asked if I could take you out for a drink?"

A flicker of shock mixed with excitement settles into her features, and her entire face lights up like the Rockefeller Center Christmas tree. "So, like...a date?" A smile spreads across her face, and I swear I've never seen anything so beautiful in my life. "I'd say sure."

I grin at her. "Good. That's good to know."

"Just so I'm clear, was that a hypothetical? Or something else?"

"Definitely a something else." I wink at her. "See you around...?"

"Eleven o'clock," Chella says.

"I'll be here."

"Me too." She claps a hand against her forehead and rolls her eyes. "That was stupid. I mean, obviously, I'll be here."

"Until eleven."

"Until eleven," she repeats, backing toward the dining room with a dazed look on her face. She lets out a soft chuckle and turns her back, practically skipping toward one of her tables.

Crazy, sexy, and fucking adorable at the same time.

A fucking trifecta.

I know it's not the best timing, considering I have a bunch of people to maim in the meantime, but hey, I need to find some kind of work-life balance.

May as well start tonight.

I take a deep breath and head back outside, jogging over to the Range Rover. With blacked-out windows, I won't be able to tell who's inside until I am.

And that should worry the fuck out of me.

Suddenly, the saying 'keep your friends close and your enemies closer' has a fuck-ton more meaning to me.

And I now have a date that I'd very much like to make it to alive.

I grip the door handle, pulling it open and finding Tony behind the wheel as expected. "Where's Dario?" I ask.

Tony nods his head toward the backseat.

"Okay, pop the trunk."

Tony lifts an eyebrow. "Paranoid much?"

"If you had the week I did, you'd understand why I'm asking."

"And you really think I'd let someone hide back there?" he asks. "I could just as easily make sure they're at the warehouse when we get there. That'd be easier and way less messy than in a vehicle," he says with a wink.

I roll my eyes. "Thanks for painting that picture." Did I mention he's a sarcastic fuck, too?

Tony snickers and I walk around to the back of the car. I'm the behind-the-scenes guy, the one who orchestrates this kind of shit. Of course I'd ask him to pop the goddamn trunk! It opens slowly, revealing absolutely nothing. I close it quickly after catching a glimpse of Dario wiggling around in the backseat, gagged with duct tape. I jump into the front seat and close the door behind me.

"Happy?" Tony asks.

"Satisfied," I say. "For the time being."

"It's not easy being the boss, is it?" he asks.

"I have a fucking permanent crick in my neck and a chip on my shoulder," I grumble.

That's all we say for the rest of the short ride. There's a deserted warehouse in the Meatpacking District we use off West Street to handle situations like Dario.

That kind of damage control is my specialty.

He whines and cries through the duct tape because, while he may be stupid in most situations, he knows exactly what awaits him at that warehouse.

Well, at least, he thinks he does.

What he doesn't know is that I'm not going to kill him…right away.

Tony drives down the desolate street, finding parking right behind the old, dilapidated building. There are a few in this area, close to Pier 26 and the Hudson River.

But that won't be his final resting place.

I crack my knuckles before getting out of the car, a rush of adrenaline coursing through me as Tony drags Dario out of the backseat and toward the large metal door. The whole area is unlit, making it that much more ominous. I'm sure Dario is shitting bricks right now, and rightly so.

He just contributed to one of the biggest heists in our organization's short history here in Manhattan. Whether or not he knew he was being duped is irrelevant. He humiliated me by letting himself get lured away from his responsibilities.

Obligation and loyalty always trumps pussy.

Always!

And because of that, he will pay the very steep price of his negligence.

I get out of the truck and jog over to where Tony wrestles Dario just outside of the door. I pull it open and shove Dario inside. He stumbles, face-planting on the cold, hard cement. I kneel down next to him and yank his hair, pulling his head backward. "Get up," I hiss into his ear.

He staggers to his feet, his eyes red and wet with tears. They plead with me to untie him, to pull off the tape covering his mouth, to let him beg for my forgiveness.

He's gonna be begging for a whole lot more than that.

I look around, my trust in Tony creeping up a few more notches. No cartel ambush, no indication of an impending coup.

A couple of shadows appear at the end of the corridor and my spine stiffens.

Motherfucker…

My hand goes directly to the gun in my waistband, my palm wrapped around the handle. "Who the hell…?" I mumble.

"You're gonna need transport once Dario is handled," Tony says in a low voice. "To the site in East New York. I didn't think you'd want to be the one to take him there."

"Obviously," I reply quickly. See, this is one of the reasons why I like Tony so much. He thinks of shit I don't. I can't be the one dragging a body to East New York.

I need to stop thinking like an enforcer.

I need to think like the fucking king.

Not that I need to admit any of that to him.

A couple of guys from the club appear once we get closer. They don't say much, just a few grunts are exchanged. I really don't need them to speak. Not now, anyway. I just need them to watch and take this very colorful story back to the others under my rule.

By now, everyone already knows how splintered our organization is and how easy it was to infiltrate under my control.

I need to grab back some of that control, making Dario a pawn in the process.

One of the guys drags over a rotting, wooden chair and I push Dario into it. He shudders, his eyes wide as I hover over him. My fingers tug at the corners of the tape and I peel it off with one quick tug. He screams, and I slap him across the face, holding up a finger to my lips.

"Shut the fuck up," I growl. "You know nobody can hear you, and if you have any hope of walking out of here, you'll listen real good and *then* speak when I tell you to. Not fucking before." I close my hand around his throat. It's not too tight that he can't breathe, just tight enough that he knows I can choke him if he doesn't cooperate.

And I have other tools in my arsenal if the hand doesn't do enough to scare him.

"I want to know exactly what happened tonight. Who was the girl who came for you?"

"Camille or Camilla," he sobs. "I don't know. She had nice tits and a great ass so, you know, I just—"

I squeeze his throat and he sputters, floundering in the chair. His hands are still tied behind his back, so it's not like he can do anything to stop me. "You just ignored your responsibilities and dipped your wick into a pool that was off limits, that about right?"

He nods. "Y-yeah, boss."

I straighten up, releasing his neck. "Boss," I repeat, pacing around him like a lion about to pounce on his prey. "That's a really important word, do you know why, Dario?"

"B-because…because…" Another sob explodes from his chest and he whimpers before finishing his thought.

I crouch in front of him. "The answer is because I *am* the fucking boss! Do you understand that, Dario? I am the boss, and I gave you an order, which you ignored so you could get sucked off by some slut bitch who was working with one of our enemies!"

He is in full-blown hysterics right now.

Poor fucking Dario.

It's about to get a whole lot worse for you.

I pull out my gun and smack him on the side of the head with it. "Shut the hell up!"

"Boss, I swear, I d-didn't know she was working with an enemy. I just figured—"

"You just figured that you must have won the fucking lottery because a hot piece of ass actually wanted you, right?" I shake my head. "And you thought getting off was worth the risk of exposing my drugs, yeah?"

"It wasn't long," he whispers. "Maybe half an hour. I didn't think anyone would notice—"

"Well, because of your needy cock, we're out a lot of cash. Do you know how much?" I seethe into his face.

"No," he whimpers again.

"Five-hundred-thousand dollars, give or take," I say, pulling away and crossing my arms over my chest. "So how do you think I should punish you for this gross negligence? Hm? Should I shoot you five-hundred-thousand times? Pound five-hundred-thousand nails into your flesh? Slice off your skin and pour five-hundred-thousand fire ants onto you?" I walk around, tapping my finger against my chin. "So many options. I could even mix shit up, you know? Do a little of each?"

The guys waiting to haul a dead body away exchange a look.

Good.

I want them to know how fucking sick I can be.

I want them to take that back to the rest of the crew so they know who they're dealing with if anyone gets any ideas about crossing me ever again.

Slap me once, shame on me.

Try to slap me twice, and I'll cut off your goddamn arm before you have the chance to swing it in my direction.

I stop circling Dario and narrow my eyes at him. "Nah," I say in response to my own questions. "I have a better idea." I look at the guys standing behind him. "Take off his pants."

One of them holds Dario down, and the other pulls off his pants. I stick my gun back into the rear waistband of my jeans and pull out a knife from its hiding place, wrapped tight around my ankle.

I press the button to extend the stainless steel blade, resting the tip against my cheek.

"It's only right that you are punished in the same way as you committed your indiscretion."

Another scream pierces the air and I shake my head. "Dario, I sure hope you got fucked real good, since you're never gonna feel the inside of a pussy again."

The next few minutes are a blur. Perspiration drizzles down the column of my spine as my hand slashes and slices, white noise between my temples muting the earsplitting sounds expelled from Dario's mouth as I morph into my vengeful and vicious alter ego. My pulse throbs against my neck as my insides flood with a rush of heat.

The once-spotless blade is stained with the sins of deceit and betrayal when I'm finished with Dario.

Seeing red is a gross understatement.

My line of sight—along with my clothes—is completely drenched in it.

Occupational hazard.

When I said I wanted the guys to relay a colorful picture, I wasn't kidding.

I hope they take pictures.

I want everyone to know exactly what will happen to them if they abandon their responsibilities under my rule.

I want them to fear the consequences of their deception.

I want them to understand that no amount of money is large enough, no pussy is tight or sweet enough, to warrant the kind of torture and torment that I will bring to them.

I step away from my masterpiece, my shoulders quaking, my breaths coming in heavy pants.

Dario is barely conscious at this point, which is actually too bad.

I grit my teeth. He needs to realize that the misery I just caused him isn't the end.

His head rolls back and forth after a few minutes, his eyes open a crack.

My phone buzzes in my back pocket and I pull it out, silencing a groan when I see Matteo's name flash on the screen.

Anxiety consumes me as I regard Dario.

I made the right move.

Fuck, I had to do this! I had to prove to everyone who and what I am, dammit!

A nagging voice in my head reminds me that the king doesn't carry out the executions.

He only orders them.

I hate this second-guessing shit! I did what I had to do to protect the family and our interests!

Whether or not Matteo will agree is another story, but I don't have time to relay the grotesque tale right now. I decline the call and stuff my phone back into my jeans.

I look up at the expectant faces of the men standing in front of me.

They're looking for direction, for strength, for leadership.

So I give it to them.

"Finish him," I say through clenched teeth, abruptly turning around and storming out of the warehouse. My phone buzzes again and I stab the Accept button when I see Bobby's name flash on the screen.

"Boss," he says. "We've got Salvatore. And the name of his partner."

Tiny hairs on the back of my neck prickle. "Tell me," I growl."

"It's one you know well from back home," Bobby says with a deep sigh. "Frankie Amante."

My throat tightens.

My ex-best friend.

Here in fucking Manhattan.

Screwing me years later, just like his father did to mine back in Sicily.

And the brother of my date at eleven tonight.

Chapter Four
MARCHELLA

I stand next to the bar at the end of the night, counting my tips. I do well enough most nights, but tonight, the cash take is amazing. I actually want to cry out with glee. The five, crisp hundred-dollar bills that the sexy stranger, who also happens to be my date tonight, left on his table before dashing out of here are safely tucked away in the front pocket of my pants, not to emerge until I've gotten home and can slip them into my safe, along with every other dollar I manage to squirrel away for a rainy day.

I just never anticipated that I'd be living in the middle of a never-ending monsoon.

I take a sip of water from the glass in front of me, my mind tripping back to the fiercely handsome guy who literally barreled into my life tonight, only to disappear just as quickly. A shiver runs through me and I glance down at my watch. It's eleven o'clock now.

I bite down on my lower lip, hugging myself in anticipation. How ridiculous! I don't even know his name, although there's something about him that's so damn familiar.

Speaking of names, I wonder how he'll react when he hears my last name. Will he be like all of the others who disappear into thin air when they find out the truth about my family? I mean, it's not like guys are lined up to beat down my broken-down door, not with the patriarch of my family tree rotting at the roots in prison.

For murder.

At twenty-four years old, I have no prospects…of anything.

I tug at my ponytail.

Maybe I can write a book.

I took courses in creative writing, and Lord knows, I love to read. These days, it's my only escape from my otherwise dismal reality, whether it's reading stories to the little neighborhood kids or smutty romance novels to myself.

How hard could it be to write one of my own?

At least I'd be able to use my name in a way that would benefit me instead of making me cringe as it so often does.

My eyes sneak a glance toward the door. It's still a couple of hours until last call, so he'll be able to get inside.

But the past year has taught me that things have a tendency to go sideways more often than not, and getting your hopes up prematurely is the surest way to be disappointed.

I see Jimmy, my boss, walk over. I straighten up and flash him a bright smile. "Hey, Jimmy! Great night, huh? And tomorrow will be even better, I'm sure! That party will bring in so much business! I'm really excited for you!" There is an exclusive event on the schedule for tomorrow night hosted by some socialite here in lower Manhattan. It's to celebrate the launch of a new artist who is debuting at the Whitney Museum of Art this weekend. The guest list is sure to be filled with A-listers, and I'm hoping that'll mean big bucks for the servers.

Namely, me.

"Thanks, Chella. It should definitely be good for the restaurant." He returns my smile, but it doesn't quite reach as high as it normally does. It almost looks…forced. A knot of fear constricts my heart.

Oh, God. Why is he looking at me like that?

Jimmy clears his throat. "Listen, Chella. I don't think I'm going to be able to use you tomorrow night after all."

I furrow my brow, my breath hitched. "I don't understand. I've been on the schedule since you booked the event. You said you needed your most experienced servers here."

"I know what I told you, but…" His voice trails off and he averts his gaze, rubbing the back of his neck. "Things have changed."

"What kind of things?" My voice rises slightly and I hate myself for it, but I need to work this event. I can easily make a few hundred dollars in only a few hours, and it will hold me over to next weekend when I work here again.

He leans toward me. "You know this event is high-profile."

I nod. "Of course."

"That's exactly why I can't risk upsetting any of the guests. The people who run in this circle can crush my business if they recognize you. I took a risk taking you back after all hell broke loose with your family, but negative publicity at that level will crush my business. I just can't take that chance." He backs away. "I hope you can understand."

I swallow the gaggle of tears in the back of my throat and nod quickly. "Sure, Jimmy. I totally see your point. And I am so thankful to be back here. I'd never want to be the reason for anything bad to happen to your business."

"Thanks, Chella. You know I think the world of you, and I'd do anything in my power to help you. But I need you to sit this one out. There will be others in the future and hopefully, when the stories die out, you won't be under such scrutiny."

I force a quivery smile. "Right," I whisper, gathering my tips and stuffing them into my pocket. "I guess I'll just see you in a couple of days, then."

Jimmy's lips curl into a rueful smile. "Take care of yourself."

"Thanks, you too." My voice is strong, but on the inside, it's choked with sadness and dejection. And there isn't much I can do other than to walk out of the restaurant with my head held high. I give a little wave and scurry outside before the tears stinging my eyes slip down my cheeks.

I clench my fists as I stare up at the sky.

No little stars twinkle down on me. It's just a thick haze, kind of like the one I feel hangs over me day in and day out. So obscure, you can't see a single glimmer of light in the distance.

I want to scream and yell and cry. I want to punch something, break something…anything! For the past six months, I've tried to battle against the negativity surrounding me on a daily basis. I've tried to keep my glass half full with the knowledge that this, too, shall pass.

When? When will it pass exactly? Well, that's the freaking magic question.

I've worked hard, kept my head down, and tried to figure out how to put the jagged pieces of my life back together. With barely any prospects for a real job, and diminishing opportunities at my current one, I'm grasping at the frayed ends of my sanity.

And Frankie—

My phone buzzes. It's the one luxury I allow myself, and it's barely functional as a smart device. But my brother's track record requires me to be reachable at all times.

Speaking of the devil, it's a text from him that lights up my screen.

Where are you?

I let out a sigh and stab a response.

He replies almost instantly.

Go home now. No pit stops.

I roll my eyes.

Damn, you mean I can't go out clubbing?

I'm serious, Chell.

I chew my bottom lip as I walk toward the subway station, fumbling in my handbag for my pepper spray, and tucking it into my sleeve as I bring my hand out. What the hell has Frankie so spooked?

I actually have a date. Where are you?

Don't worry about me. And who the fuck are you hanging out with?

A smile tugs at my lips. *Just a guy I met at work. I won't be late.*

There's a long pause before he responds.

I don't like you being by yourself with a strange guy.

I roll my eyes. *Well, lucky for me, you're not my keeper.*

Just lock up tight when you get home. Make sure nobody follows you. I'll see you soon.

If that doesn't sound comforting...

And make sure the jackass keeps his hands to himself.

I snicker and lean against the wall next to the front door. I look left and right, but my mystery date is nowhere to be seen. A few minutes later, I frown at my watch. Still no sign of him.

It was silly to think that maybe I could experience a little sliver of normalcy. A hot guy, asking me out...that's just not my life.

Not my reality.

Not anymore.

I give him another five minutes because it's not freezing out, but as each one passes, my 'reality' becomes more and more clear.

I let my resting bitch face slide into place as I get onto the subway a short while later. It's filled with university kids, most of them drunk, high, or both. And none of them seem to have a care in the world, other than getting wasted or laid.

How lucky they are to enjoy their evenings without giving a single fuck about anything.

That used to be me.

I ride to my stop and then get off the train, sure to keep an eye behind me as I jog up the steps to the street. I stuff my hands into my jacket pockets and keep that fierce look on my face as if to challenge anyone who dares get too close. I pass the bars and delis and storefronts in my shitty neighborhood, looking straight ahead as cars zoom past me in the road. I turn my head every once in a while, a knot in my gut warning me that there is always calm before a storm.

But nobody follows me.

Nobody speaks to me.

And nobody—

I yelp, my foot getting caught in a sidewalk crack. I put my hands out to brace my fall, landing on the pavement with my full weight on my wrists. Bits of gravel and grit scratch up my hands, and my knees scrape against the sidewalk, tearing a hole in one pant leg.

Fuck.

I sit back on my heels, a sob rising in my throat.

That's when it hits me.

No matter how hard I try to keep my head up, no matter how much time I put into planning for a better life, reality is always back to smack me in the face.

And it fucking sucks.

I drag myself to a standing position, whisking the dirt off my jacket and pants. I examine my hands, the thin cuts on my palms already bleeding. I let my hands fall to my sides and turn to my right, catching a glimpse into the overflowing tavern. A song by the Dropkick Murphys interrupts the pity party in my mind, girls and guys singing and drinking and dancing.

I wish I was one of them.

Come to think of it, I wish I was anyone other than who I am right now.

I should feel guilty for thinking that, for despising my father for unraveling what remained of our family after Mama died, for wishing I could just run away to a place where nobody knows who I am, a place where I can get a fresh start and a new lease on life since my current one is about to expire.

Maybe it already has.

After a fitful night's sleep, I wake up to a lot of banging. Cabinet doors, closet doors, pantry doors. I lift my head from the pillow, rubbing sleep out of my eyes as I pull myself into a seated position. "Frankie?" I call out, my voice groggy. "What the heck are you doing out there?"

But he doesn't answer.

I'm just greeted with more banging and heavy footsteps pounding around the apartment.

I swing my legs over the side of the bed and reluctantly launch myself off the bed. I said we'd go for a run, so maybe it's better to get up and at 'em early.

I catch a glimpse at the time on my phone and groan.

Seven o'clock?

Ugh, I was thinking more ten-ish.

I pad into the kitchen, running a hand through my sleep-tousled hair. Frankie is dressed and thumping all over the place, piling things together by the front door. I furrow my brow as I take it all in.

"How was your date?" he grumbles when I come into the kitchen.

"Didn't happen. And I don't want to talk about it, so please don't ask." I nod at the pile of crap he's assembled in the center of the apartment. "Going somewhere?" I ask, heading for the cabinet where my favorite coffee mug resides. I frown at the coffee pot and then at my brother. "Couldn't you have started the coffee while you packed?"

Frankie lets out a huff. "There isn't time," he grumbles.

I furrow my brow. "You want to tell me what's going on? Are you okay?"

He runs a hand through his hair, letting out a frustrated sigh. "I'm fine." His brown eyes twitch at the corners, and I know immediately that he's holding out on me. "For now."

"What are you talking about?" I narrow my eyes, forgetting all about the coffee. "Did you do something last night?" I look around again at the mess on the floor. "Why are you pulling all of your crap out here?"

"Look, Chell. I don't have time to go into detail, but we need to get out of here."

"Why?" My eyes widen. "Oh my God, how many times have I told you to stay away from those fucking scumbag gangsters you insist on hanging around? When are you going to learn? After everything happened with Papa, after the mess he caused for us, the loss of everything we ever knew, how could you let yourself get caught up in that shit again?"

"Stop being so judgmental! You know it's my job—"

"It's only a job if you get fucking paid," I shout.

"That's the problem," he says, stopping short. His shoulders slump and he raises his pained expression toward me. "I did get paid. Big."

"What did you do for this payment, Frankie?" I ask, my mouth suddenly bone-dry. I swallow hard, but the growing lump in my throat almost chokes me.

"Something bad. Something," he says, walking over to one of the windows that faces the street. "That can hurt us, way worse than anything we've experienced before. The shit with Papa would feel like a picnic in comparison."

I storm over to him, pushing him against a wall. I wag a finger in his face, my voice quivering with anger. "You'd better tell me exactly what you did that can hurt *us*," I hiss.

"It's more the 'who' than the 'what' that's the issue," he mutters.

"I don't like playing these games with you," I say. "Tell me what happened!"

Frankie averts his eyes. "Look, I'll explain everything, but in the meantime, I just think we need to get out of the city for a while. Just lay low somewhere where nobody knows us until I can figure out—"

His cell phone rings and we both jump. He pulls it out of his pocket and stares at the screen for a second before answering. I can't see the name or number but judging by the fact that the color in my brother's normally tan face fades more and more with each passing moment, I know it's not a call he wants to take.

But he answers because the look of resignation on his face speaks volumes.

"Yeah?" he barks into the phone. Always the tough guy. Always the fucking troublemaker!

My breath hitches, and I nibble on a hangnail as he continues his terse exchange. It must be a burner phone, even though there isn't a whole lot of detail exchanged.

God, I hate that I even know what a burner phone is…

He finally hangs up after a few minutes, but he looks somewhat settled after whatever he was just told. He drops the phone back into his pocket and sinks onto the couch, combing his fingers through his hair.

I sit across from him on the edge of the rickety coffee table, wringing my hands together. "Who was that? More importantly, do I even want to know?"

"It's not important," he grunts. "What is important is that it looks like we're clear for the time being."

I clasp my hands together and bring them to my lips, squeezing my eyes closed for a second. I say a silent prayer to God that whatever Frankie did isn't as bad as I think. "Frankie," I say, struggling to keep my voice even. "You are jeopardizing our lives by sticking with whatever thug crew you're working with. I don't care what they've promised you, but it isn't worth what you'd be giving up if you ever got caught doing their dirty work. Do you understand that?"

"We're not starting this again, okay? This is what I know! It's all I know! This life is it, it's all we've got." He turns away. "Chella, if we wanna make fast cash, big money, this is the only thing I can do to help."

"You can't make money if you're dead, Frankie!"

"I know, I know!"

"What the hell did you do?" I ask, my voice shaking.

Frankie puts his hands on my shoulders. "I can't give you any details, except I *did* do something bad last night, but the good news is, nobody knows I was involved. The guys I was working with didn't sell me out. That's what they just told me. So we're good. We don't need to run."

"Yet!" I say, throwing my hands into the air. "And what happens next time, when someone does sell you out or worse, you get caught? Huh? Then, what?"

"You've gotta take shit a day at a time. But today, don't sweat it. We're gonna get paid big, okay? I'm talking a huge chunk of cash that'll take care of a shit ton of bills with enough left over for us to enjoy a little bit. To move outta this shit hole and into a better place."

I shake my head. "Frankie, I can't get caught up in another downward spiral, do you get that? You know what Papa's conviction did to my career, my life. Both of our lives!" I spring up from the coffee table and start pacing around Frankie's belongings. "Last night at work, Jimmy told me he couldn't use me tonight for a huge party because I might bring bad press to the restaurant."

Frankie scoffs. "That's bullshit!"

I shrug. "Is it? I mean, Papa is a convicted murderer, a known mafia enforcer. Jimmy would get a lot of flack for employing me. On a normal night, it's not a big deal, but there will be a lot of press at this event. They'd sniff me out like a piece of meat rotting in the kitchen. It would crush Jimmy's business."

"Well, you don't have to worry about working there tonight because it's payday!"

I cover my face with my hands. "You don't understand. What I'm saying is that my life is one step away from complete destruction if someone else in my family gets pegged by the media for some boneheaded scam to make a quick buck," I say with a pointed look. "And just so we're clear, that 'someone else' is *you*."

Frankie claps a hand on my shoulder. "Chella, I know how hard you have been working. Can't you just accept this and let out a sigh of relief that I finally came through for us?" He walks over to me and pulls me in for a hug.

"I'm still a little afraid to breathe," I mutter, laying my head on his shoulder. "Are you going to tell me what happened last night? Don't keep me in suspense, especially if we need to flee the city in the middle of the night."

"I'd rather not," Frankie mutters.

I pull away and clutch his arms, shaking him. "All of your earthly belongings are piled in the center of this room. You were ready to run somewhere, anywhere far away from the city out of fear that whoever you screwed over was going to come for you and do God only knows what. I think I have a right to know what we're up against!"

"You're not up against anything," he growls. "This is all on me, Chella. I won't let anything happen to you."

"Do you really think that's your choice?" I ask. "I mean, these guys go after everything and everyone, Frankie. After all of these years, haven't you at least learned that?"

"Yeah, well, nothing is gonna happen to you. I made sure of that. And this afternoon, I'm gonna meet the guys I was working with and collect my cut. It's gonna help us out. I wanna help us, Chell. It shouldn't all be on you, especially since…" Frankie's voice trails off before he finishes his thought.

"Since what?" I ask.

He shuffles over to his pile of clothes and grabs them off the floor. "Nothing. Don't worry about it. But we're okay. I promise."

"Okay, well, how about you promise that you won't do anything risky or stupid again?" I grab an armful of his stuff and trudge back to his room with it. "Then we don't have to worry about making a quick getaway."

He smirks at me. "But I'm so good at this shit. How can I just walk away?"

"If they break both of your legs, you won't have a choice."

"I don't plan on getting caught. The guys I'm working with know they can count on me."

"Translation: they know you'll do just about anything for a fast buck." I graze his arm. "It's too dangerous. Not worth it. We'll figure this out. I'll come up with a plan to make the money we need somehow."

"How many more nights of waiting tables are you gonna have to suffer through to pay that money?" Frankie shakes his head. "I've proven myself. Let me pull my weight."

"It's a bad idea. And what if they're going to pull one over on you? You said you're going to collect your cut. What makes you think they're going to give you a cent? How do you know they aren't about to screw you?"

Frankie chuckles. "You really have no faith in me, do you? I'm fucking *in*, don't you get it?"

"You shouldn't go to your meeting spot alone," I say. "I'll come with you."

He lets out a loud guffaw. "You're insane. I'm not taking you with me!"

I don't argue. I'm the last person who could help him in a shady situation and he knows it. I can't even stand the sight of blood. I get queasy and lightheaded. And aside from the pepper spray, I'm probably the least street-smart person on the planet, other than when I use my resting bitch face on the subway.

It's kind of ironic because I've grown up in a family firmly ingrained in the mafia. I was always kept away from the nitty gritty, though. Papa never saw me as a protégé. That was always Frankie's role. I was the book smart one, the reader, the dreamer, the one who was going to do great things, the one who started to…well, that is until her plans came to a screeching halt.

Frankie always said Papa's enemies would be back for us, something I probably should have prepared a little bit better for. I guess the past six months of nobody lashing out has given me a false sense of security. Either they can't find us, or they just don't want to bother looking now that my Papa is behind bars.

I really don't know what I'd do if they came for me, if I could even get away. I'd try, sure. But that world is pretty foreign to me. I never wanted anything to do with it growing up, and after the fallout with the trial, I detest the idea of it. That lifestyle stripped me of my own success, everything I had planned for my future. And while I get that Frankie has never been the studious type, I really wish he'd found a different niche, one that didn't involve drugs, guns, or a gaggle of thugs who can't even pronounce two-syllable words.

Maybe this will be the wake-up call he needed. Take the money and run, Frankie!

Anything to get him away from the thug life! My God, I would have so many words for the leader of the fucking shithead pack he runs with!

"Can you take Chase or Johnny with you?" I ask. Those are two of Frankie's friends, ones who didn't desert him after Papa was convicted. Ones who'd always been there and refused to walk away from our family because of the bad press. I trust Frankie more when they're with him.

"It's not really a place for them, Chell," he says, rubbing my arm. "I've gotta do this on my own. But it'll be quick. I'm just going uptown, nowhere crazy. I'll probably be home for dinner. We can order pizza, my treat," he says with a wink.

My heart thumps hard and fast when he smiles. I want to believe him, but the overwhelming sense that something is about to go very wrong washes over me, consuming my whole being. Maybe I'm just being overly protective. Or maybe I'm right on target with these feelings. Nothing is ever quick—even death—with the mafia.

"Do you, ah, have a gun?" I ask.

He rolls his eyes. "Course I do."

I nod. "Okay, well, don't forget to bring it. Just in case."

"I'm telling you, it's going to be fine. Besides, I wasn't even the ringleader. Salvatore handled all of the heavy shit. And he's the one who called me about coming to collect my cut. He's the one they would have gone after, not me. But they obviously don't know it was us who pulled the job." He squeezes my shoulders. "What'd I tell ya? Good things are starting to happen, Chella. This is only the beginning."

And that's what I'm afraid of — and also that my and Frankie's interpretations of 'good things' don't exactly match up.

Chapter Five
ROMAN

My blood bubbles in my veins as I hear Salvatore on the phone with Frankie. That slimy little bastard. He's been here for years, and I've only been in this position for months. He waited a damn long time to exact his revenge against my family.

But he doesn't get the last word.

The Amantes are done screwing over the Villanis.

This is our town, and no punk-ass prick soldier is gonna take what we've built!

Maybe it's payback for running them out of Sicily.

Maybe he needs the cash since his father keeps making bad choices that get him closer and closer to death.

Or maybe he's just goddamn stupid.

"You did real good, Sal," I say, circling the chair where he's tied up. "That was very convincing."

Sal nods quickly. "And he'll be there, too. He needs that money. He's in a pretty shitty place right now."

I stop circling and drop to my knees, dragging my gun down the side of his bloody and bruised face. "Frankie and I were best friends back in Sicily. Our fathers were business partners a long time ago back in Sicily, at least until his father screwed mine out of a real estate deal. And then my father forced the Amantes out of the country. Did you know any of that?" I rise to my feet and sweep a hand through my hair. "So now Frankie sees his opportunity and decides to get his revenge, yeah? He figures he can come after what my family has built and take his share." I hover close to Sal's twitching face. "But he can't. And he fucking won't get away with it. He betrayed my family for the second time. You know how that feels?" I tap the gun on the side of his face again. "Like you're getting ass-rammed. *Dry*. Nothing to prep the assault."

"Roman, look, I know you're angry, but—"

"But what, Sal?" I thunder. "You were pissed off, you had a beef with my family because we fired you, so you figured you'd come up with a plan to come back for what *you* thought was yours, yeah? That alone was stupid. Then you team up with Frankie Amante to help. You know how that makes me look, Sal?" I hiss into his ear, yanking it so hard, he lets out a piercing yelp. "Makes me look like I've got my head up my ass, that I didn't see it coming. Not a good look for a boss, is it?"

"N-no," Sal whimpers.

"But you made sure to wait until Matteo was outta the picture to enact your little plan, didn't you? You figured you'd get away with our money if I was the one in charge, right? Lemme ask you something," I say, shoving my face right into his and yelling at the top of my lungs, "Is this how you imagined things would turn out, you cocksucker? Huh? With you beaten within an inch of your pathetic life, tied to a chair, with a cinderblock chained around your ankles?"

Sal doesn't answer. His chin quivers and his shoulders quake as the tears spill from his beady eyes.

I shake my head. "If you weren't such a goddamn pervert, things mighta gone differently, you know? Like if you'd left your disgusting hands off Zoe instead of handing her off to your dipshit crew to send us a message, you might not be sitting here right now with your dick hanging out. But that's why we fired you in the first place, isn't it, Sal? Because you never could stick to the plan. You always had to put your own fucking spin on shit, and it bit us in the ass plenty." I smirk. "Looks like old habits die hard, for you and your buddy, Frankie. That apple sure as hell doesn't fall far from the tree in the Amante family!"

Sal sputters and wiggles in the chair, and I narrow my eyes at him. "You could've told him it was a setup. You know there's no way out for you," I say. "Why didn't you?"

"Because why the fuck should he get away with all that money?" he sneers. "I did my part! I just got caught! I shouldn't have to lose everything to him!"

"Another reason why you'd never make a good leader," I muse. "Captain goes down with the sinking ship. You've heard that, yeah?" I furrow my brow. "But this…Captain sinking the fucking ship with everyone still on it…that's a new one."

"If I don't make it out, nobody does!" Salvatore smirks. "You might wanna look up Frankie's sister, too. You never know. We mighta pulled this job on you before and you didn't even realize it. She might have some of the money we stole. Just sayin," he says with an ominous chuckle.

My spine tenses.

Frankie's sister.

The date I missed.

How the hell could I have gone back to the restaurant, knowing it was her brother who stole all of that blow? How could I look her in the eye, knowing I was hours away from skewering him?

I couldn't face her.

I couldn't stomach the thought of looking at her, if I'm being honest.

That Amante blood runs through her veins, too. And as hot as she is, I don't need any more toxins seeping into my goddamn life.

"Selfish prick," I mutter, rolling my eyes at Bobby and Ray who dragged Salvatore's fat ass over here, same place where I popped Dario barely twelve hours ago. "Sellin' out everyone and his fucking mother on his way out," I grumble.

"What are you gonna do?" Ray asks in a hushed whisper.

"I'm gonna hold his hand and read him a story…just before I put a bullet between his beady-fucking-eyes. Cushion the blow a little." I snort. "What the hell do you think? I mean, the guy's already anchored, for Christ's sake."

Ray clears his throat and gives me a pointed look. "Boss, can I have a second?"

I walk away from the guys, leaving Bobby to handle Salvatore's angry spewing. "What is it? We don't have a lot of time for small talk," I mutter, the reality of what Sal just said knotting my gut. What if he's not bluffing? What if they really did pull shit like this before? I thought I'd only snoozed on five-hundred thousand, but maybe it's more. Maybe it's a lot fucking more!

"Are you sure this is the best way to handle this?" he asks. "All this blood. Have you spoken to Matteo? He wouldn't—"

I narrow my eyes, hairs on the back of my neck prickling. "First, don't ever fucking question me, you got that? Second, Matteo gave me orders to keep shit running smoothly while he's gone. I don't have to check in with him for every little dipshit thing. And third, I haven't even been home yet. I'm tired, angry, and hungry. So don't piss me off more with this crap, okay? If your conscience is a problem, take it with you and sit in the goddamn car while I handle things here."

A look of shock flickers across Ray's face.

Fuck.

I didn't mean all of that.

Most of it, yeah.

But not all of it.

Ray's on my side, and the last thing I want to do is alienate anyone. Especially now.

I let out a frustrated breath. "Listen, Ray—"

He holds up a hand. "No, boss. It's fine. I shouldn't have challenged you. Just tell me what you need."

I lean my head back against the wall. "You're right. It's too much blood." He doesn't need to know why I'm so desperate to spill it, but I think enough has been done to prove that I can steer a tight ship.

Sal's out.

There's no way he survives. He's an arrogant prick, a sellout, and a slimy, two-faced bastard who only pollutes the world we live in. He can taint even the most vile places…case in point, the Hudson River.

But Frankie…I could show him some mercy. He was my best friend at one point. Besides, there is a big problem that still needs to be addressed and he can help with that.

I need legitimacy.

I've shown these guys that I can rule with an iron fist, but does that make me a good leader? Am I that much better than fucking Sal?

I need to show them that I can get what I want and not have to use brute force to grasp it.

So I won't kill Frankie. Yet.

I'll use him, instead.

He's gonna find the guys who financed Sal and his crew to pull off this heist and he's gonna get back everything he stole. They have our drugs, and my pride, in their fucking back pockets. I just need a plan to force Frankie into cooperating with me.

Or leverage.

"Sal has to be punished," I grunt. "He can't get away with this, especially after he was fired by Matteo. He can't walk outta here. He needs to be carried out. In a fucking bag."

Ray nods.

I stroke my chin. "But Frankie…I have a different plan for him. We need him to find out who orchestrated this whole thing. Let's face it, Sal ain't that smart. Someone else is behind it, and Frankie can find them."

"How do you know he won't cut and run?" Ray asks. "If he knows what you did to Sal and Dario, he won't wait around for you to take a crack at him."

I glance at Sal who is slumped over in the chair, bawling like a baby.

"Frankie's sister," I murmur. "She may be just the bargaining chip we need to win this whole game."

Ray nods. "Great, how do we find her?"

"Sal will do just about anything right now to stay alive. I'm gonna make him a deal."

"What kind of deal?"

"A deal where I dangle freedom in front of his ugly ass face in exchange for information…and cooperation," I say, a plan hatching in my mind as I speak. A sinister smile plays at my lips.

Oh, yeah, it's *my* game now.

I rake a hand through my hair, my brain now fizzling with ideas as if I've just been injected with some serious caffeine.

I stop in front of Sal. "So you want the rest of your crew to go down in flames, huh?"

He glares at me, his eyes red and puffy. He couldn't lead a crew out of a goddamn paper bag. But I'll humor him. For now.

"They deserve it. I didn't steal anything. I just fucked around with one of your girls."

I jab a finger at his chest. "You organize this shit show, Sal?"

"No! It was Frankie, I swear!" he cries out. "And I already made sure he'll be at that meeting spot you gave me. If you let me go,

I'll help you find whoever else he was working with! Let me show you that I can be loyal to you again!"

Wow, this guy has really done a complete one-eighty in the past few minutes. Now he thinks he can actually have his job back, too? Does he really believe I'd ever go along with that? Eh. Fuck it. Let him believe what he wants, as long as I get my drugs and handle the traitors quickly and somewhat cleanly.

"I want what was stolen, too," I say through gritted teeth. "All of it."

"I can get it for you," he says. "Please, Roman. Give me a chance to make this right!"

I pretend to think about it before responding. "Okay, Sal. I'll give you a shot. But you know what's going to happen if you fuck up, right? Do I need to show you—?"

"No!" he yelps. "I've got it. And if Frankie needs some more convincing, his sister works at the Grammercy Tap Room. I've only seen her once in the whole time I've known Frankie. He doesn't let any of us get near her. I only know where she works because I saw the caller ID on his phone one night when she was working."

Frankie is the one I want to punish most, that cocksucker. I want to do it for Matteo, for my family, but especially for my father. My former best friend is now my mortal enemy, and he's the one who will pay the steep price for this betrayal. And if I know Frankie, he will definitely try to run as soon as he gets the chance. So I need my leverage.

Sal is singing like a fucking fat canary right now, and I should be happy. Thrilled, even. He's about to sell everyone out, and he's practically paving a path back to my money.

But a knot in my gut tightens when I hear her name, and I'm suddenly back at the restaurant with booze puddling in my lap as I gaze up at her snarky grin and get lost in her blue-green eyes.

Marchella.

Chella.

And just like that, the elusive bargaining chip falls right into my lap.

I needed an incentive to get Frankie to return my money, and now I have one.

Except she just happens to be the girl who got away…literally. She's the girl I fantasized about for the better part of my teen years. Hell, I did more than fantasize about her, too. But I was smart enough to know back then that if I got too close, the sparks I felt between us would ignite and the flames would swallow me whole.

And that's in addition to what Frankie would have done to me if I even dared look for too long.

All of the memories burst between my ears, swirling through my mind as I scrub a hand down the front of my face. I need to get my head on straight. This is my job! I can't let these crazy feelings take over when I have so much at stake, like the loyalty and respect of my family and organization. I need to show them all the consequences they'll face if any of them decide to pull a similar scheme, how I won't tolerate deception and if they test me, they'll pay with their lives. And not only them, but everyone they love.

Just like Frankie.

My throat tightens and I clench my fists.

And Marchella.

Fuck.

I turn to Ray. "Make sure Bobby meets Frankie at the meeting spot Sal gave him." My jaw twitches. "And get me a location for his sister."

Chapter Six
MARCHELLA

A heavy feeling in my gut weighs me down as I finish straightening up Frankie's room. We are not running away from our lives. Our reality is bleak right now, but dammit, I'm going to figure out a way to make it better. There has to be something better out there for us.

I thought we hit rock bottom when Mama died. I had no idea how much deeper hell went.

But, as they say, when you finally do crash, you have nowhere to go but up.

So that's my glass-half-full perspective for the day.

My mind wanders back to my shift last night at the bar and the mystery man who left me hundreds of dollars as a tip for pouring liquor into his lap, then left me high and dry after my shift.

His eyes had been so captivating, it reminded me of another time…a happier one where I was carefree and in love. Sure, some might have said it wasn't real because I was only fourteen, but I know what I felt.

It's strange. The man from last night was rough and cocky and arrogant, but those eyes…they gripped me in the same way. I'd have followed him just about anywhere while caught under his salacious spell. There had really only been one other guy who'd elicited this kind of response, but that was such a long time ago, in a different life, one where we danced around our feelings for years because the danger overshadowed the future.

And then a worse danger seeped into our lives, poisoning any chance of us being together.

I was young but I knew what I wanted, what I needed.

Then I was yanked away forever, and what I wanted was shoved into the dark recesses of my mind and heart, to the point where it almost felt like a figment of my imagination.

Like it wasn't ever real.

Like it never could be again.

Fast forward to the present.

I let out a deep sigh. Dating and sex…those are luxuries I haven't experienced in a very long time. Most guys aren't too thrilled about hanging out with the daughter of a convicted murderer, and an infamous gangster to boot.

My shitty past just insists on dictating my future. It's like the quintessential re-gift that just keeps fucking looping with no end in sight.

Too bad, because some mind-bending sex is exactly what I need to get my mind off of our dismal circumstances. I thought I was on the path toward it last night, but oh well.

I bite down on my lower lip, the memory of his scent infusing my senses yet again.

So strong, so heady, so masculine.

God, I'd love to have broken my dry spell with him. We wouldn't have had to exchange names, so there'd be no risk of him freaking out once he found out who I was. It would be pure carnal bliss…sweaty, hot, and—

"Thanks for helping me pull my shit together," Frankie says, jerking me from my wanton daydream. He zips up a hoodie and twists his baseball cap around so the bill is backward. It's his classic "I take no shit" look.

"No big deal. I had the time," I say in a rueful voice, shrugging.

"What are you gonna do this afternoon?" he asks, and I furrow my brow. He sounds way more interested than normal in what I have planned for my low-budget day.

"Maybe I'll go for a jog, something we were supposed to do together, remember?" I say, wagging my finger in his face.

"Tomorrow," he promises.

"Yeah, well, I won't hold my breath."

I walk into the kitchen and pull open the refrigerator door. It's dismally empty, save for a six-pack of beer, a gallon of orange juice, and a few eggs. "You said pizza for dinner?" I ask with a quick grin.

"You got it," he says, giving me an affectionate punch in the shoulder. "Hey, ah, since it doesn't sound like you have anything really pressing to do, why, um, don't you take a ride with me? I was planning to make a stop before I head over to my meeting."

I narrow my eyes. "And where exactly are you going?"

Frankie rubs the back of his neck. "To visit Papa. Wanna come with?"

"I'd rather donate an eye and pluck it out myself with a pencil. Besides, I don't relish the idea of running home from Rikers so you can take your meeting."

"Chella," Frankie says. "You really need to see him. To talk to him. It's been too long."

"I have no interest in talking to him," I grumble, slamming the refrigerator shut.

"I really think—"

I spin around, my lips twisted into a grimace. "Look, I get that you had a special bond with Papa. But we never had the same connection. He let you in on things, gave you guidance, tried to prepare you for this life. I never got the same attention. He could never talk to me the way he did with you. He could never teach me things he taught you. But he could have made an effort. I tried and failed. You know what? I needed him, too, especially after Mama got sick. And he faded away more and more once she died until he was finally gone. Literally."

"I always thought it was because it haunted him, how much you look like Mama. How you have a lot of her mannerisms."

"You don't think that haunts me, too?" I say through clenched teeth. "And you see it, too. Did you toss me aside because you couldn't handle it? No! But that doesn't even come close to explaining why for years before that he cast me aside."

"He's not a bad guy. He tried to do what was best for us, and for Mama when she was here. He made a lot of mistakes, yeah. But he always took care of us."

"Until he got put away and made our lives crumble around us *again*. He did it once and we had to find a new life in a different country! Then he did it a second time when he killed that guy and left us to pick up those pieces, Frankie. We had to take care of each other because there was nobody else to help us!" I hold up my hands. "Wait. Stop. I don't want to do this right now. I'm already nervous enough for you to go to that meeting. I don't want to go down this road with Papa. I can't. He made his bed."

"Okay," he mumbles. "I just think that maybe it's time to figure out how to move past things. He *is* all we have left."

I shake my head, smoothing down the front of my t-shirt and pulling my hair into a low ponytail. "I'm not ready, Frankie. I'm hurt. And angry. And frustrated. I don't know when all of that is going to blow over, if ever."

"You can't hold a grudge forever," Frankie says softly. "He's still your father."

"Yeah, well, right now, he's just a guy who's responsible for ruining my life. *Twice*." I slip my apartment key into one of my sneakers before sliding my feet into them.

"Okay, well, just consider making a visit someday, Chell. He always asks about you. He knows he fucked up, and I think he wants to make it right."

I press my lips together into a tight line. "Just please, please be careful, Frankie. Call me. I'll have my phone glued to my hand in case you need anything."

"And who you gonna call if heads start to roll?" he asks with a smirk.

"Ghostbusters," I say with a chuckle. I pull him close, burying my head in his cologne-spritzed neck and inhaling deeply. This is what comfort is to me. My brother, the one person in my life who believes in me. The one person I want to take care of. The one person I know truly cares about me. I have to do right by him, to fix all of the shit that's gone wrong in our lives. He's hurting, too. I have to find a way to heal us both.

I pull open the door and turn to look at my older brother. Tall and handsome with a grin that can get him pretty much anything he wants. I've seen it in action. My shoulders slump for a second. He could be anything he wants. He has so much zest for life, so much personality. Why would he want to demean himself with this kind of gangster work? Any job that makes you look backward more than forward to make sure nobody is chasing you with a machete isn't worth it, in my opinion.

"Why don't ya take a picture? It'll last longer," he says with a snicker.

I flip him off and shut the door behind me, silencing the giggle that almost escaped. Can't do anything to alert Mr. Raynor. Although, this sports bra pushes my boobs up pretty high and gives me some good cleavage. I might be able to buy us another week if I have the unfortunate experience of running into him.

But luck is on my side today.

I make it out of the building without so much as a glimpse of him.

The sunshine warms my face as I step onto the pavement. I rub my hands down my arms as a cool breeze slithers under the moisture-wicking fabric. I begin my jog — crossing over Sherman Avenue and heading in the direction of Inwood Park. When we went apartment hunting after the bank foreclosed on our home, this was one of the only locations we could afford that would actually give us our own space. It's not glamorous by any stretch, and there's no way on God's green Earth that I'd go for a jog in the park after dark — even though daylight is oftentimes sketchy — but it's home for us.

For now.

And so I carry pepper spr—

Shit.

I forgot my pepper spray.

I got so rattled by Frankie's invitation that it went out of my mind completely.

I do have the key in my shoe, though. If I can manage to not hurl all over an assailant, I could get the sneaker off and impale him or her with the tip.

A snicker slips through my lips.

As if.

I pull in a deep breath as I jog along Seaman Street, and everything gets a little greener, a little more lush and fresh. I love this slice of nature. Maybe because it's an escape from the hustle and bustle of everyday city life. I can come here and lose myself in the foliage, leaving all of my problems back with the hectic street traffic which never seems to calm, regardless of the hour. The Harlem River greets me, the water rippling in the breeze. The top of the water glitters as the light hits the peaks and I break into a run.

I take one of the paths, passing a Little League baseball game on my left as I navigate my way around the park. A twinge of sadness makes my heart clench as I watch the kids running and screaming and cheering for their teammates. I miss being around kids so much. Two hours a week at the community center is not nearly enough for me. My students' enthusiasm and zest for learning made me excited to go to work every day, to teach them and watch their little faces light up with joy when they connected the dots I'd lay out for them. But I can understand my parents wouldn't want their kids instructed by the daughter of a convicted murderer. I hate leaving that legacy in my wake, and I'm determined to change it.

Somehow.

People walk their pets, little girls pass me on pink roller skates, and things feel, at least for a little while, normal.

I crave that normalcy every day. It's one of the reasons why I come here. I don't care much for the exercise, but it gives me something to do while I people-watch and wonder about their circumstances. My situation isn't great, but I don't think I'm the worst off by any stretch.

We're all struggling in some way.

That's another reason I love this park.

The silent camaraderie.

It's comforting and proves I'm not alone in my struggle.

My feet pound harder on the concrete, my shoelaces loosening and flapping against the ground as I run, faster and faster until my lungs feel like they're going to explode. It's a welcome release from the stress cloud hanging over me. The muscles in my legs tense and tighten with every step, a cramp in my side warning me that the end is near.

I slow down, collapsing against a chain link fence, wheezing because I never remember to breathe in through my nose and out through my mouth. I turn so my back is plastered against the fence, and I lean my head back as my breathing calms. It takes a while but then again, I have plenty of time.

Regrettably.

When I finally drag myself away from the fence, I tighten my ponytail and head toward the park exit and back to the craziness of the city and my life. This little slice of bliss will be here when I get back.

I remember running through Washington Square Park back in my college days when life was bright and promising and there was no need to escape anything.

I wish I had a damn time machine. A DeLorean. I'd easily find a road where I could hit eighty-eight miles per hour and get the hell out of…well, hell.

I psych myself up for the next leg of my run when I can finally breathe again. I gather speed as I dart through trees in a quieter area of the park. A flash of black catches my eye and I divert from my intended path, cutting around some bushes in pursuit of the perked-up ears that just trotted past me.

The area is a bit more wooded, so I have to sidestep trees and rocks to find the skinny stray who is bent on evading me. It finally peeks its head out and I jump from one rock onto a larger one right next to the puppy, the sole of my foot skidding and then slipping on the smooth top. I fly into the air, my arms flailing as I brace for my fall.

"Ahh!" I shriek, my body sailing forward as if in slow motion. I throw my arms over my face, in preparation for the impending crash, but instead of jagged rock, I collide with something else as a strong arm pulls me back to solid ground.

Something that smells like Prada cologne and has massive muscles gathers me tight. My heart thuds with increasing force as I gaze up at what…or rather…who…cushioned my fall.

Holy crap on a cracker. It's the guy from the bar last night.

The big tipper with the delicious body and eyes I could stare into forever.

The guy who stood me up.

Joe.

But when those crystal blue eyes focus on me, I momentarily forget all about my search-and-rescue mission and my wounded pride. That is, until…

"Aarf! Aarf!"

I jerk my head around with a gasp, scrambling to regain my footing as the black puppy takes off like a shot, scooting out of the park under a broken bit of fence.

"Oh, no!" I moan.

"Your dog?" Joe asks.

"No," I reply. "I think it was a stray. But I'm sure its owner must be looking for it."

I look around at the park behind us. We're so far off the beaten path, I don't even know how I missed this guy hanging out back here. We're in the most desolate area of the park.

Tiny alarm bells go off in my mind.

Nobody…except this guy who occupied most of my dreams last night…is around?

He's here…but he didn't show up back at the restaurant after my shift…

Something feels weird.

I bite down on my lower lip, his arms still grasping me. "You stood me up," I say, narrowing my eyes at him.

How sick is it that I don't want him to let me go even though he could be a total stalker? I mean, what are the odds we'd be here in the same place at the same time?

"I know. I'm sorry."

I wait for more of an explanation but nothing comes. "That's all you have to say?"

"I can tell you I fell asleep, and when I woke up it was three a.m."

"Would that be true?"

"No," he murmurs, his lips lifting slightly. "But it's easier to swallow than the real reason."

"And you just happen to be wandering around here in the most secluded part of this park, perfectly positioned to save me from face-planting in the rocks?"

"Fucking fate, huh?" he says.

I furrow my brow. "This isn't exactly a place that the Village crowd frequents."

"Who said I was part of the Village crowd?"

A tingling between my thighs makes me slam my knees together. This guy could be a total psychopath and here I am, craving his fingers, his mouth...*everything*. "So you're saying this run-in is just a coincidence?" I say with a nervous laugh.

"I don't believe in coincidences, Marchella." His gaze darkens as he stares down at me. "I came here for you."

Chapter Seven
ROMAN

Holy Christ.

What in the ever-loving fuck am I doing here in this shithole park, holding the woman whose world I'm about to shatter? She's already had enough shit to deal with over the years, and here I am ready to dish out some more?

My gut twists. I wanted to see her again last night…so fucking badly.

But I would have done things…bad things…things that would have come from a dark place inside of me. The place where my need for vengeance festers.

I was afraid I wouldn't be able to stop myself from taking what I'd wanted for so long and then justifying it because of what her asshole brother did to me.

The rage would have ignited and incinerated everyone in its path.

I was smart enough to stay away last night.

Not so much today.

After finding out Frankie led the charge on the robbery, and then when the plans to snatch Marchella came together, I knew I had to see her one more time before all hell broke loose and swallowed her whole.

So I drove all the way up here and waited for her.

I knew it was only a matter of time before she'd step outside of that dingy apartment building where they live. It was too nice of a day to stay inside, and as far as Frankie knew, nobody was coming after him, so he'd never have warned her to lay low.

Fucking idiot.

I followed her into the park, managed to keep up with her frantic jog, even though running isn't my chosen form of cardio, and saved her from cracking her head on a boulder while she chased a stray.

Now she's in my arms.

And pretty soon she'll be sprawled in my trunk.

I told my guys to hang back, that I needed to check out the scene first to make sure it was safe for us to move forward with our plans. But it was all bullshit. I had to see her again. The spark between us sizzled from the second I left her at the restaurant, and the aftershocks kicked up whenever I'd picture her face in my mind afterward.

It's almost as if she was a sliver of sanity and I needed to grasp onto her to ground myself.

All of the teenaged lust came rushing back with an unparalleled force, and the things I dreamed of doing to her and with her consumed my conscience when I wasn't thinking about jamming an ice pick into Frankie's eye.

The events of the past couple of days fester under my skin like an infection that can't be killed with even the strongest antibiotic. Shit is slipping away from me — my credibility, my ferocity, my power — and even though I've tried to yank it back, it keeps eluding me.

I guess I felt like I had one last lifeline to grasp onto — *her*.

I know I'll never have her the way I want her. It's not like I could ever act on it, not after what Frankie pulled, and not with our family history.

And after I 'handle' Frankie, I'm pretty sure she'd never come near my with a ten-foot pole...unless she had one to swing at me.

"You came here for me," she repeats, a look of disbelief flitting across her features.

"Is that so hard to believe?"

"You blew off our date," she says sharply. "But then again, you *did* leave me a pretty generous tip, even after I dumped a highball full of scotch into your lap," she says, her full pink lips lifting.

"I did." I look around. We're still alone for the immediate future.

Safe. Guarded. Protected by all the damn trees.

I don't have long to get this out.

"I came here to apologize for missing our date," I say.

Her eyebrows shoot upward. "Seriously? It wasn't that big a deal."

I lift an eyebrow. "Really."

She twists her ponytail around her finger and takes a step backward, a smirk on her face. "It's not like I don't have guys hitting on me all the time."

"Ouch. I came here to apologize. Now you're just kicking me while I'm down."

"You didn't have to make the trip. You could have found me at the restaurant."

"You're right, but then I'd have had to wait to see you again. And you aren't working tonight."

Her eyes pop open even wider. "Wait, who told you that?"

"The girl who answered the phone when I called the bar."

"You called, asking for me? So, what are you, some kind of stalker? You figured you gave me that tip and now you're entitled to…" she stumbles over a branch as she takes another step away from me. "Hey, wait a minute. Did they tell you where I live? How would you even know—?"

"I make it a point to find out what I need to know when I'm interested in a woman, Marchella," I murmur. I don't move toward her because right now, she's like a petrified little animal. One false move, and she'll dart.

And I don't feel like running any longer.

I need her to stay right here.

With me.

I've never felt this conflicting tug of emotions before, and I don't know if I ever will again. What I do know is that Marchella is my bargaining piece. And as much as I want her to be anything but, I can't change the circumstances.

Hers *or* mine.

I have to save face.

I have to prove my worth to the organization.

And I cannot fucking crack!

I stare at her, watching her expression soften the tiniest bit. "I have a can of pepper spray in my pocket. I will use it if you come too close."

"I don't want to hurt you," I say.

This is one-hundred percent true.

If this was another life and we didn't have a history, I'd have wanted to hunt her down and violate her in as many ways as I could imagine, all while her asshole brother watched, tied up and gagged. I would have wanted to punish her, all because she's an extension of Frankie, the man who completely fucking emasculated me in the eyes of the underworld.

And my own family.

I would have wanted to make an example of her, of both of them.

But it isn't a different life, and all of the feelings that percolated last night…all of the X-rated fantasies…came bubbling to the surface once again.

I have to hurt her. There's no way around it.

Once I move forward with my plan, she'll hate me forever.

And for us, forever was never an option for anything more.

"Good," she says, twisting her head left and right and then narrowing her eyes at me. "So why don't you tell me why you were so desperate to see me that you had to follow me into the park? You weren't just hanging out here. You had to have tracked me."

"What if I did?"

"Well, that would be hella freaking creepy! Especially since you could have seen me last night but chose not to come back."

"You're right. But you have to believe it was for a good reason. Besides, you're not running away from me now," I say. "If I'm so creepy, why are you still standing here?"

She shrugs, her long ponytail cascading down one shoulder. "Probably because I'm stupid and naïve. But maybe because…" Her voice trails off.

I take a tentative step forward. "Maybe because…?" I ask.

Her hand slides into her pocket, which is totally flat, by the way. She has no pepper spray. It was a bluff. But I did see her run, and she's got some pretty powerful legs, legs I don't plan to have near me unless they're wrapped around me. "Maybe because I'm kind of glad you came looking for me in some weird, twisted way."

"Why does that make you weird and twisted?"

She rolls her eyes. "Not me, dude. *You*."

"I've been called worse," I say with a smirk. "And if that's the worst you can say, then I'll stick around to hear some more."

A smile plays at her lips. "What makes you think there *is* any more?"

I take another step. "Because, like I said before, you're still standing here. I take that as a good sign."

The electricity cracking between us…she can feel it, I know she can. But how the fuck doesn't she know it's me? How can she not see me the way I see her? How can she not remember?

Unless the hate runs so deep, she won't acknowledge what's long been buried.

Pretty soon, she won't have much of a choice but to unpack it all.

She clears her throat and tucks a stray hair behind her ear. "Yeah. So, um…*Joe*," A nervous giggle slips through her lips. "What happens next?"

A loud ringtone pierces the air and I grab it out of my pocket.

"Yeah?" I say, dragging my eyes away from Marchella.

"Boss, Frankie's on his way. We have to do this now."

"Okay," I grunt. "I'll meet you at our spot." I gave them the address of her apartment building under the guise that we'd tail her from there.

Dammit, I didn't get enough time!

Why'd she have to run for so fucking long?

I click off the phone and stuff it back in my pocket.

"So, I, uh, guess you have to—" she starts to say, but I don't let her finish. I close the space between us and snake my arms around her waist, crushing my lips against hers to silence the rest of her thought.

I drink her in, the taste of spearmint so sweet on her lips. I plunder her mouth with my tongue as I press my fingertips into the small of her back. A tiny moan slips from her mouth, her arms tightening around me, her fingers tugging at the hem of my shirt. Fuck, I want to sprawl her out on the ground and tear off her clothes so I can feast on her, tasting every inch of her frenzied body. Our tongues twist and tussle, coiling heat igniting the flames of passion deep in my gut...flames that I've never felt singe me, much less incinerate my insides.

This is what I needed to experience.

This is why I came.

This is what I had to know...at least for a few fleeting moments before her life completely implodes, courtesy of me and her dear dipshit brother.

I pull away, breathless, dragging my thumb and forefinger down the sides of her flushed face. Her eyes sparkle with lust and excitement, all signs of fear completely erased from her expression.

That'll change soon enough.

She cocks her head to the side, a shocked expression settling into her features. "Wow," she whispers.

I graze her lips with mine one more time. "Ditto," I say, a smile tugging at my lips as I back away.

"Wait, that's it?"

I run a hand through my hair. "Yeah."

"You seriously are going to just walk away after *that?*" she exclaims, throwing her hands in the air.

My smile fades. "You'll see me again, Marchella. I have a nasty habit of turning up when people least expect me."

And with that, I turn away from her shocked expression and jog toward the nearest exit.

I have a job to do.

Chapter Eight
MARCHELLA

My head is spinning so fast right now, the only way I can make sure I don't land face-first in the dirt is to climb down the trunk of a tree so I can sit down to rehash the crazy, fucked-up events that just took place.

I went from chasing a stray to being stalked to thinking I was going to be murdered to being kissed senseless.

And now I'm alone again.

It all happened so quickly, I could convince myself that it was all part of my daydream fantasy loop.

But the heat pooling in my belly and between my legs is enough to convince me that he was not, in fact, a mirage. That gorgeous yet nameless man's hands grazed my lust-filled body, his demanding fingers pressed into my flesh, his lips crushed against mine, and his devious tongue launched a delicious invasion on my mouth.

It really happened.

Then, without warning, things ended just as fast as they started.

But damn, it was intense and oddly, so…familiar.

Powerful.

Blissful.

And way too fleeting.

I press my fingertips to my temples, my skin prickling from the memory of his touch. I lean back against the rock, flinging a hand over my forehead, every cell in my body on high alert.

How am I supposed to just pick myself up and walk away like it never happened?

Because that's exactly what he did.

He took off faster than a shot, phone call or not.

I should probably be second-guessing my actions, wondering why he mysteriously flitted into and out of my life twice in the past twenty-four hours, but the endorphins coursing through me just keep that stupid smile plastered across my face.

Like I don't have a care in the world.

An alternate reality.

Maybe that's why I don't want to break the spell.

Maybe that's why I subconsciously know that if I leave, it will shatter and I'll be plunged back into my actual reality.

I take in a deep breath, knowing I can't escape forever but a few more minutes to bask in the feeling of euphoria that has commanded my body and mind can't be bad, right?

Let's call it therapeutic.

When I finally drag myself up from the rock, I tighten my ponytail and head toward the park exit and back to the craziness of the city and my life. This little slice of bliss will be here when I get back. And I will go back, just to relive those stolen moments and hope that I may get a chance to claim a few more like them.

He came to find me.

A shiver rushes down my spine.

He likes me.

And I like him, too.

I rub my hands down the sides of my arm and cross back over Seaman Avenue, the gravity of Frankie's predicament washing over me as I put distance between myself and the delicious little tryst I just shared with my sexy stalker, Joe.

A deep sigh expels from my mouth as I trudge back to my apartment. I know this isn't hell. I mean, it's definitely worse than purgatory. But I have Frankie, and we have food and a roof, albeit questionable since the plaster chips incessantly over our heads.

We have hope.

I may get jaded, but I haven't completely lost that hope.

And dammit, I have a degree from one of the best universities in the country!

I can fix this!

Running always empowers me. Makes me feel like an in-control badass, and even if it's total bullshit, it makes me smile. I furrow my brow as I pass a quiet side street. A tiny whimper makes me do a double-take, and I duck down the street in search of the source of that sound.

Oh my gosh, it sounds like…

I walk gingerly down the sidewalk, searching for any movement. I strain my ears to try and hear the sound again. A car zooms past and I jump, startled by the noise and annoyed that the coughing muffler might have scared the animal away.

When it's quiet again, I keep walking, twisting my head left and right when I gasp, clapping a hand over my mouth. A furry paw peeks out from one of the run-down buildings. It disappears as quickly as it steps out, and I jog over, falling to my knees when I see the tiny puppy cowered against the cement wall. It looks up at me with big, sad brown eyes and lets out another cry. This time, it doesn't look like it has the energy to run away, which makes sense since it must have run all the way here from the park.

My brow furrows.

How insane is this?

The puppy, the Stalker otherwise known as Joe.

What are the freaking odds that I'd see them both…twice…in the most unlikely of places?

I reach out tentatively, smoothing down its matted fur. A little peek at its back confirms it's a girl. She's almost all black, except for a small white patch around her neck.

She doesn't look like a typical stray, especially around here. I wonder if her owner brought her to the park for a visit and she got away somehow. I bite down on my lower lip. I think it's a Boston Terrier. I cup her chin in my hand and tilt her face upward to see if she's wearing a collar. Not that I needed to move her head. She's so little, it would be hanging down like a necklace.

My gut twists.

Of course.

Her collar probably slipped off. "It's okay, baby," I whisper. "You're okay."

But she's not.

So I decide that second to add her to my list of blessings.

I said I loved the silent camaraderie, but I'll take it in barking form, too.

But the dog doesn't bark. She just ventures toward me, one slow step at a time. I hold out my hand so she can sniff me, and it isn't long before she's licking my entire arm. She's not completely comfortable yet. I guess she's still sizing me up.

"I don't know your name, puppy," I murmur. "But how about we call you Bella? My mama used to call me that all the time. It means 'beautiful'." I wiggle my fingers under her chin. "You sure are beautiful. And I'll bet my mother led me right to you because she knows that I need something soft and cuddly more than ever right now." I smile, feeling lighter than I have for a long time.

I feel like someone is looking out for me, like I'm not alone.

I let her lick me for a few more minutes as I contemplate my next move. Much as I want to take her home with me, I have to take her to the police station. They must have a way of tracking down her family. She must have a chip they can scan. Maybe the family has already reported her missing. The thought of giving her over to the cops makes my heart clench, though.

Maybe I can keep her overnight. I can give her a bath, feed her, play with her, give her a nice warm bed. At least she can have a good night's sleep before I take her to the station. Who knows how easy it is to find dog owners anyway? What if they need to put her in a shelter while they investigate? That would be horrible!

Bella takes a few more steps toward me, close enough that I can scoop her up. She nuzzles her head against my leg and I stroke her back a few times. When she's close to climbing on top of me, I reach around her gaunt body, about ready to pick her up when a searing pain shoots through my shoulder. My body lurches forward and Bella darts out of the way as my hands fall to the pavement, planted on either side of me. I clench my teeth, the pain crippling the muscles in my arm. I crawl toward the side of the building to use it as support, and Bella follows me. I smack my hands against the brick, clawing at it as I struggle to my feet.

I make it up halfway before a cold, numbing sensation spirals up my right calf and I collapse back onto the ground with a loud moan. Bella is now on top of me licking my face, and my head feels like it weighs a hundred pounds, way too heavy for me to move it around. I let out a pathetic whimper, my energy supply depleting at an alarmingly rapid rate.

"What's wrong with me?" I moan, my voice thick and heavy. My face slips down onto my now-immobile hand. I can vaguely feel bits of gravel sticking to my cheek and I want to brush them off. I want to be able to move my hand. But the numbing spreads to my left side, paralyzing my limbs. I manage to flip myself onto my back before my eyes droop closed for good. I force them to stay open, to see someone…anyone…who might be responsible for this.

For killing me.

Because if this isn't me loitering at death's doorstep, I don't know where the hell else I could possibly be.

Just before my eyes float closed for the final time, I see something familiar and my throat tightens, emitting only a gurgling sound instead of a full-fledged scream.

Holy fuck.

Those eyes...

I try to cry out.

But my mouth can't form words.

My lips won't move.

And my voice is silenced.

My eyes float open and I see white.

White and glaringly bright, recessed ceiling lights.

I swallow hard.

Fuck, is this heaven?

I squeeze my eyes shut for a second to adjust, then crack them open a bit once again, this time remembering not to stare. I roll my head gingerly to the right and left as I take in the space. I can see a desk and a few chairs in one corner of the room. Stark white walls. Covered windows. My hands run over a soft, buttery leather texture beneath me.

Okay, if it *is* heaven, then I must be in some angel's office.

Or maybe God's…

I rub a hand over the spot in my shoulder that feels like it's on fire and my fingers graze a bandage of some kind. I squeeze my eyes shut, bringing my hands to my temples and cringing when a sharp pain shoots down my right arm.

Where am I?

And why am I here?

My brain struggles to focus, to make sense of the images wallpapering my mind. Splintered memories scatter behind my closed eyes and I take a deep breath, trying hard to focus.

Little things begin to make sense.

The sunshine. The Little League game.

I remember running. Fast and hard.

To escape.

Almost like I knew what was going to happen...

I try to raise myself up to identify any other clues about where I might be, but my body is sluggish, my limbs lethargic. It isn't cooperating at all with my frenzied mind. Gripping the sides of the leather cushion I'm sprawled out on, I push upward, a woozy feeling crashing over me. Bile rises in the back of my throat and I squeeze my eyes shut, praying for the nausea to pass. I swallow a few deep breaths and that seems to settle my stomach.

But then again, I still don't know why I'm here in the first place or who brought me here.

That realization alone is enough to send my belly back into upheaval.

I shudder against the back of the couch, voices in the hallway getting louder, closer, and more heated.

My ears prick up at their words. They obviously must think I'm still asleep.

One of the voices sounds vaguely familiar, although I can't imagine how I'd know it.

I struggle to hear more.

"…meeting…Sal called…be here in an hour…kill them both…"

I let out a little gasp, fear clutching me. Kill who?

Me?

I try to swing my legs around the side of the couch where I'm lying, but they barely graze the floor. I have to try harder. If they don't know I'm awake, there's a chance I can get away. True, I have no clue where they've taken me, but a chance is a chance and I have to take it.

When I press my feet into the hardwood, my ankles buckle and I fall forward onto my knees, crashing onto the floor. I swallow a scream because the impact hurt like a bitch. My hands fall next to me on the floor and I crawl toward the door, listening against it for any indication that someone is still out there.

Silence.

It's golden in this case.

Dizziness assaults my mind, but I fight through it, knowing the opportunity will pass if I don't take it.

I reach up and twist the knob ever so gently, pulling open the door. It's heavy and I have barely any strength, so I grit my teeth while I work it. I only need a sliver of space to slip through. I puff and pant to create my escape, my heart thumping harder and faster with each passing second. I shimmy through the space, face planting onto the carpet in the hallway and gasping for air after all of the work I've just made my body do.

"You need something? You could've just yelled for us."

I yelp at the voice, rolling onto my side to catch a glimpse of one of my kidnappers, when my heart damn-near stops.

"You?" I croak, my pulse throbbing against my neck. "What the hell is going on, Joe? You just...you just...you kissed me!"

He drops to his knees next to me. "I told you I have a knack of showing up when people least expect me. And my real name isn't Joe."

"Then who are you? Tell me your name," I rasp, barely able to speak. My head is heavy, my mind thick with cobwebs.

He stares at me with those piercing eyes, and even in my thick fog, the familiarity takes hold again. "You don't recognize me, do you?"

"Sorry, I'm a little woozy right now," I snip. "After all, I was fucking drugged and kidnapped!"

He lowers himself next to me, staring intently as I try to focus. "Even after that kiss," he hisses. "You still don't know?"

My pulse throbs against my throat and I desperately try to focus. Who the hell would do this to me? Is he someone my father screwed over? Someone Frankie messed with? What the hell do *I* have to do with any of that?

"Your father tried to crush my family back in Sicily," he growls. "And now your brother is trying to do the same to me."

"Oh my God...*Roman*?" I choke out the name, a mix of fear, anger, and lust clutching me tight. "Roman Villani," I repeat in a strangled whisper. "You fucking asshole! How dare you come anywhere near me! You ruined me. You and your family ruined everything!"

His dark eyebrows furrow but he doesn't respond. Instead, he reaches for me, snaking his arms around my back.

I swat his hands away. "Don't touch me, you bastard! I don't want your hands on me ever again!"

"You're gonna have a hell of a time getting back on that couch," he says in a threatening voice.

"I have no intention of getting back on that couch!" I shriek. "I don't know what kind of sick game you're playing, but I'm leaving! We have nothing to say to each other! And if memory serves, you were too much of a pussy to say anything to me before we got forced out of Sicily!"

Roman rubs the back of his neck. "Yeah, see, that's not how the whole kidnapping thing goes. The way it works is that you stay put or I hurt you. And I really don't want to hurt you, Marchella."

"Fuck you!" I struggle to make my voice as strong as possible even though panic slithers through my insides. "Why would you need to hurt me? Why am I even here? And why the fuck would you come after *me* in the park when you're supposed to be running your illicit criminal businesses?" I pant, my breathing labored. "I don't have anything to do with you, nor do I *want* to have anything to do with you! Ever again!"

"Oh, you have plenty to do with me, *Chella*." My throat tightens at his use of my nickname. "And you have a lot of power right now, not that you know it. But I know it and that's what is important."

My head spins like a top at his words. I can't make any sense of this whole thing. "I hate you!" I scream. "Your family ruined our lives!"

He captures my chin in his hand and holds it tight so I have no ability to turn my head away from him. "Your father ruined your life," he hisses. "We did what we had to do to protect ourselves. I don't know what your piece-of-shit father told you, but he's the one who destroyed everything because he was a greedy bastard. Still is, from what I've seen in the news."

"You don't know what the hell you're talking about!" I screech.

"Don't I?" He glares at me. "You know exactly who and what he is, Marchella. You always did. And you knew Frankie would turn out just like him."

"And look at how things played out," I seethe. "Now you're the scumbag jerkoff who's in the business of destroying lives. I always thought you'd turn out a little more civilized."

"I guess you thought wrong," he grunts.

I roll onto my other side and claw at the wall for leverage, trying desperately to pull my body to a standing position, but as soon as I manage to get part way upright, my knees wobble and I collapse to the ground with a loud thud. I groan, rubbing my ass bone as it slams against the floor, which thankfully, is carpeted.

This time, Roman doesn't ask to help me up.

He scoops me into his arms while mine flail about, punching and scratching him with an energy I thought had been completely drained out of me. Tears sting my eyes as I fight to free myself from his grasp. I fail. Miserably.

I curse, scream, and spit, but nothing makes him flinch.

His jaw is tight, and when he shifts me to kick open the door, my face falls against his chest. And despite myself, I drink in his spicy scent, melting into him as it infuses my being. So dangerous and delicious at the same time. I want to breathe him in forever…and hate myself for even thinking that.

Then my back hits the couch cushions again, and my reality slaps the shit out of me.

I glare up at him. "I want to know why I'm here and why you drugged me! What does Frankie have to do with this? And where is that puppy?"

"You really have no idea what went down the other night, do you?" he says in a harsh voice, pinning me to the leather with his storming blue irises.

How is it possible that only a short time earlier, I'd found myself drifting away into those clear, calm pools of blue?

They're so different now — turbulent and full of rage.

Pure fire.

How the hell didn't I see the person behind that gaze? Was I that scarred by losing who I *thought* was the love of my life that I couldn't recognize him until he shot me with a tranq dart?

And hard as I try, I can't make any sense of this whole thing, including my role.

I grit my teeth. I don't want to give him an inch, but from the sound of things, it seems like I'm the only one behind the eight ball. "Frankie said something about a job," I mumble. "And when I saw him this morning, he was nervous that it might have gone wrong. But then he got a call and all was well again." I shrug, glaring at Roman. "That's all I know!"

"That's all he said, huh?" Roman leans toward me, his breath hot against my face as he seethes his next words. "Let me set you straight right now, Marchella. Your fucking brother robbed my organization of five-hundred grand worth of blow and I want it back. That's why you're here."

I gasp, pulling away. "No, he didn't. Frankie would never do that! You were best friends!" But even as I squeak out those words, the truth settles into my mind. I don't want to believe it, but the look on Roman's face tells me I have no choice. Suddenly, Frankie's avoidance of my questions, his unwillingness to give me straight answers…it all makes sense now. The puzzle pieces are falling together and the completed picture makes my gut knot.

Frankie fucking lied to me, that goddamn jerk! He's the reason why Roman came looking for me and toyed with me in the park! Frankie is the reason why I got snatched! Why I'm about to get—

Oh my God…

Why the hell did he bring me here?

I writhe against Roman, struggling to escape his piercing gaze.

He reaches out, his hand grasping my throat. "Oh, but he did. And it wasn't coincidence that he robbed my club. It was revenge against me and my whole family, and now he's gonna pay," he growls through clenched teeth. "He pulled that job and there's only one reason why he's not dead right now. But that can change very quickly if you don't cooperate, do you understand?" His hand tightens just enough to make me work harder to pull in a quivering breath.

I dig my fingernails into the thick skin of his wrists but he doesn't wince. He just smiles. It's a sinister smile, one that makes every hair on the back of my neck stand on end. Goosebumps shoot up my arms and down my legs as the chill in his gaze settles deep in my bones.

"You can't hurt me, Chella. But rest assured, I will hurt *you* if you pull another stupid stunt like trying to escape," he hisses. His eyes are dark now, dangerous and menacing. I shift against him, wiggling under his muscled chest. He only presses himself farther into me, and fuck me if I don't feel a tingling sensation between my legs.

That traitorous bitch!

I despise this man! How on God's green Earth am I even remotely turned on by having him plastered against me?

I narrow my eyes at him, watching as the anger in his volatile gaze battles with another emotion…lust. My breath hitches and he evidently realizes it too because he lets go of me, pulling away. His face is a mess of conflicting expressions, and he looks exactly the way I feel right now.

My hands fly up to my neck and I slide away from him, using my feet to propel me as far away as I can get. "What are you going to do to me?" I yelp.

"If you behave, nothing," he grunts, getting off the couch and turning his back on me.

"W-what about Frankie?" I ask, my voice barely louder than a whisper.

Roman folds his arms over his chest and lets out a deep sigh. "He will have one chance to make things right."

"What if he can't?" I ask, my throat tight, a gaggle of panicked tears in the back of my throat.

Roman turns to look at me, his eyes icy, piercing my heart as he speaks his next words. "Then someone dies."

Chapter Nine
ROMAN

That fucking bastard!

Frankie did this! He put me in the position where I need to hurt him by hurting his sister!

It was stupid to go after her in the park like that, to toy with her, and to torture *myself*!

Frankie Amante humiliated me, did the same thing to me that his old man did to mine! He challenged my ability to lead and pulled the rug right out from under me, making me look like a fucking incompetent idiot in front of the men whom I'm supposed to manage. Those are the men who need to respect me, the ones who need to fear me, dammit!

Now when they look at me all they'll remember is how Frankie pulled one over on me, how he was able to infiltrate my kingdom, how I am responsible for him getting away with all of that coke.

I basically invited our enemies inside and let them ravage my fucking home!

And if Matteo hears about this before I have a chance to tell him…Jesus.

It'll be a goddamn bloodbath because of our history with the Amantes.

I rub the back of my neck, walking over to my desk and sinking into the chair.

"What does he need to do, Roman? How can he fix this?"

Marchella's voice ripples through me in a way that has me doubting my ability to restrain myself since every time she speaks, every time she parts her lips and stares at me intently with those soul-piercing eyes, the urge to fuck her senseless grabs hold — just like it did in the park.

Talk about a serious conflict of interest.

And I still need to figure out what the hell to do about Frankie.

I haven't had much time to think since I've basically been running from one maiming to the next since I left the Grammercy Tap Room the night before. Doesn't leave a whole lot of time for planning my next move.

And now that I have her here…now that my leverage is lying on a couch in my office, fearful that I'm about to end not only her life, but Frankie's, all I can think about is burying my head between her legs and feasting on her soft pussy.

Which is exactly what I wanted to do from the second I knocked into her at the bar last night.

Fuck! I need to concentrate on more than just getting off right now!

I can't keep avoiding her question. She's rolled onto her side, her long ponytail snaking over her shoulder as she stares at me, an unspoken plea for mercy in her gaze. "He gets one shot," I grunt, shoving back the chair and standing straight up. My mouth twists as I send the chair crashing into the desk.

"And what will you do with me in the meantime?" she asks. I can tell she's trying to keep her voice even and strong, but I hear the waver she tries desperately to hide. And I get it. I'm a brutal killer and I shot her with a tranquilizer gun so I could kidnap her and possibly murder her.

If I were her, I'd be shitting a brick, too.

But there's already been too much blood spilled. My family name can't be stained with any more, not on my watch.

I need to assert my control in another way and Marchella is going to help me.

And her question ignites fierce flames of desire deep inside of me because while there are endless possibilities for what I'd like to do with her in the meantime, I can't give into a single one of them. My priority is getting the organization back on track after that ambush, not obsessing about a hot piece of ass who just so happens to be lying on my couch in tight black Spandex.

My cell phone pings, and I pull it out of my pocket, peering at the screen. My eyes burn from lack of sleep and I blink fast to clear my vision.

Where the fuck are you?

Dante. That's his way of expressing concern.

I send a reply. *Still at the office. Don't wait on me for dinner.*

You work too hard. And you need to eat.

I roll my eyes. Food. There's a luxury I can't seem to squeeze into my day.

Order extra pizza. I'll have some later.

In a few seconds, he sends a reply.

Okay. And bring home some Jack Daniel's. You're out.

Freaking lush drank me dry already?

I shove my phone back into my pocket. When I finally do get home tonight, there will definitely be a lot to explain to my brother. He comes to New York to escape his own slice of hell, and now I'm about to plunge him into a different one.

None of us could escape the shit show that choked us in Sicily, and my whole family still carries that hate for the Amante family even though we came out on top.

A strangled sob jolts me from my inner turmoil and I look over at the couch. Chella's eyes are closed, but I can see a single tear slip down one flushed cheek. "I told him to find legitimate work, something that would keep him out of trouble. But he didn't listen. He said he could make good money, that we would be taken care of." Her eyes float open and she slowly sits up, gripping the arm of the couch for balance. A dejected expression shadows her face as she pins me with her rage-filled gaze. "That was always *my* plan. To take care of us, since my father gave up on that responsibility a long time ago."

Jesus Christ, when did this turn into a therapy session? Do I look like a goddamn shrink?

But I remain silent, letting her continue her tirade since I need time to process all of this shit anyway.

"Mama was gone so everything fell on me. And that was fine!" she says, her voice shaking. "I didn't mind because I had goals for myself and my life! I was going places!" She digs her fingertips into the leather, her knuckles turning white. "I had a plan,

Roman. A fucking life and it was finally headed in the right direction! I worked goddamn hard for it, too. And then everything went up in smoke."

"Wait, what about your mother?" I ask.

Chella's face darkens. "She died six months ago. Cancer."

I swallow hard. Fuck. "I didn't know," I mutter. "I'm sorry."

"It devastated me. All of us. And everything unraveled like a cheap rug once she passed." Chella moves to the edge of the couch, pushing herself off of it and rising to her feet on wobbly legs. "I'm so tired…of feeling…helpless and alone!" she rasps. "Tired of working…my ass off at some dead-end job, living paycheck to paycheck…to pay off our family's debts and medical bills and not able to enjoy…a single fucking penny of my hard work!" She inches toward me, grabbing onto everything she can to keep her from crumbling onto the floor in front of me. "And just when I thought things couldn't get worse, I get fucking sexually assaulted in the park by my childhood crush, and then kidnapped by him because my idiot brother can't keep his hands to himself! Because he's always looking for an easy way out, but there isn't one! Not for us!" she screams, seeming to use every last bit of strength in her to force out those words. Her chest heaves harder with each labored breath as she sways into a chair. "Things were so perfect in Sicily. So much…hope. And then it went up in smoke. And you didn't stop it…or me. I…hate…you!" Tears spring to her eyes once again as she takes her final step toward me. And just as she swings her fist out to hit me, her legs give out and she collapses against my chest, wilting in my arms like a dying flower.

For a split second, she's quiet, save for the soft whimpers slipping from her mouth.

"I really hate you," she mumbles with a sniffle. She tries to push away from me, but I keep my grip around her waist tight, knowing she'll crumble to the floor if I let go. "I hate everything you stand for, the way you hurt innocent people, the way you try to make them fear you. You turned into your father. I saw it happen when you chose your family over me years ago. You never cared about me. You only cared about making your family happy. You're evil and vicious, just like them, and you don't give a damn about anything but money and power." she says, the tears now streaming down her cheeks.

"I'm just trying to do my job, Chella. If people cross me, they get punished. That's how this works. Your brother fucked me over, plain and simple, and now he needs to deal with the consequences. Our past doesn't factor in. This is about me and Frankie. It has nothing to do with my family or what happened in Sicily."

"He was desperate," she says, her voice pleading. "He was just trying to do the right thing for us."

"And in doing the right thing for you, he screwed me pretty damn hard. Caused a lot of problems for my organization that I need to fix. He created a huge goddamn mess, Chella. A big one. If he wants to keep you alive, he's gonna have to figure out how to clean it up. Fast."

Her puffy, red-rimmed eyes make my throat tighten and my resolve falters.

She doesn't deserve this. She didn't make the asshole decision to dick me over, Frankie did.

He's the one who needs to suffer, not her.

And hearing her tell me that she hates me…that stings. Yeah, I let her go because what the hell choice did I have? Was I supposed to run off with her at eighteen and get cut off by my family?

Family always comes first.

Always.

I hated like hell to see her go, but I had no choice.

And I never stopped loving her either.

Clearly, she doesn't carry the same torch for me.

As I stare down at her, overdosing on her raw beauty and vulnerability, I realize what I need to do…how I can make things right for everyone involved.

Frankie will pay, but so will I.

Chapter Ten
MARCHELLA

So much suffering. When the fuck will it ever end?

Roman helps me settle back onto the couch but I shove him away. I don't need his help. I need his mercy.

But everything he just said confirms one thing.

He's still my enemy.

My head falls into my hands, the sobs exploding from my chest.

I hate that I'm crumbling in front of this man. I hate that I'm so emotionally broken that I'm allowing myself to lose my shit in front of someone I loved to the ends of the Earth who has just basically threatened to kill me and my brother if he doesn't get what he wants.

Because the truth is, while my situation is dismal at best, I still manage to pop out of bed in the morning. I still have some shreds of positivity left in me. I still have hope, dammit!

But everyone has their breaking point, I guess.

And since I'm already fractured, I guess it was only a matter of time before I cracked open completely.

God, what I wouldn't do to feel my mother's arms around me, to hear her soothing and syrupy-sweet voice whisper that everything will be okay…that this, too, shall pass.

I have clung to that saying for the better part of the last year and you know what?

Shit's only gotten worse! Nothing has gotten better!

Case in point, I'm sitting on a couch in my captor's office awaiting a sentence of his choosing because Sticky Fingers Amante couldn't get a real goddamn job!

"I'm sorry your brother put you in this situation," he grumbles.

"And I'm sorry you're such a fucking insolent and controlling asshole who assaulted me, drugged me, and dragged me away from something that actually needed my help! Did you even care that I was trying to save that stray dog? Was it even a thought? She needed me, but did you care, you selfish bastard?" I know I'm rambling now, but I can't stop the anger flowing out of me.

I wished to have my mother's arms around me, but I'm convinced that when I found Bella, I had a little piece of Mama in my grasp before they tore it away from me.

I drag my hands down the front of my face, sniffling loudly. I'm crumbling like a freaking house of cards right now and I don't really think I can stop it.

Maybe it's a good thing. Maybe he'll think I'm completely nuts and let me go because keeping me would be more trouble than it's worth.

Since nuts are prone to cracking.

Roman's jaw tightens and his fists clench tight at his sides.

"Are you going to hit me now?" I hiss. "Haven't you done enough to me already?"

In a flash, his fist whips past me and crashes against the wall, putting a dent in the sheetrock.

My mouth drops open. "You're a sick bastard."

He turns his fiery glare at me, his eyes shooting white flames. "I didn't hit you, did I?'

"You've clearly got a lot of pent-up rage," I mutter.

"Who says it's pent-up?" he growls, shaking out his hand. The impact must have done some damage, although he doesn't give any indication that he's in pain.

I guess he's just so used to causing it that *feeling* it doesn't quite register.

"Lucky guess." I narrow my eyes at him. "Tough guy got taken, so now he needs to prove he still has a dick swinging between his legs, right?"

When he launches himself at me, I am completely caught off-guard.

"Don't make assumptions, Chella," he snarls, yanking my ponytail so that my head is tilted toward his, giving him the upper hand. "You don't know shit about me anymore. And you don't have the right to judge what you don't understand."

"What I understand," I sputter. "Is that you have no regard for anything but yourself and your reputation. That's why I'm here. And that's why you're gonna snatch Frankie. You need to make examples of us to show your thug peons what happens when the great Roman Villani gets a dose of his own medicine. Tell me," I seethe through clenched teeth. "How many times did you pull a scam on someone you worked for to get ahead, huh? How many times did you fuck over someone else to get yours?"

He pulls my head back farther, his lips hovering over mine. "How many times isn't the question you should be asking."

"Oh, yeah? Well, then, enlighten me. What's the right question?"

"The right question is did I ever get caught? And the answer…" he says in a low, gruff voice. "Is *no*."

I swallow hard. His forehead is pressed against mine, his powerful body plastered against mine as the heat in his gaze snakes through my insides, charging me up like I've just stuck my finger into an electrical socket.

"Do you know why?" he continues, his eyes shooting white hot flames. They're dark and clouded now, filled with a twisted mix of emotion that I can't even begin to process.

I grit my teeth, not backing away. Fuck him if he thinks I'll cower!

"Because I was—"

"Boss!" A deep male voice calls out from the other side of the door. "They're here."

Roman hovers over me for a few final seconds, his nostrils flared. It's almost like we're playing a twisted game of Chicken.

"I don't give a damn why, by the way," I hiss. "You might be great at your job, but you're a piece-of-shit mobster who has zero decency or morals."

"I don't need either," he seethes. "Because I have something more valuable. Power."

"You have nothing!" I screech, hurling my hand at his smug expression.

He catches my hand in mid-air...fucking again! I really need to work on my timing.

"Wrong," he grunts. "I have *you*, Marchella."

"You're no better than Frankie or my father!"

And with that, he backs away with a grim expression on his face, smoothing down the front of his t-shirt. But he doesn't say another word. I drag my eyes away from his bulging biceps. The fabric stretches tight over his broad chest, and I can see his pecs ripple as he moves toward the door. I swallow hard.

He kidnapped me and pretty much threatened death and yet, here I am, admiring his ripped muscles?!

Jesus, I really am a headcase.

Roman pulls open the door and moves aside as Frankie pitches forward onto the floor at his feet. His face is bruised and bloody, and the front of his shirt is stained bright red. A loud groan escapes his lips as he moves into a fetal position, clutching his midsection.

"Frankie!" I scream, adrenaline flooding my veins with an energy that I was certain had been zapped from my body. But that fight-or-flight instinct kicks in and I dart over to him, collapsing on the floor and covering his body with mine. My gut twists at the sight of all the blood, but I hold him tight and somehow manage to hold myself together.

"What did they do to you?" I weep, my face pressed against his arm.

One of Roman's guys yanks me away from Frankie and shoves me back onto the couch. I land with a gasp, twisting around toward Roman. A glimmer of fury in his expression morphs into a raging inferno, and he grabs the guy by the jacket and slams him against the wall. The pictures hanging on either side of him crash to the floor, shattering on the hardwood.

"Don't you fucking lay a hand on her unless I tell you to!" he roars, letting go of the guy and then slamming his head against the wall a second time, I guess to make sure he really drove his point home.

Well, that was somewhat chivalrous in a sick sort of way.

The guy groans, rubbing the back of his head. He mutters an apology and backs away as the other guy with him stands still with a stoic expression on his worn face.

Smart. I'd stay still, too.

Roman kneels down next to Frankie who is still crying into the floorboards. He pulls off his baseball cap and fists his hair, yanking his head off the floor. "Frankie," he says in a low, menacing growl. "Do you know why you're here?"

"Yes," he wails, still holding his midsection. "And I'm s-sorry, Roman!"

"Sorry for what, exactly? For stealing from me? For fucking me over? Or for getting caught? Which is it, Frankie?"

"For all of it!" he groans. "I needed the money and it wasn't coming fast enough. So when Sal came to me with the job, I figured it could help. I didn't know we were gonna hit your stash."

Roman punches him in the jaw, and I yelp.

"Stop that! Can't you see he's already hurting?" I scream.

But he just ignores me, pulling Frankie's head closer to his mouth. "You're a fucking liar! Your friend Sal sold you out. He told me the job was your fucking idea!" A vein in his neck twitches. "You knew exactly what you were doing, who you were doing it to, and you were banking on me not finding out, you cocksucker." He lets go of Frankie's hair and his head drops to the floor like a rock. "Did you really think I was gonna let it go? I'm not my father. I do things *my* way! I'm not gonna run you outta Manhattan. I'm gonna run you into the core of the fucking planet!"

I cover my mouth with my hand, tears streaming down my face. I have to do something! I can't just sit here while they kill him! "Please don't hurt him!" I plead. "Give him a chance to make this right. You said you would. He's not a bad person. He was just desperate to do something to help us." I turn my eyes to Roman. "Don't you understand that? Haven't you ever felt that before, that you just need a chance to prove yourself?"

Roman walks over to the couch, falling to his knees in front of me. He cups my face with his rough hands, bringing it close to his own, searing my insides with those molten eyes. "Don't challenge me," he rasps. "Or my decisions. Otherwise, you will be punished."

"I'm willing to do whatever it takes to protect my brother from you," I say, my voice quivering. "He did a stupid thing, but he doesn't deserve to die."

The electricity sizzling between us is so intense, my nerves are on the brink of short-circuiting, maybe for good.

But still I hold my ground. Frankie is an idiot. He knows better, yes, but look at the role model he had! It's up to me to help him out of this mess.

If Roman will let me.

"Okay, then." His voice is rough and gravelly and I find myself longing for his strong hands on my prickled skin.

"Okay, then...what?" I ask, my mind glitching as I stare into his stormy gaze.

"I said one chance, yeah?" he grunts. "Here it is. Frankie gets my drugs and I keep you until he finds them."

"Keep me?" I repeat. "What the hell are you—?"

"Listen, Chella. If I let you both go now, he'd take you and flee the city."

I swallow hard. Shit.

"So to keep him on task, I'm keeping *you*. You'll stay with me until he gets back what he stole." He turns to Frankie, whose black and blue eyes are almost swollen shut. His body shudders as Roman approaches him on the floor and he rolls onto his side to protect his busted-up midsection. "You're going to go back to the assholes you worked with and steal it back."

"But...but I can't! They'll never let me have the drugs back!" Frankie sputters. "And I don't even know how to find them! They came to me!"

"Well, those are big problems, aren't they?" Roman hisses. "Looks like you've got a lot of work to do, especially if you don't want to end up like your friend, Sal, who's recently been sunk to the bottom of the goddamn Hudson River!"

I gasp. "If he tries to steal the coke from them, they might kill him!"

Roman turns slowly, regarding me with his penetrating gaze. "I guess he's gonna have to come up with a stellar plan, Marchella. That is, if he doesn't want you to be plunged into a watery grave just like his pal, Salvatore."

My throat tightens. "You're a fucking monster!"

He doesn't respond right away, but his lips pull into a tight line, his face a mess of anger, regret, and disgust. "I am," he growls. "And you'd be smart not to test me." He nods toward Frankie again. "You have one week. I want my drugs or the cash equivalent, and I want the fuckers who thought it was a smart idea to take it from me. You deliver on all that, you get your sister back. You try to fucking cross me again, and I'll tie you to a chair to watch me violate her before putting a bullet between her eyes. Then, once *you* think you've suffered enough, I'll make sure you suffer even more before I plunge a knife into your skull. You'll beg and plead for death by the time I'm done with you."

Frankie struggles to his feet. "Don't you fucking lay a hand on her!" he bellows with as much strength as he can muster.

Roman grabs him by the shirt collar to hold him back. "Then do your fucking job, dick. Otherwise, death will be the least of your concerns." He eyes one of his guys. "Get him the hell out of here." He lets go of Frankie and gives him a smack on the cheek. "Don't get any ideas, Frankie. I'll be watching. If you make any moves, you know exactly what I'll do."

"Fuck you, Roman!" he yells.

"Frankie, stop!" I scream. "Just do what he says and stop—"

But I don't even have time to finish my thought before Roman punches him, sending Frankie flying to the floor again, clutching his already-shattered jaw. "I don't appreciate the tough-guy act. And if you try it again, I'll make sure you go home with every finger broken."

I watch as Roman's guys drag Frankie out of the office, leaving a trail of his blood behind him. Bile rises in the back of my throat, making me gag. I know the dark red streaks are just the beginning. There will be puddles if Frankie doesn't deliver to this madman.

When he walks toward me, my spine stiffens. How could I ever have felt anything but disgust and disdain for this man? My God, could I be a worse judge of character? He is a savage and sadistic pig, for fuck's sake! And I let him kiss me!

"What if he can't meet your demands?" I ask. "If he doesn't know how to find those people, how can he find your drugs? He was your best friend! How can you do this to him…to me?"

I see a flicker of remorse in his eyes before they ice over once again. "Frankie is a resourceful kid. They found him once. I guarantee they'll find him again," he says gruffly.

"But you only gave him one week! What if—?"

"People in my line of work don't sit around on their asses planning their next big moves. They strike while the iron is hot. And this time, it's fucking scorching. If they think they found a weakness, they'll come back to hit it again." He narrows his eyes at me as he approaches.

"Don't you come near me, you sonofabitch," I say through clenched teeth. "He's all I have left, and if you try to hurt him again—"

"What are you gonna do?" he murmurs, backing me against the couch cushion. "Huh? Are you gonna hit me? Stab me? Kill me?"

"I'll do worse," I say, my voice quivering. "I promise you that!"

"Good." He nods. "Then I'll have something to look forward to."

Chapter Eleven
ROMAN

I pull up to my building about half an hour later, stabbing the security code into the keypad of my private parking garage. The engine of my Bentley hums as we wait for the gate to lift. When it finally does, I slowly drive into the darkened space, pulling around the side to my regular spot. I shut off the ignition and turn to look at Marchella. She's still stewing, but at least she's smart enough to know that if she wants to keep her brother alive, she needs to cooperate with me.

I want to tell her not to worry, that I have no intentions of killing her or Frankie. But as long as the threat hangs over her head, she's under my control. And right now, that's where she needs to stay.

I get out of the car and walk around to open her door, but before I can grab the handle, she opens it herself, shoving the door into me. I jump back but not in enough time and she swings the door into my gut.

"Oh, I'm sorry," she says in the fakest sweet voice I've ever heard. "I didn't realize chivalry is still alive and well in your domain."

"Don't press my buttons, Marchella," I seethe, pushing her against the door. My head gets a little fuzzy at her nearness, her sweet scent intoxicating me even as repressed anger bubbles in my veins. She's always had that spark inside of her. I guess recent events have really made them ignite, and fuck me if I'm not turned on by the woman she's become. "You won't like what happens if you do."

She tilts her head to the side. "Well, let's see. You've already stalked me, kidnapped me, drugged me, and threatened my life. What's left? And let's be real. You aren't going to kill me…yet, anyway. You need me alive to make sure Frankie delivers, right? I'm the incentive." Her eyes shoot white-hot flames. "So guess what? I'm going to push, push, push — harder and faster than you ever thought possible," she seethes, trying to sidestep me. "I'm not the same girl you remember, Roman. Never forget that."

I grab her wrist, yanking her back so she's forced to look at me. "Let's get something straight. You're here because your brother fucked up. And until he makes things right, you'll stay here, next to me, under me, on top of me…any which way I want, understand? You're fucking mine until I say you're not."

My pulse throbs as her gaze becomes decidedly more murderous, although I'm pleased to see a bit of shock settle into her expression as well. I want to keep her on her toes. I want her to wonder what I'll do next.

"Let's get another thing straight. The only way you'd ever have me on top of you is if I was about to impale your heart with a steak knife. And the only way I'd ever be under you is if I was comatose or dead."

"I like a challenge," I growl, breathing her in, letting her rage infuse me. As if I need any more of it. "Game fucking on."

I move away, letting her stomp away from me. I have to forcibly drag my eyes away from her Spandex-covered ass as it swings left and right while she stalks toward the only door visible. It leads to my private elevator. This is bad news…bringing her here, having her so close to me. I follow behind her, sticking my key into the door as she stands next to it, her hands over her chest.

I lead her toward the elevator and stick my key into the lock next to it. Lots of security is required in my line of work. When you blank out on safety precautions, shit goes sideways and you end up being robbed of five-hundred grand worth of blow.

Cue the fucking irony of that one.

The elevator door slides open and she just stands there, staring straight ahead, as if getting in will mean she concedes to this whole thing. The reality is, she conceded once she got into my car. Resisting now is kind of futile.

"You getting in or what?" I say after a few seconds. My patience is wearing thin, and I have a lot of shit to deal with once we get upstairs.

She clutches the sides of the elevator, her shoulders quaking. I furrow my brow, knowing that the alarm will sound unless the doors are allowed to close.

"I c-can't," she rasps.

"Look," I sigh. "I already told you, play your cards right and all of this will be over before—"

She shakes her head. "No," she whispers.

"Unless you try to fuck with me—"

"No!" she thunders. "No fucking elevator!"

I lift an eyebrow. "You got a problem with elevators?"

Marchella turns to look at me, her face pale, her eyes swirling with sadness. "Yes." She pushes past me. "Now, where are the stairs?"

I fist the sides of my head, following her as she walks deeper into the basement parking garage, pulling open another door. I can see her shoulders relax when she's greeted by the cement stairs. All five flights of them.

By the time we get to the top, I'm out of breath and sweat trickles down my spine, making my t-shirt cling to me like Saran Wrap. I collapse against the door and stick my key into the lock. I own the whole building, and the other apartments are about to undergo some serious renovations when I combine all of the floors into one, five-story living space. But for now, I'm staying on the top levels.

With Dante.

I silence a groan, twisting the knob and pushing open the door. I'd better come up with a way to spin this to him and fast.

Marchella turns a critical eye at me. "You really need to build up your stamina."

"Are you offering to help with that?" I rasp, my heart still beating hard and fast against my chest from the impromptu exertion.

She flips me off and walks into the apartment, stopping short in the foyer.

It's pretty damn impressive, if I say so myself. Not that I had much to do with the décor. I paid a very expensive decorator to handle all of that. It's an open floor plan without doors. Sunlight streams into the space through the large windows that line the perimeter of the apartment. There are two floors in my apartment, the top accessible by a set of tempered glass stairs in the center of the living area. Stainless steel railings glimmer in the dusky light, and polished porcelain tile floors bring a touch of modern glamour to the space.

At least, that's what the decorator told me when she presented me with the hefty bill for her services.

The entire place is painted, white which makes it look even grander than it is. And carefully curated pieces of abstract art in bold colors are strategically placed to offer pops of color and brightness. And the view?

Fucking outstanding.

I've got every high-end piece of electronic equipment, a gym, and a top-of-the-line Viking kitchen that would give celebrity chef and personal friend of mine, Tommy Marcone, a hard-on.

Everything.

None of it makes me happy, though. Not when I know one wrong move can shatter my perfect and expensive-as-hell bubble.

People think this stuff gives them legitimacy. I guess I did, too, when Matteo first put me in charge. I figured I needed all of the components to really be the part I wanted to play. As time went on, I realized how fast the rug can be pulled out from under you, and material things don't do shit to cushion a steep fall from the top of the food chain.

You'll just crash...hard.

And the possessions won't do you a damn bit of good if you're in traction.

Or dead.

People may be impressed by all of this, but to me? It's just more to lose, more hanging in the balance, more of a noose around my neck.

More pressure to not fuck up, worse than I already have, that is.

A sharp pain shoots down my arm from the stress.

How fast your life can go from being great to being hell.

Speaking of hell, I'm sure Matteo will be calling at some point and he's gonna want an update on his organization, the one I've just shrunk down by about five-hundred grand.

"So, this is my gilded cage for the foreseeable future, huh?" Marchella says, stepping into the apartment, her sneakers squeaking on the floor. "Or are you going to keep me locked up in some dungeon?"

I toss my keys onto a nearby table and wave a hand around. "You see any doors?"

She folds her arms over her chest. "I'd say you have great taste, but I'm pretty sure it's not your taste I'd be complimenting."

I shrug, leaning against the stairway. "I'm not offended. I know the skills I bring to the table, and interior design ain't one of them."

"Yeah, that's right," she says darkly. "I believe murder and kidnapping are two of those said skills."

"Whoa, those are some harsh words." Dante struts into the foyer with only a towel wrapped around his waist. He nods at

Marchella. "Who put the rusty nails in her Cheerios this morning?"

I roll my eyes at my brother. "You couldn't have put on pants, Dante?"

"You're lucky I have on this towel. I prefer to be free as the day I was born, but I wouldn't want to offend your guest...or make her jealous." He gives a long, appraising look at Marchella, and the skin on the back of my neck prickles.

"I'm not a guest," she hisses, although it takes her a second to respond since she's focused on Dante's pecs. A little too focused for my liking, actually. "Your brother here kidnapped me. And if memory serves, we're old family friends."

Dante gives Marchella a long look and lets out a whistle before raising his eyebrows at me. "Damn, Romo. Looks like you left out a few details on the phone last night. You that hard up for a date that you had to kidnap your old girlfriend?"

"Fuck off," I huff, raking a hand through my hair. "This isn't social."

"That's an understatement if I ever heard one," she mutters.

Dante looks between us and finally his eyes settle on me. "Sounds like there's a story here. I could use a drink, but oh, shit. You didn't bring me the Jack I ordered."

"Sorry, I didn't realize laying low was a requirement when you're on vacation," I snap. "You've got legs and cash, yeah? Couldn't you have DoorDash'd that shit?"

"Ouch, some host you are," Dante grumbles at me. He grins at Marchella. "I can see why you're a little prickly about him. He's become kind of an acquired taste, you know? Like sushi."

Her eyes widen. "Actually, he's more like a fucking lethal poison, the kind that paralyzes you and slowly and tormentingly kills you, shutting down one organ at a time as it infests your body."

"Wow, that's…graphic," Dante says, nudging me. "You hear that, Romo? She's definitely not your biggest fan *anymore*. You're gonna have to do lot of work to get her on her back, bro."

"He's not getting me on my back!" Marchella yells, her fists clenched. "He's not getting anything from me except a fucking right hook if he dares to come too close! He's a slimy, derelict thug bastard who drugged me, beat up my brother, and kidnapped me! And the only reason I'm here right now, the only reason why I haven't clawed out his eyes with my fingernails, is because of Frankie." She turns to me, her chest heaving. "Trust me, though, *Romo*. I am fucking stabbing you with a hot poker in my mind right now!"

Dante turns to me with an eyebrow lifted. "What the fuck does Frankie have to do with this?"

"Long story."

Dante looks between us. "I've got time." He walks over to the bar. He pulls a bottle of tequila off of one of the shelves and pours three highball glasses of the clear liquid. "Since you have no more Jack," he says with a pointed look at me.

"Next time you invade my space, I'll make sure I have a fucking case," I grumble, turning the glass away when he tries to hand it to me.

Marchella takes hers, though. She tilts her head back and gulps it down before Dante has a chance to raise his to his lips. Then she grabs my shot and guzzles that one, too. Her face contorts as the liquid fights a path down her throat. She then holds up her empty glass, pointing it at me. "He had one of his goons shoot me with a freaking tranquilizer gun!"

Dante pours her another shot and she drinks it down, her lips twisting yet again. I can tell Dante is enjoying this little show, especially since he's not the one in the line of fire. He smirks at me, leaning against the bar, still in his fucking towel. "I'm waiting for more. I have a feeling this is gonna get good."

"Do you know what he had the nerve to do before shooting me on the street while I was trying to help a tiny little stray dog?" she says, a little slur lacing her words since she probably has nothing in her stomach at all. She walks toward me, holding out her glass and pointing. "This sick bastard stalked me in the park and sexually assaulted me! In public!"

"Tsk-tsk, Romo," Dante says with a shake of his head. "Have I taught you nothing?"

"Oh, for Christ's sake! I didn't assault her! I kissed her!" I focus my glare on Marchella's now-flushed face. "And if I recall, you loved it! It's not assault if you were begging for it!"

"*What?*" she shrieks. "Don't flatter yourself, dick! I didn't beg for any of that! You saw me and took advantage of the situation! I should have dumped that whole bottle of scotch on your lap last night at the restaurant!"

I stomp toward her, my jaw twitching because I have so many more words to hurl at her, but more than yelling, I want to pin her against the wall and run my hands down the sides of her trim torso. I want to feel her body plastered against me, her lips crushed against mine.

Again and again.

Luckily, before I can act on any of it, my phone vibrates in my pocket. I pull it out to see Matteo's name flash across the screen. I can't send him to voicemail again, so I stab the Accept button.

"Romo, what's going on? I tried calling you before. Why didn't you call me back?"

I rub the back of my head "I, ah, was in the middle of a meeting. I was gonna get back to you tonight. How's Heaven?"

My sister-in-law, Heaven, is about eight months' pregnant right now, and from the looks of her, ready to pop any day. That's the reason why they decided to stay in Vegas for a while longer. She hasn't been able to fly, and they have a pretty posh setup at our family's hotel, The Excelsior. Matteo is using the time to his advantage, working hard to expand our businesses out West along with a few other mafia families of Red Ladro, the syndicate we formed a little over a year ago.

"She's good. Crankier than usual."

"Keep her away from her gun," I say with a snicker. Heaven is famous for her red-hot Irish temper and has been known to let off steam by firing off a few rounds whenever she gets the urge. She's controlled herself throughout the pregnancy, but it sounds like she might just snap like a rubber band, and it's only exacerbated by the fact that she can't down whiskey right now either. "But keep your fridge stocked with those chocolate tarts she loves so much from Bouchon Bakery."

"I know. She can eat her weight in those damn things." He chuckles for a second. "How's everything going with the clubs? You haven't had any issues with the suppliers, have you?"

I let out a small sigh of relief. He obviously isn't plugged into what's been happening out here.

Looks like my actions against Salvatore, Dario, and Frankie—rash and vicious as they may have been—gave my crew the jolt they needed and resurrected some respect for me and my role. Maybe there is something to be said for using brute force to command respect.

"No issues," I say because there was no issue with the suppliers. They brought exactly what we agreed upon. The issue is with the bastards who are still faceless and nameless until I can get my pal Frankie to sell them out.

But what Matteo doesn't know won't hurt him. It may kill *me*, but that's not for him to worry about. It's for me to fix.

"Good. I was afraid I'd have to crack some skulls. I know I've been gone for a lot longer than I originally said, but it's been good to build relationships out here. And I know you've got things covered in the city."

"Yeah," I say, my throat tight.

"By the way, there is another reason for my call. There's an event tomorrow night and I need you to go in my place. It's some charity ball sponsored by a bunch of stuffy politicians who we need to keep in our back pockets. It'll be good for you to get out there and network. I know you've spent a lot of time behind the scenes, but it's time to get you out and rubbing elbows, you know?"

I nod. "Yeah, sure."

"I'll text you all the details. You think you can find a date between now and then?"

My eyes unconsciously flicker over toward Marchella, who is about to shoot another finger of tequila. Jesus, I need to get some food in her or she'll be hanging over my railing, puking her guts up within the hour.

"Never had a problem finding one before."

Matteo snickers. "No, you haven't. Okay, I'll talk to you in the next couple of days."

"Sure," I croak, clicking off the phone.

"Doesn't sound like you gave him the scoop," Dante quips.

"He was preoccupied with Heaven," I mumble.

"And what have you never had a problem finding before?" Dante asks.

"Christ, man. Do you have to eavesdrop like a fucking spy all the time? Do you ever just tune shit out?"

"Nah, not when it gets your dick in a twist like this." He grins. "So. What does he have you doing for him this time?"

"He wants me to go to some charity event tomorrow night. He asked if I could find a date."

"Ah," Dante says with a nod. "So, kidnapping with a purpose. Nice."

Marchella narrows her slightly drunken eyes at me. "Are you thinking that I'll go with you to this thing?" she screeches. "Because, oh hell fucking no to that!"

"You don't have a choice," I growl.

"Really?" she snaps. "Then you're gonna have to shoot me with another dart to get me anywhere near that event!"

"That can be arranged," I say darkly.

"Why in the world would I ever do you any favors? You're holding me captive! What kind of sick and twisted person would even think it's okay to ask me to go? I mean, hello! I'm your fucking hostage! Taking me out in public isn't an ideal scenario."

"She does have a point," Dante says. "It is a little weird. She's not your employee, she's your ex-girlfriend."

"Stop saying that! Whose fucking side are you on?" I yell.

"Well, to be honest, I don't know. You show up here with the chick you pined for back in Sicily who claims you beat the shit out of her brother, your former best friend, and kidnapped her. That to me screams a little hard up for some female companionship, but hey, I don't judge."

I clench my fists tight, my pulse throbbing against my neck.

"Yeah, why don't you tell him the whole sordid story?" Marchella seethes. "Let him judge for himself!"

"Salvatore Giaconne and Frankie Amante robbed us last night," I grunt. "Worked with a crew to ambush us. They got away with five hundo worth of blow." I jerk my head toward Marchella. "My ex-best friend fucked us up the ass just like his father did to Pop back in Sicily. The grape doesn't fall far from the vine." I glare at Dante. "So, yeah, I took her as leverage while Frankie gets our drugs back."

"Damn," Dante mutters.

And he doesn't know the half of it, the rest of the blood staining me from head to toe. The hairs on my arms prickle as I crack my knuckles one finger at a time, a throbbing sensation between my temples making my head ache.

Dante looks at Marchella. "Your brother was always an asshat."

"S-screw you! Your family is a bunch of scumbag pigs!" Marchella staggers over to the couch and leans against it. "But whatever. So now you have me and I can't work so I'm just going to s-sink further into debt. I'll probably lose my job, the only job I could even get after everything hit the fan with Papa…"

She keeps rambling and I don't know what any of it means, but one thing sticks.

She's my bargaining chip, yeah. But she didn't have anything to do with the stunt her brother pulled. And she didn't have anything to do with what her father pulled years back. She's been the one to suffer through all of it. I don't want to fuck her for his bad judgment.

I mean, yeah, I wanna fuck her, but not that way.

I rub the knot forming at the base of my skull. "Just stop talking, okay? You're giving me more of a goddamn headache right now." A frustrated sigh slips from my lips. "Dante is right. I should pay you if I want you to come with me." I can see his eyes widen and he probably thinks I'm off my nut, but I keep going. "I'll pay you for your lost work time, okay? In return, you come to this event with me." I walk to the couch. "You be the perfect date and I'll make sure you have the money you need for your bills."

"Oh, so what is this-s, *Pretty Woman* with a little gangster twist?" she mumbles. "I'm not gonna screw you, Romo. And I don't kiss on the mouth."

"Yeah, well, that ship's kinda sailed."

She leans back against the couch, rolling over the top of it and landing face-first into the seat cushion with a little yelp. "You lost my puppy. My Bella," she murmurs. "Jerk."

I peer over the top of the couch and sure enough, she's passed out in what seems like seconds.

"Cheap date," Dante says. "You sure know how to pick 'em, bro."

"Tell me about it," I groan.

"What'd you do to her puppy?"

I roll my eyes. "That's the only question you have for me?"

"We can start there." Dante saunters over to another couch and sinks into the leather, draping an arm over the top.

"Are you gonna get dressed tonight or what?"

"Hey, I usually air-dry at home, so consider yourself lucky that the towel is still on."

I let out a frustrated sigh and collapse into a chair opposite him.

A loud snore comes from the opposite side of the room and I sigh, pushing back my hair. "I guess I can talk freely since she's on another planet right now." I lean forward, my head in my hands. "Frankie stole those drugs. He hooked up with Salvatore Giaconne, who had a beef with us. But he claims he can't get the blow back, that 'they won't let him have it.' He also said they found him and not the other way around. He says he doesn't know how to get to the drugs or the dipshits who have them." I let out a sigh "Sal didn't give me any names either. It's all on Frankie. I think he's full of shit. He's working with an enemy of ours. I know it."

"Maybe you're looking too deep," Dante says. "Maybe it really was a revenge plot, Sal getting you back for firing him, Frankie getting you back for running them out of Sicily and humiliating their family."

"I don't know. But I don't trust Frankie," I mutter.

"So what's that got to do with Sleeping Beauty over there?" Dante's forehead creases. "You kidnapped her as leverage, but for what? Is it just to get the drugs back?"

I shake my head. "I want the drugs, yeah. But, for all I know, we'll never see them again. The bigger problem is taking care of the bastards who made off with our stash. I need to make sure they never pull the same job twice."

"And that's why you went insane, drugged your ex, and snatched her off the street?" Dante lifts an eyebrow.

"No," I say tersely. "I did all that to prove to my guys that I'm not some pussy who's gonna let anyone walk all over me. I did it as a show of strength, as a way to keep their respect since I lost a ton of it when this went down.

Dante nods. "Okay, so where's Frankie now?"

I shrug. "I don't know. I gave him one week to get me what I want."

"And you restore everyone's faith in you and you jump into Matteo's number two spot because you've made the empire whole again."

"Exactly."

Dante shakes his head. "Romo, what if you're spinning your wheels looking for an enemy who isn't there? What if you miss the real ones, Frankie and Sal, because you're chasing a fucking figment of your paranoid imagination? You always think people are trying to cut you down, to undermine you because you're the youngest. Matteo left you out here to run things because he trusts you. Don't fuck with that, bro. Do your job. Don't make problems where none exist."

"I'm not imagining it!" I say, standing up and pacing across the floor. "And now I need Frankie to get me the guys who were behind this. Once he does that…" My voice trails off as I sneak a glance over at Marchella's limp body.

"You give her up? Again?"

I swallow hard. "Yeah. That's how the story ends, Dante. I close the book on the Amantes for good."

"Can we talk about the puppy now?"

I groan. "Bobby got Marchella with the tranquilizer dart while she was trying to help a stray puppy. Same one she was chasing in the…" My words drift off as I recall my arms wrapped tight around her in the park, right after she almost wiped out on that rock. "…in the park."

"In the park. And is that where you, ah," he grins. "Sexually assaulted her?"

"I admit, it wasn't my smartest move," I grumble.

"This is your problem, Romo. You don't think. You just do."

"Says the guy who takes his sniper rifle to bed almost as often as his whores."

"Easy, bro. No need to judge."

"Look, you run your life and I'll run mine, okay?" I shake my head. "In the meantime, I have to figure out how to make the next week as painless as possible for myself." I nod at Marchella. "She can be pretty brutal."

"Judging by the way she sucked back that tequila, I'd say you should stock up if you want any peace."

I nod, staring out at the skyline.

There might be something else I can do.

You know, for the sake of keeping peace.

―――

I hold open a bag of some horrid-smelling things called Nudges that I found in the pet aisle of a nearby Key Food supermarket, hoping the scent alone will have Bella running to eat out of my hand. I grabbed a few other necessities like a leash and some wipes because stupidly, I was hopeful I'd actually be able to find her. But now it's been three hours since I left my apartment and it's starting to get dark. Pretty soon, I won't be able to see her even if she is skulking around these streets.

I wander up and down the streets around the park, knowing that once darkness falls, I'll be fucked in this neighborhood. I've got my gun, but if I get jumped by a group of thugs with something to prove, it'll be damn useless.

I wind up back in the spot where Bobby shot Marchella because the little alleyway is the last place where I saw Bella. I guess I'm hoping she'll come back around. I sink to the concrete next to the old brick building, tall, overgrown weeds on either side of me. My shoulders slump and I lean my head back against the side of the wall.

Why in the hell am I even here?

Do I really think that I'm A) gonna find the dog, and B) gonna be able to ingratiate myself with Marchella even if I get lucky and she comes sniffing around?

My cell phone buzzes and I grab it. "Is she up yet?" I ask.

"Nah. In fact, I think she's actually drooling a little. You finish your little errand?"

"Not yet." I sigh. "I'll be home soon. Hopefully."

"Okay. Don't forget the Jack."

Jesus Christ. "Is that all that's on your mind right now?"

"Nope," he says. "My mind is on your little captive right now. She's got some mouth on her. I'm thinking about what else she can do with it."

"Did you put on pants?" I say through gritted teeth.

"Negative. I figured easy access, you know? If she wakes up horny," Dante adds with a snicker. "I mean, she clearly hates you, but I figure I'm fair game."

I grip the phone tight. I will kill him if he lays a finger on Marchella. Kill him fucking dead!

"Relax, Romo. I know you still like her," he sing-songs. "But ya know, it's gotta be her choice. That's only fair."

"Screw you," I hiss. "And I am long fucking over her. You think she'd be interested in you, go for it. I don't need her brand of hell in my life."

"Thanks for giving me your blessing," he says. "My dick appreciates it."

I hate him. I hate him. I hate him!

My stomach rolls as I raise the bag of Nudges to my nose. I'm starving but not dying.

"I'll see ya later," I snap, clicking off the phone.

My brother. What a dick. He rode my ass incessantly about her back in Sicily because he was the only one who actually paid attention and saw what everyone else missed.

Of course he'd try to make a run at Marchella just to fuck with me.

Like he needs to. The guy can get any woman he wants, whenever he wants.

But he also loves a challenge.

And Marchella is just that.

I stagger to my feet. This manhunt is useless. I'm not gonna find—

Something winds around my ankles and I jump, looking down at the ground. I really hope it's not a sewer rat. They're the size of cats here in the city, with thick tails about a mile long.

Scary as fuck, not that I'd ever admit that.

But whatever it is nuzzles the side of my leg without making a peep. I lower myself to the ground and the ears perk up, standing at attention. Big bug eyes stare up at me…or rather, the bag of Nudges in my hand.

"Bella," I whisper, a smile tugging at my lips. I didn't spend too much time studying the dog Marchella was with, but I remember small, black, and those big eyes. This has to be her.

I reach down to stroke the underside of her chin but she backs away, creeping back toward the small alleyway between the buildings.

"Shit," I mutter, pulling a Nudge out of the bag and holding it out, whistling at her. Her eyes widen and she takes a few steps toward me. She moves gingerly and I don't make any quick moves, just in case she gets spooked and takes off like a shot.

Speaking of shots, we need to get the hell out of here.

Immediately, if not sooner.

Bella inches toward me and turns her head up toward the steak-like looking thing in my hand. I fight the bile rising in the back of my throat.

It sure as hell doesn't smell like a side of beef to me, but hey, it got her out here.

She must be fucking starving.

I look around, hearing faint yelling in the distance. I start to back away from the brick, urging Bella to follow me out far enough that I can scoop her up. I tiptoe backward, holding out the treat, whistling at her as she creeps closer.

"Come on, girl. Just a little more," I murmur. My car is right around the corner, my gun tucked into the back of my jeans. She finally makes her way out into the open and I hold out the treat to her. She jumps for it, capturing it with her teeth so fast, I almost think I imagined it.

She must swallow it whole because it's only a split second before she puts out her paw, looking for more. I take a quick look around and hurriedly hand over a second one. This time, I put it on the ground and gently put my arms around her as she scarfs down the treat. She wiggles like crazy, but I don't really have time to comfort her. I've got an expensive car sitting out on a street known for gang violence and general obliteration of anything out of the ordinary.

She can eat the whole damn bag in my front seat, but we've gotta go now.

I hold her as tight as I can without squeezing her too hard and start hoofing it back to my parking spot. Just as I'm about to round the corner, a loud shattering sound pierces the otherwise still air. I jump back with a gasp, peering around the side of a building. A car alarm sounds and I turn away from the mess of shards glittering on the concrete around my Bentley.

Why in the ever-loving *fuck* did I take my own goddamn car?

I could have found a piece-of-shit Honda or something to drive up here but no.

Take the Bentley!

Make yourself a target!

I let out a frustrated breath. Can't very well go to it now. They'll fucking skewer me for whatever I have on me, which includes a lot of cash and my grandfather's Rolex.

Sonofabitch!

I look down at Bella. "Don't bark, whatever you do," I hiss.

The derelicts who busted into my car aren't the least bit scared off by the alarm. They keep ransacking the thing. My E-Z Pass is in there, but I never keep registration or insurance in the glove compartment. I always carry that on me.

The stereo will be torn out, but who gives a damn about that?

I rack my brain for anything incriminating, but nothing registers.

I'm not stupid enough to leave weapons in the car while it's unattended.

Same thing with cash.

I just hope they leave enough of the car that I can drive it the hell outta here once I get a chance.

I almost cheer when I hear police sirens approach, but I also don't have time to sit around and file a report. I can handle my car business myself.

If I can get to said car.

I peek around the side of the building again to see if the sounds startled them enough to leave the crime scene. One guy is hard at work on getting my rims off, but jumps away when the sirens get louder.

"Yo, Boom, we gots ta go! I ain't endin' up in the clink again for your sloppy ass!"

The one called Boom jumps out from the hood, screaming and cursing at the group of guys who take off running down the street. "You fuckin' pussies! I almost had the battery!"

"Fuck it!" Another one of them yells over his shoulder. "I ain't waitin' to get pinched!"

Boom runs after them, still bitching.

I don't wait until they're out of sight, just that they're far enough away that I can slam the hood closed and jump into the car before the cops show up. I pull open the door and roll my eyes. They demolished the steering column, I guess to try and hotwire it. Must have been a bunch of low-level thugs since they abandoned that plan and went for the battery instead.

Idiots. If they were part of my crew, I'd have kicked their asses for leaving their fingerprints all over everything *before* leaving the car as evidence.

I'll worry about that tomorrow.

In the meantime, I turn on the car and stomp on the gas, zooming down the street. I can still hear the sirens, but they sound a little farther away now. Either I made a just-in-time escape, or something else caught their attention.

In this neighborhood, it's probably the latter.

Forty minutes later, I'm lugging my heaping bag of pet crap in one arm, and Bella in the other, as I jog toward the elevator of my building. I shift the bag to stick my key into the lock, collapsing against the back wall as the doors close.

The bell dings once we reach my floor and I stagger across the hall toward the front door. I twist the key into the lock and practically fall into the foyer, I'm so spent from my 'errand'.

I drop the bags onto the floor and the open bag of Nudges spills onto the floor.

Bella sure isn't complaining.

I lean back against the door. I wonder how many of those she should have. I definitely don't need a stray dog shitting all over the place. But when I asked about that at the supermarket, one of the workers told me to pad train her. I have no idea what the hell that means, and I didn't really have time to chat with him, so I bought a box of pads he recommended. I'll guess I'll just wallpaper the place with them and hope she knows where to go.

My eyes drop to the little black puppy who seems to have way more energy now that she's eaten half a bag of treats.

She looks up at me and lets out a high-pitched bark. Then she takes off, racing around the room so fast, she becomes a black blur. My eyes can't track her fast enough, and I see black darting around tables, chairs, couches, and potted plants.

But she never crashes into anything.

A few more high-pitched barks pierce the silence, and Marchella lets out a loud groan as she resurrects from her face-down position on the couch. Slowly, I see her sleep-tousled head rise from the couch cushion, red marks lining the sides of her face where they were pressed against the pillow seams. Her eyes are heavy and a little bloodshot, but when Bella leaps onto the couch next to her and attacks her with her tongue…fucking gross, by the way…she gasps and an expression of pure joy settles into her features.

Only, I'm used to the look of disdain and disgust, so this is new.

And much nicer.

If I have to keep a hostage, I'd like her to be at least somewhat agreeable.

She grabs Bella and holds her up, squealing with excitement. Bella obviously feels it, too, because she lets out another bark.

Marchella looks over to me, a bright smile on her face. "I can't believe you did this. How did you…oh my God, where did you even find her?"

I shrug. "It's like I said before. You didn't do anything to deserve this, Marchella. You shouldn't be the one to suffer. And this dog obviously meant something to you. So I went back to Inwood."

"You went to Inwood," she repeats to herself, almost disbelievingly. "At this hour? And you found her." Marchella shakes her head, whispering. "I figured she'd be gone forever…"

"It doesn't matter." I point to the bags on the floor. "I got you stuff you'll need for her. I think your first stop should be the bath, though. She fucking stinks."

With eyes that shine a whole lot brighter than they did when I left her a few hours ago, she holds the puppy in the air and spins her around, talking to her in a baby voice. Marchella doesn't seem to mind the smell either.

I fold my arms over my chest. "So I guess you're a dog person."

She lifts an eyebrow at me. "And just like that, we get personal? This isn't a sweet reunion, Roman."

"I was just trying to make conversation. Look, you don't have to tell me anything you don't want to. Hell, we don't need to speak for the next week. But don't mistake my questions for congeniality. I'm not looking for a friend here. I'm looking for my product. And you being here is gonna get it for me."

"Wow, you're a real charmer. I guess some things never change," she says sarcastically, continuing to dance around with the dog. "You must need a stick to fight off all the ladies, huh?"

I push myself off the wall, my stomach grumbling. "Like I said before, this ain't social, Marchella."

"You know, it would be a lot easier for me to figure out how to deal with you if you weren't so inconsistent."

I pad into the kitchen, swallowing a yawn as I pull open the refrigerator.

Almost completely empty.

Dante.

I slam it closed and turn to look at Marchella. "What's that supposed to mean?"

She nestles the puppy against her shoulder and walks toward me. "Well, let's see. You purposely avoid telling me who you are, then you stalk me, kiss me like I've never been kissed in my life, drug me, and kidnap me. Then you have my brother beaten to a pulp, threaten us both with extreme torture before death."

The corners of my lips curl upward and I let out a chuckle. "Like you've never been kissed by in your life, huh?"

She rolls her eyes, flipping her hair over her shoulder. "That *would* be what you caught. I should have known," she mutters.

"No, no, keep going. I wanna hear the rest. Don't leave me hanging."

"You basically hired me so I'll go with you to that event, in essence paying me to sit tight so that my brother stays on task to get your money back. Then you rescued this puppy because you knew she meant something to me." She shakes her head. "Completely inconsistent."

"Well, I'm not a total dickhead, much as you'd like to believe otherwise," I say. "Besides, it gets cold at night. The puppy should be inside. Christ only knows what she sees, or just barely escapes, when she's creeping around Inwood at night."

Marchella narrows her eyes, the blue much darker than it was only a few minutes ago. More turbulent, like a violent wave that's about to consume everything in its path. "I came here hating you with every fiber of my being."

"And so what now? Did I score any points?" I flash a half-smirk.

"Not enough to make a difference," Marchella snips. "I just wanted to point out that your behavior for a mafia thug is bizarre as hell."

"So I basically risked my life going into your neighborhood for nothing? Not even a fucking 'thank-you'?"

She recoils, her eyes now wide. I guess the thought didn't occur to her. Then her expression is eclipsed by the pent-up anger at her situation. "Let me tell you something, Roman. If you want me to kiss your ass because you did a couple of somewhat decent things after shooting me up with a drug that could have killed me, as well as making me your captive for the foreseeable future, you're crazier than I thought!"

I grit my teeth, my hands balled into fists at my sides. Of course, she's right. I did some pretty shitty things today, like stealing her freedom. Did I really think that finding the puppy would make her forget that I'm a vicious and somewhat unhinged killer who slapped a target on her beloved brother's back?

Still, a little gratitude wouldn't hurt. I did risk my life *and* my car.

That's the heated side of me, the irrational side that tries to justify all of the bad.

The side that doesn't give a damn about anything but being close to her.

I stomp across the room, my jaw tight as the puppy jumps out of her arms. She gasps as I put my hands on her hips, my fingers digging into her flesh. The puppy stares up at us as if she knew to get the hell outta dodge, then trots into the kitchen.

Electricity crackles between us, my insides sizzling at her nearness. "I don't normally give a damn about people's feelings," I growl, tightening my grip on her. "People serve a purpose to me. They're a means to an end. Period."

"Why are you telling me that?" she says, her teeth clenched. "Do you think I'm some kind of an idiot? I know how your world works. I know you only care about your money. And I know you made this grand gesture to get on my good side so I don't mess up your event by telling everyone what you've done to me, my brother, and our lives. You're using me. Manipulating me!" She struggles against my grip, her sinful body rubbing against me in the process. It makes my blood boil, except it's desire, not anger, coursing through me.

My pulse throbs against my neck as we glare at each other, death wishes co-mingling with a hunger that proves we share the same inner conflict.

The longing infused with hatred.

The craving that battles the disdain.

Our lips are so close together that I can almost graze hers with my tongue.

The all-consuming lust blinds me, clouding my judgment and my objective.

"I'm doing what I need to preserve my organization," I hiss. "You're only alive right now because of what you can do for me. And you'll go to the event as my date because I'm paying you to. But, like your brother, if you decide to fuck around, you'll suffer the same fate as him. So don't test me, Marchella." I force out the words because I need to do something to show her I'm not some pathetic excuse for a leader. It's the only way I can preserve my place, and I need to remember said place unless this whole plan goes up in smoke.

I can't let myself be distracted by her gorgeousness, her smart mouth, or her fiery will.

All of those roads most definitely lead to hell.

Her eyes widen for a split second and she takes in a sharp breath.

Yeah, I surprised myself with that little speech, too.

It may fuel her hatred but it'll keep me in control.

"You're a fucking asshole," she whispers.

"I know," I snarl. "Always remember that. You'll survive longer."

Chapter Twelve
MARCHELLA

His blue eyes glitter with the threat of danger, but instead of making my gut clench, his gaze makes me tingle in places that have no business being awakened by this sick lust coursing through me.

How can his egocentric words actually turn me on?

He has a bounty on my brother and complete control over me as a result.

He shot me, for fuck's sake!

I want to punch him so badly. To land a right hook against his beautiful, stubbled jaw, shattering it like he did my life!

But most distressing is that despite everything he's done and said, I still want to feel his lips on me, to have his devious tongue tussle with mine, to drink in his villainousness because for all of the hatred he generates, my pent-up desire trumps it all.

And the flickering embers in my belly roar to life as his eyes drink me in, telling me in no uncertain terms that he feels the exact same way.

Just like I always believed he did.

But screw him if he thinks I'm going to do anything about it.

"Ooh," I say in a mock scared voice. "I'm so scared." I shove my good shoulder against his thick, muscled chest and of course, it doesn't do a damn thing. He stays rooted to his spot and presses his fingers deeper into my flesh.

My heart thumps, blood rushing between my ears as the overwhelming urge to kiss him grabs hold of me. The line between lust and disgust…my God, it's almost invisible right about now.

"Don't make me prove it to you," he grunts. "Because I will, and you won't want me to stop once I get started."

I gasp. "You're sick!"

"It's the only way to thrive in this world, sweetheart," he says, letting me go with a smirk playing on his lips.

Aarf!

I peek around him where Bella is standing next to his sneakers, not bothering to bite back the grin that spreads across my lips when I see the puddle next to his kicks. "Yeah, well, I'm sure that there's more to it than that. Like dry shoes."

He furrows his brow and follows my amused glance to where Bella created her own indoor facilities.

"Fuck!" he groans. "That's my favorite pair, for Christ's sake!"

"I guess she didn't like the way you were talking to me," I say, folding my arms over my chest. "Girl power or whatever."

He narrows his eyes at me and I flash a bright smile in return.

"I guess your gesture of goodwill kind of backfired."

We stand there, staring each other down, like a battle of the wills. There's a man inside of this brutish, menacing jackass, one who is fighting against his rough exterior. The years may have been kind to his appearance, but they've created a monster façade. That's why I didn't recognize him at the restaurant and at the park. I don't know this menace that he's become. I believe that the real Roman is still trapped inside. I can see it more clearly now…not only in his eyes, but in the little things, like going out to find Bella. But the guy on the outside can't let him out for too long, not in the mafia world, or else things might spiral out of control.

And I know that guy on the outside well.

He's my father.

It's true, Papa and I never had the kind of tight-knit relationship he has with Frankie, and that's in large part because I resisted his 'job'. I had no desire to be anywhere near his work, and our relationship grew more and more strained over time because of it. But I saw how he'd let his true self shine through for my mother. There was a softness, a deep love, an open heart reserved just for her. It didn't happen often because heaven forbid, the big, bad mob enforcer showed the world that he could be a sensitive guy.

Roman has definite shades of my father, which makes me equally drawn to him and fed up with him. On one hand, I want to scream at him and unleash the rage he's caused to knot deep inside of me. And on the other hand, I want to fling myself into his arms and feel them wrapped around me again.

It's the quintessential push and pull.

Roman breaks away from my gaze and stomps into the kitchen for a roll of paper towels and a bottle of spray cleaner. He's back a second later, muttering a string of colorful expletives in Italian.

I bend down to help him, reaching out for the spray bottle as he's about to grab it again. It's just a brush of our fingers, but my God, the shock that zaps my insides makes me visibly shudder.

He turns his ice-blue eyes toward me, and I can see a flicker of surprise in the depths, as if he felt the same thing and has no idea how to process it. Well, yeah! I *am* his captive, so there are parameters.

I guess…?

I've never been kidnapped before, so I'm not super familiar with the protocols. But I am pretty certain that lusting for your captive is bad.

So is lusting for your *captor*.

Yikes.

I bite down on my lower lip, tearing my gaze away from his. My pulse thumps against my throat as I spray, spray, spray… anything to keep my focus off of Roman.

Because regardless of what lies beneath the surface, he's still a fucking animal.

And I'm his prey.

I mop up the cleaner with paper towels and scramble to my feet before I get too close to him again. He's still lamenting his sneakers, so I use that as an opportunity to dash into the kitchen and get my head screwed on straight.

This man had Frankie beaten to a pulp! How can I have any feelings other than nausea for him?

I clutch the sides of the counter, my stomach clenching as Bella rubs up against my leg.

An exasperated sigh makes my throat tighten, and I can't figure out if it's due to Bella's accident, or my rapid disappearance.

How sick is it that I'm hoping for the latter?

"You must be starving," he says.

I nod, continuing to stare at the floor because I'm petrified he's going to mistake my admission to hunger for…well, *hunger.*

"There's nothing in the fridge. Dante ate pretty much everything," he grunts.

"Let me take a look." I push past him and pull open the refrigerator door. "You have plenty of stuff in here," I exclaim, rifling through the shelves and drawers. "Eggs, English muffins, bacon, cheese…I mean, as long as none of it is expired, we can have breakfast for dinner?"

He smirks. "So you're gonna cook for your kidnapper?"

"Well, you're paying me, right?" I turn around, my eyebrow lifted. "But I have one condition."

"I didn't realize employees negotiated with their bosses," he mumbles.

"This is important. You have to let me call Frankie. He's all alone now and he's hurt. You have to let me see if he's okay. Please, Roman." I swallow hard. "Look, I have no way of reaching him other than to ask your permission. Which," I'm quick to say. "Absolutely sucks. But I'm not too proud to ask because he's my brother and I love him, even if you do want to skin him alive."

He looks at me for a long minute, and just when I think I might spontaneously combust because of the heat generated by his panty-melting stare, he shakes his head. "No."

My jaw drops. "Why the hell not? I only want to find out if he's okay. What if those guys found him? What if they know he was with you? They might hurt him, or worse!"

"Do you understand that I don't give a damn if he's okay?" he yells. "Your brother took what didn't belong to him! And if 'those guys' fuck his shit up, then good! He deserves it for what he did! Thinking he could get his revenge all this time later. He took enough. I owe him *nothing*!"

A gaggle of tears knots in my throat. Fuck, this is too much. I can't see my battered brother, I'm alone with this crazy, paranoid thug, and now I have all of these other toxic memories from my past bubbling up from the deep recesses of my heart.

I have to get away from Roman, away from everything he's dredged up over the past few hours.

Christ, I was practically living in poverty a few hours ago, but it was a hell of a lot more tolerable than this shit show Roman has cast me for. My shoulders quake and I hurry to scoop up Bella before stalking out of the kitchen toward the second floor.

"What happened to breakfast for dinner?" he asks, his jaw tight.

My mouth drops open and I turn to look at him with as much disdain as I can conjure up. "Are you serious? Because if I'm anywhere near a scalding hot pan right now, there is a hundred percent chance it'll be smashed against your face!" I take a deep breath, stopping on the stairs. "But don't let that stop you from enjoying your meal." I stomp up the steps, hissing loud enough for him to hear. "I hope you fucking choke!"

I clutch my mother's hand as we wade into the clear blue water in Turks and Caicos. The sand feels so soft beneath my toes, like a thick carpet warmed by the sun's rays. I let the gentle rippling waves wash away the angst, the uncertainty, and the sadness. I tilt my head backward to stare up at the cloudless sky.

It's a perfect day because we're together, creating a memory I will cherish for years to come.

Mama's thin and fragile hand grips mine tight as we wade deeper, the water rising higher and higher until I take a final step, my foot no longer finding the sandy floor. I gasp, unprepared for what lies ahead...what lies beneath the surface.

My arms and legs flail about as I sputter. My head bobs up and down like a buoy, and the resort is in the far-off distance. How did I drift so far away?

And where is Mama?

I don't feel her fingers laced with mine!

"Mama!" I gasp, the waves getting more turbulent by the second.

The sky, which was a bright cerulean only moments ago, is now dark. The sun, once bright, is now eclipsed by thick, ominous clouds. A heavy wind catapults my body through the waves and I scream, struggling for breath. My lungs constrict with panic, my limbs struggling to keep afloat.

But the volatile water has other plans for me.

A rumbling wave gathers speed and height, capturing me in the swirling curl as it hurls itself toward the resort miles and miles into the distance. It rises, higher and higher like an all-consuming tsunami, dragging me along for the ride, certain devastation in my near future.

I try to shout, to warn everyone on the shore who is seemingly oblivious to the impending danger. But nobody looks up...nobody, not even my family.

I wave my arms in the air, trying to catch their attention, but they are too busy laughing. Mama, Papa, and Frankie, playing Frisbee in the sand, no clue that their entire world is about to be shattered.

And I can't do a damn thing to change the outcome.

I have no control...

My world goes black right before the impact strikes and I blink fast, reaching out for the handrail in the stuffy elevator at Memorial Sloane Kettering. I clutch the metal tight, trying to steady myself, but the dizziness assaults my body, sending me crashing to the floor in a cold sweat.

"Chell," *Frankie whispers on the ground next to me.* "You've gotta get up. It's time."

"But I can't," *I say, my eyes stinging with tears.* "I'm not ready. She's not ready!"

"We have to go," *he whispers, a single tear slipping down the side of his face.* "She's waiting for you. Don't let her wait anymore..."

He helps me up as the doors open and I hang onto the handrail for balance. Fear grips me, the gravity of the situation making my knees wobble as I gingerly step forward, tumbling into a thick patch of foliage at Washington Square Park as my dog Princess darts past me in hot pursuit of the pink Frisbee I just tossed.

"Get it, girl!" I squeal, clapping my hands as my mother lets out a breathless wheeze from the bench nearby. I turn to look at her, gasping as she falls over onto the side of the bench, her face ashen.

"Mom!" I shriek as her eyes flutter closed, her body spasming. "Somebody, please help us!"

EMTs appear from out of nowhere, gathering her onto a gurney and loading her into an ambulance that skidded to a stop right in front of our bench only seconds after I let out that bloodcurdling yell.

I clutch the sides of my head, an empty feeling in the pit of my gut making me shudder. I catch a glimpse of my pink Frisbee laying on the lush green grass in the distance.

A dark green minivan careens around a corner and big, sad brown eyes stare at me out the side window, a tiny paw slapping against the glass.

"Princess!" I shriek, clutching the bedsheet tight in my fists. "No!"

Chapter Thirteen
ROMAN

I throw off the comforter, jumping out of the bed and grabbing my gun off the nightstand. I stumble in the darkness, stubbing my toe against the leg of a chair. I swallow a yelp, creeping toward the door with my hand outstretched. I pull it open, careful not to make a sound since I have no fucking clue what the hell is happening beyond my bedroom.

Luckily, there isn't any more screaming.

Sounds like tortured sobs have replaced the piercing shrieks that just jolted me from the X-rated dream I was having about my gorgeous captive.

I take a step out of my room and turn my head in the direction of the crying.

"What the fuck is that?"

My heart jumps, the force practically launching me off the floor. "Dante, for fuck's sake!" I say in a loud whisper, pointing my gun at him.

He throws up his hands, jumping backward. "Jesus Christ!"

"I could have shot you, moron!"

Dante grins. "Eh, you'd have missed. Besides, why the hell do you need the gun? The alarm didn't go off. Your girlfriend just had a nightmare."

"She's my hostage, dammit!" I whisper-shout.

"Yeah, but you still have a hard-on for her," he teases. "Don't try to deny it."

I roll my eyes. "Go back to bed."

"I'm hungry," he whispers. "I didn't eat before I passed out. I want a snack."

"Can I please check things out without having you on my ass?" I hiss. "Go back to bed!"

"You know, being a murderous kidnapper has turned you into more of a prick than you already were."

"You wanna see murderous?" I growl. "Then stick around!"

Dante lets out a soft snicker. "Okay, okay. Go 'comfort' your girlfriend. Then when you're done, I'll invade your fridge."

"You already did that, by the way," I mutter as he backs into his room.

I sweep a hand through my hair, dropping the hand with the gun clutched in it. He's right. There's no intruder. I'm being overly paranoid right now.

This kidnapping shit is new for me.

Usually I just slash and walk.

I can usually rid myself of my victims pretty fast.

This one will be with me for a while. And I've already pissed her off enough for one night. After she stormed out of the kitchen, I heard the shower in the bathroom run for a good half an hour. Then, silence.

Not even a single bark.

I figured she let Bella into my room to shit in the rest of my sneakers but surprisingly, they were spared. Of course, she might have hidden a little steaming surprise for later.

It's what I would've done in her position.

I hold out my fist and softly knock on the door before pushing it open a crack.

I can see Marchella's silhouette as she stands by the window, staring out at the moonlit sky.

She turns with a gasp, the beams of light dancing on top of her dark hair like a halo.

The angel and the devil.

How friggin' ironic.

"You okay?" I say in a low voice, my eyes adjusting to the darkness.

She stares at me, tears streaming from her eyes as she shakes her head. "No. I haven't been okay in a really long time, as a matter of fact."

I take a tentative step into the room, then stop short as Bella leaps to her feet and growls at me from the foot of the bed.

I furrow my brow. She's staring at me like she wants to tear me to shreds with her sharp little chompers and I have to admit, even though she's tiny, that guttural sound makes me take a step back.

I hear a hint of a giggle and sneak a glance at Marchella. Despite her sniffles and tear-streaked face, she's actually smiling. The sight makes my dick tingle.

Ah, shit.

I guess I *am* that twisted.

"She doesn't like you."

I lift an eyebrow. "I'm an acquired taste."

"In other words, if at first you have to choke it down, sputtering and gagging, try, try again?"

My lips curl upward. "I've never had any complaints about anyone choking anything down."

She lets out a frustrated huff, turning back to the window. "You're gross."

"Yeah, but in a few days, you might actually find me tolerable. It can happen just like that." I snap my fingers.

"Right now, I find you insufferable," she whispers. "I don't understand why you couldn't let me call Frankie. He was hurt badly and you wouldn't even let me check on him."

"Chella—"

She spins around, holding up a finger. "No, don't call me that. We're not friends. Only my friends call me that."

"I don't want to be your enemy," I say, stepping forward and risking Bella's wrath. "I never did."

"You created this situation, Roman." She sniffles. "You don't get to choose how I feel about you!"

"I'm trying to do my—"

"Your job," she snips. "Yeah, yeah. I know all about it. Your loyalty. Sorry to pile on more work for you."

"You know, I did a very nice fucking thing when I went to get that mutt off the streets."

"Yeah, it was nice," she says. "And what was your motive, huh? Because let's face it, guys like you always have one."

"I didn't have an agenda," I grunt. "I didn't need to go into that shithole neighborhood and get my goddamn car busted up! I went to do a nice thing!"

Her brow furrows. "Your car got busted up?"

I lean against the wall. "Yeah. Some guys broke into it and stole my stereo. They were about to steal my battery and rims, too, before the cops showed up."

She lets out a chuckle. "Serves you right. Ever hear of karma?"

"Trust me, if that's the worst to even blow back on me, I'll consider myself damn lucky," I mumble. I sigh, pushing away from the wall. "And now that you've had some fun at my expense, I'm going back to bed. Next time I'll know to stay the fuck out."

My eyes flit over her lithe body, covered only by a thin white t-shirt she must have found in one of my drawers. I wonder if she's wearing panties, but the t-shirt is long enough that I can't tell.

I only came in here to check on her because she was upset, and now she's got my dick in a complete twist. How the hell am I supposed to sleep now?

I want to say something else. I want to tell her why I really went back for Bella. I want to tell her that even though I'm holding her captive, I've never been as turned on by a woman as I am by her.

But the walls surrounding her are too high and thick to scale.

It ain't worth it.

This is the life I chose, and they don't come with happy endings.

At least, not in the literal sense.

It's why I had to ignore my feelings for her in the first place.

I don't bother to say goodnight. I just square my shoulders and walk out, trying to maintain some degree of dignity.

I fist the sides of my head and stalk toward the kitchen. I pull open the refrigerator door since I didn't eat either. I don't know why I had to pull that power play bullshit with her before. Was it because I didn't want her attention on anything but me?

I could have let her call Frankie. I could have been a decent guy.

But then I wouldn't be me.

I scan the contents of the refrigerator, and the meal Marchella was planning sounds a lot better than what I know I can do with the same ingredients. Besides, my stomach is knotted like a pretzel right now.

I opt for a beer and collapse onto the sofa, facing the window. I don't bother with any lights. I just stare out into the night sky. It looks and feels heavy and thick since there are no stars twinkling back at me.

Then again, what'd I expect? This is Manhattan.

I take a swig from the beer bottle, setting it down on the table in front of me. I rest my head against the back of the couch and let my eyes drift closed. A soft pattering across the floor makes me jump a few minutes later.

"Hey," Marchella says softly, tucking a strand of hair behind her ear.

"Hey," I reply shortly, my jaw tight. This time, I don't let my eyes wander. I keep them focused on hers.

She nods toward the empty couch cushion next to me. "Mind if I sit?"

"You're kind of my guest, so…" I shrug.

"Thanks," she says, sinking down next to me. I expect her to speak but she just sits there, quiet, a pensive look on her face. "I shouldn't have been such a bitch to you before. I know you were just coming to make sure I was okay."

I shrug. "I didn't deserve the welcome wagon."

"True," she agrees, a hint of a smile on her face. "I just…look, it's been a rough year for me. Way worse than anything we dealt with back in Sicily. I have a lot of things swirling through my brain on a daily basis, things that haunt me every day. Sometimes they decide to destroy my nights, too." She toys with her hands. "I guess all of the stress from today triggered my mind, making it spin out of control."

My lips stretch into a straight line. "You have every right to be pissed off at me," I mutter. "No need to apologize."

"You have to understand how fucked up this is, Roman. You're planning to keep me here like I'm a bird in a gilded cage until my brother delivers for you. And based on what I know of mafia families, there's no out for Frankie. You'll never let him go. You'll never let me go. Because guys like you are too concerned with watching your backs. You can't have weak links floating around, threatening your livelihood." She rubs a hand down the front of her face. "Believe me, I know," she whispers.

"Your dad?" I ask. I assume she's talking about his prison sentence. He was always a fucking loose cannon. It didn't shock me that he finally got caught, not that I paid too much attention to the news. He was always the guy who went overboard more often than not. He never followed instructions, always thought he could do things best without anyone else's guidance. He had his own way of doing things and if he didn't like someone else's plan, he cut them out of it. It made him a lot of enemies back in Sicily, aside from my father, and I'm sure he made plenty here over the years.

She nods. "I know how you guys operate," she says softly. "I know you don't allow risks to impact your businesses. You crush liabilities. Frankie is a definite liability. Why would you ever let him walk away once he does what you ask?"

I grab my beer bottle and take another gulp. I can't argue with her. You always handle liabilities. It's part of the job. Eliminating threats to the kingdom is the only way to survive and thrive.

It's why my father got rid of the Amantes.

"I never told you I was gonna kill him," I say. This is true, primarily because I really don't want to kill him. I want him to hand over the schmucks whom he's working with and let them kill him. He can be bought, I already know that. It's his weakness.

But I also know I'm opening myself up to a lot of hell if I don't ice him.

The truth is, if I kill him, I'm gonna have to admit to Matteo that I fucked up and that I let our family get taken for a second time by an Amante. It's gonna tell him I don't know how to handle a situation without using brute force. And leaders need to figure out different ways to get what they want.

He'll never take me seriously if I can't fix this without bloodshed.

I thought by sparing Frankie's life I was being strategic, but the jury's still out on that.

I don't trust him, and if he crosses me, there will only be one way to fix this.

I can't risk another blow to my authority.

"You didn't have to say anything," she murmurs. "I know he's a live wire. He's always been that way. I think that's why he and my dad were always so close. He's exactly like my father."

"And you're your mother. I mean, from what I remember."

A faraway smile brightens her face. "Yeah, I definitely am. We both loved so many of the same things, we shared so many of the same personality traits. We were incredibly close. She was like my best friend." She sighs. "I miss her so much. I felt like once she was gone, I'd lost that parental connection. My dad and I don't exactly mix. And now that he's in jail, it's like we're not even part of each other's lives anymore. I feel like I've lost them both."

"You don't go and visit?" I ask.

She shakes her head. "No. I can't."

"Why not? I'm sure he misses you."

"I don't miss him," she whispers. "I mean, he's the reason I'm trapped here with you."

"Ouch," I say, clutching a hand to my heart. "That's cold."

"Well, it's true. If he hadn't gone to jail, I wouldn't be scraping together pennies to pay all of our bills and support what's left of our family. But he made a mistake, the biggest one, and now we're all paying the price." Marchella lets out a humorless laugh. "I had a life, Roman. It wasn't extravagant but it made me happy, as happy as I'd been in Sicily. And then everything came crashing down around me like massive dominoes. Sometimes I wish they'd have just crushed me when they tumbled. Then at least I'd be out of my misery. Trying to keep your glass half full is fucking exhausting."

She hugs her arms around herself, dipping her head low. My fingertips tingle with the urge to pull her close and trace a path over her bare skin.

"I'm, ah, sorry about all of that," I murmur. "I didn't know."

"How could you?" she says, turning her head toward me. The pain flickering in her gaze makes my chest tighten. "How could you possibly know that my life is in shambles right now? She gives her head a quick shake. "I don't need your pity."

I sigh. "You know, things always get better just when you think they can't get any worse."

"I've been waiting for that sudden shift for about a year," she snips. "It's been a damn long twelve months with no end in sight." She sighs. "And now this business with Frankie...he's always been this way. Worse than when he was a kid. Short fuse, short-sighted. He never thinks about consequences. He's all emotion. But he means well, and I know he'd do anything to keep me safe. He's going to find your money, Roman," she says, twisting toward me. "I promise you he will. He won't want anything bad to happen to me."

"Are you trying to convince me or yourself?" I ask. "Because I can't tell right now."

She leans back against the couch cushion. "He doesn't always do the right thing. But he does the best he can. I just hope he figures out a smart way to get you what you want," she whispers. "Because I'm afraid his emotions may get him killed otherwise."

I don't usually feel remorse for my work.

Then again, I don't typically bring my work home with me.

But having Chella here, next to me, exposed in the literal and figurative senses, makes me realize what I've been missing out on all of these years. I thought I was just missing the sensitivity chip. Now I see I've had it all along. I just didn't care enough to channel it.

I've done a lot of bad things in my life and I never looked back once.

And now, I have another choice to make, a chance to make a strong move to restore faith in my influence.

Except I can't seem to stop looking backward at the girl who makes me feel more vulnerable and exposed than I ever have before.

It was dangerous ten years ago…and it's even more so now.

Marchella runs a hand through her sleep-tousled hair and I catch a whiff of coconut.

My shampoo…

I shift on the couch when my dick jumps at the mental images of her soaped up in my shower, naked and wet. She was gorgeous as a teenager, but now? Christ. She's all woman with curves that my hands itch to caress. My mind sticks me in the glass-enclosed space right behind her, my cock pressed against the globes of her ass. I run my hands over her tits, flicking her nipples as she moans and rests her head on my shoulder. My cock dips in between her ass cheeks and she gasps when my fingers slide into her tight pussy—

"Roman!" She snaps her fingers in front of my face and suddenly, I'm no longer submerged in the hot spray.

"Yeah?" I say.

"Did I lose you? I feel like you completely blacked out there for a second."

"No, I'm here. I was, ah, just thinking that maybe you might be, um, hungry."

Hungry. Hmm. Well, I can definitely say at least one of us is.

She narrows her eyes. "I forgot. We didn't eat before because you pissed me off."

I scrub a hand down the front of my face. "I'm sorry about that. I didn't mean for you to starve."

"Well, I had the anger to keep me sated," she says with a tiny smile.

"Are you still angry?"

"Are you still a dick?"

We stare at each other. I watch her tongue dart out of her mouth and sweep over her lips, her expression full of conflict.

I feel that conflict, too.

Fucking *everywhere.*

"I can't apologize for who I am, Marchella," I say, my voice gruff. "But I promise that I'll never hurt you. You'll be safe with me."

She nods. "That pretty much tells me what I need to know."

"What do you mean?"

"You didn't mention Frankie in that promise."

I lift an eyebrow. "I said I'd never hurt you. Killing your brother would hurt you, yeah?"

"Yeah."

"So you have to trust me, then."

"What if he can't get your money back?" she asks, her voice wavering. "If he says he can't get to it, what will you do then?"

"He's going to find it," I say. "He has you to think about. He won't want anything bad to happen. He's gonna do what he needs."

"Right," she whispers, toying with the ends of her hair. "Okay."

Now, Marchella is a smart girl. She knows as well as I do that Frankie isn't the brightest bulb in the chandelier, and that any job he does is at risk of blowing up in his face because he never thinks about his actions.

That sure as hell hasn't changed.

But yet, she's still trying to convince herself that maybe I'm not the bloodthirsty savage she originally thought I was.

And that maybe I do have some redeeming qualities after all.

That'd be a first.

I've lived my life thinking I was just beyond redemption. How ironic would it be if my captive felt differently?

Captive.

There's that word again.

Why does it have to make me so damn heated when I think of tying her up and making her the kind of captive I really want her to be?

I jump off the couch, feeling as if I need to hurl myself into a cold shower but instead, opting to open the refrigerator. That'll give me a chill *and* something to occupy my hands and eyes. I grab the carton of eggs, not sure what the hell to do with them, but knowing if my digits are free to wander, they may act on their own and do things that would be very bad.

Bad in the good way.

I can hear her feet pad into the room behind me. I swallow hard, sticking my head deeper into the fridge.

"You buzzed out of there pretty fast," she murmurs. "Why?"

I squeeze my eyes shut. I can't exactly tell her that I wanted to mount her on my couch and that I took off before my body betrayed me.

It's done that before…too many times to count.

"I, ah, wanted to eat something."

Understatement of the fucking century.

She sidles closer to me and reaches for the eggs. "Here, let me."

But when her hand grazes mine, it jolts me and the carton flies out of my grip, smashing against the polished tile floor.

Eggs.

Everywhere.

As if on cue, my stomach rumbles. But I know it's not because I have a taste for a very early breakfast. No, the hunger that has tormented me since I first laid eyes on Marchella Amante at that restaurant is manifesting itself.

Right here and right now.

A most inconvenient time.

But when is anything about my life simple?

"Dammit," she mutters, looking around with a huff. She grabs the paper towels from the counter and sinks to her knees to mop up the runny mess coating my floor.

"Here, let me. I dropped them. You shouldn't have to clean it up."

She gazes up at me, a tiny smile playing at her lips. "Well, you're paying me, right? I *am* your employee."

Good Christ.

My mind and my dick immediately jumps to the thought of what else can I get her to do for cash?

I press my fingertips to my temples, forcing out the thoughts before they percolate for too long. I've got serious issues right now.

Sex with Marchella is one I don't need right now.

It would be wrong on so many levels.

But despite that knowledge, I can't tear my eyes away from her on the floor, the way her bare thighs tighten as she wipes up the eggs, the way the hem of the t-shirt rides up giving me the tiniest glimpse of…

No.

My dick jumps.

No fucking panties.

Thank you, God…

Tiny hairs on the back of my neck prickle as I sink down to the tile and reach out to grab the paper towels. Her back is turned toward me as she stretches over to clean up a stray piece of shell. The t-shirt lifts and the curves of her ass peek out at me, taunting me, tempting me to reach out and grasp them. I want so badly to dig my fingertips into her flesh, to sink my teeth into it, to drive my palm against it as she wiggles and writhes in my arms.

She should be punished for flashing that perfect ass at me…

And suddenly, a flaming pain shoots up to my skull as she gets up, her back crashing into my nose. I tumble backward against the cabinets, my hand flying up to my face and I let out loud groan.

"Oh my God!" she says, crawling over to me. "I'm so sorry! I didn't know you were behind me!"

"It's okay," I grumble. The intense pain explodes between my temples. Okay, so clearly that was karma getting me back for lusting after her ass.

I'd better watch myself with this one, or I might end up in traction before our time is through.

"Let me see," she says in a soft voice, slowly peeling my hand away from my nose. Her face is so close to mine that her breath flutters against my cheek like feathers. "It's not bleeding." She grins. "I think you'll live."

"Good," I say, dragging one of my hands down the side of her face. I don't know it escaped my control, but it's calling the shots now.

And I'm powerless to stop it.

Marchella's eyes widen slightly, and more so when my fingertips trace a path down the slope of her neck, dragging the neckline of the t-shirt with them as they clear a path south.

She doesn't stop me, though.

And her eyes are glued to mine, searching for a reason to push me away, to ignore the spark of electricity between us.

I know. I'm searching for the same things.

But both of us come up empty because here we still are, immersed in each other and buried in this twisted little bubble of forbidden desire that I've re-created, so many years later.

I close my fingers around her arm and pull her toward me. She leans forward, still on her knees. Her lips are so close to mine, like a scrumptious meal that is just within reach of my palette.

And I'm a starving man.

I push myself away from the cabinets, gathering her in my arms, all pain forgotten and replaced by pure, carnal lust. I can feel her heart race, thumping hard as I press against her chest. She straddles my legs as I run my hands down her spine, digging my fingertips into the small of her back because I need her closer still. Her hair falls forward, tickling my skin. I slide one hand behind her head, my fingers tangling in her soft, wavy hair.

"Marchella..." I murmur before crushing my lips against hers. She wraps her arms around my neck and I lose my balance, tumbling backward against the cabinets. I plunge my tongue into her eager mouth, drinking in her desire and taking that first bite of the forbidden apple that I just know is going to be my undoing.

The coiling heat of her tongue blasts through my insides, igniting the sparks that have lain dormant for far too long. My hands slip down the sides of her torso, toying with the edge of the t-shirt. My dick thickens against my boxer briefs as she grinds her hips against me. And just knowing there's no fabric covering her sweet pussy makes my pulse jackhammer against my throat.

With a loud gasp, she pulls away, her eyes filled with dread. "No, this can't happen."

"Why not?" I pant, breathless from that kiss.

"Because it's *wrong*," she whispers. "Your brother is right down the hall. And besides that, I'm your prisoner, for Pete's sake!"

"Prisoner. Right." I sweep my hair out of my eyes, thinking as fast as my libido will allow me to. But damn, the lust is so thick, it clouds my mind. "Okay, well, what if I handcuffed you? Would a little role play make it right?"

That's when I see it.

Raw hunger. She can't hide it from me. It's an expression I know all too well.

She likes the idea of me cuffing her.

Fuck, I like it too…

"Roman," she whispers.

"Yeah?"

Marchella is still on top of me and my hands are on her waist, although they would like to be somewhere else right now.

Actually, in a lot of different places.

"I...I..." She bites down on her lower lip, the vicious battle still waging in her blue-green eyes.

Which side will win?

Oh, Christ, don't keep me in suspense.

I'm ready to fight!

And then her lips crush against mine, crowning me the victor. She locks her legs around me, rubbing her chest against mine as she fists my hair, devouring me with a voracity I've only fantasized about. Our teeth crack, tongues flailing wildly as our heated bodies entwine right on the kitchen floor. We're like two predators fighting over the same prey, attacking each other with an unbridled passion that courses through me like a raging inferno. I tug at the t-shirt, clenching the fabric in my fists, my dick screaming for release. I sit straight up with her still in my lap, grasping the globes of her ass beneath the t-shirt. A tiny mewl slips out of her mouth and she tugs at my lower lip with her teeth.

Without warning, she breaks away, her brow furrowed. "Did you hear that?"

"You mean, your body screaming at me to get you naked? Yeah, I heard that," I murmur, trailing my fingertips down the slope of her back.

She lets out a soft giggle. "No, I thought I heard someone. What if Dante is awake?"

"If he is, he's gonna get a hell of a shock if he comes in looking for a midnight snack because *we're* what's cooking in here.'"

"Oh my God, that was so incredibly cheesy," she says, giving me a playful slap on the arm. "Tell me you don't use lines like that on all the girls. I can't imagine you'd get laid if you did."

"Maybe you just bring it out of me," I growl, tugging her hair and attacking the sensitive area behind her ear with my teeth.

She melts against me and I make a mental note about her ears.

I slip my hand between her ass cheeks and squeeze before moving to her pussy. My fingers slide inside of her slick heat and I let out a moan. "My God, you're so tight…"

Her breathing becomes more labored as I plunge my fingers deeper into her wetness, caressing the soft folds. She writhes against me, her eyes squeezed shut as she rides my digits like the bad girl I'd hoped she would be.

She grips the sides of my face, attacking my mouth with a pent-up fervor that makes my toes curl, her body supercharged by my evidently magical fingers.

Wait until the next course is served…

Marchella pulls away slightly, her hands gripping the sides of my torso. "Take me to your room," she murmurs, her eyes glittering with desire. "Now."

She takes her time sliding off of me and I rise to my feet, the ache in my balls so deep and so agonizing, I want to back her against the island and bury my dick deep inside of her so I can get the release I so badly need. A chill slips down my spine as she traces the outline of my pecs with her fingertips, sweeping her tongue over her swollen pink lips.

I lift her into my arms and she locks her legs around me as I move from the kitchen to my room down the hallway. Our gazes are locked on each other, and it's a damn miracle that I didn't crash into anything in my path.

When we're inside, I close the door as quietly as possible since I know Dante will be skulking around for food any second. He's like a scavenger, for Christ's sake. And the skulking... well, that's courtesy of his job. You never know when he'll appear over your shoulder. He's stealth like that. It's a skill that keeps him alive while he's stalking his prey.

It's also a skill that can come back to bite me if he happens to see what I'm doing right now.

Violating the kidnapper protocol by fucking the captive.

My dick jumps.

Oh, yeah. I'm gonna fuck her good, too.

I lay Marchella on my bed, her dark hair splayed on the comforter around her flushed face. Her eyes sparkle in the moonlight that streams into the room, and she raises her arms over her head as I straddle her, a coy smile on her face.

I slide the fabric over her head and toss it to the floor, revealing her lush tits. "No panties," I breathe, lowering my head and grazing her lips with mine.

"I couldn't find any in the drawer," she murmurs. "Your kidnapping plan clearly wasn't premeditated."

"I guess that's a good thing for both of us," I say, plunging my fingers into her wetness, eliciting a loud gasp from her. I dip my head lower, and with my free hand I knead the soft flesh of her breast. I tease her nipple, gently tugging at it with my teeth as she wiggles beneath me, squealing from the sensations generated by my greedy mouth.

I want to taste all of her, sampling every bit of sweetness from those pouty lips to her quivering pussy.

I work my fingers harder and faster, flicking her clit at the same time. She clenches tight around them, a sharp yelp tumbling from her lips. I silence any other sounds by feasting on her puckered mouth and letting her sounds of pleasure infuse my entire being.

I back away slightly, pulling off my boxer briefs. My cock springs to attention, precum pooling at the tip. But it's gonna have to wait a little longer.

I haven't finished my appetizer yet.

I slide my tongue down the front of her abdomen as her legs fall open, beckoning me. I sweep my tongue down her slit before slipping it into her, stroking her velvety walls with every push deeper into her heat.

She grips my hair, tangling her fingers into it as I nip at her clit, flicking it with my tongue. Her legs tighten around my head and she grabs a pillow and presses it over her face to muffle the screams that urge me to rocket her into oblivion.

Not that I need an invitation to do *that*.

It's a given with me.

Suddenly, she throws off the pillow, pulling my head away from her pussy. "I need you inside of me now!" she rasps through gritted teeth, panting like she's choked for oxygen.

My lips curl upward as I reach into my night table drawer and grab a condom. I tear it open with my teeth and slip it out of the packet, but she takes it from me before I can roll it on. I didn't think it was possible for my cock to get any harder, but when she leans forward and teases my slit with her tongue before taking in the entire length of my throbbing shaft, I know I'm in serious danger of erupting. My hands grip the back of her head as it bobs up and down, stroking me with her lips and tongue. Tiny sparks in my groin make my skin prickle under her touch and I clench my teeth to hold back the groan that threatens to escape.

She pulls her mouth away from me minutes later, rolling the condom onto my shaft, slowly, maddeningly, tormentingly. And when she leans back onto the mattress, pulling me against her, all thoughts of what is horribly bad about this situation fade into the deep corners of my mind where I don't judge my actions and I don't worry about consequences.

Two things that are definitely going to bubble to the surface once I'm no longer drunk on my longing for Marchella Amante.

I'll consider them later…much later, when I'm sufficiently hungover from my carnal binge.

I position my cock at her entrance, my gaze tussling with hers as I thrust deep inside of her with a muffled groan. Christ, I wasn't prepared for this…*her*. Liquid heat drowns me upon entrance, suffocating me in the most sensuous possible way. I could die a happy death knowing I'd be rooted here for eternity.

I collapse on top of her, sliding my dick against her clit with every push and pull. I tug at her bottom lip with my teeth, my tongue delving into her mouth, wanton lust coursing through me and kindling every nerve ending.

If I were a forest fire….well, fuck.

I'd be ash by now.

Marchella's nails lance the skin of my back, digging into my flesh, deeper and more frenzied as I lunge forward. Her body thrashes beneath me, soft cries slipping from her mouth.

And, my God, I love the fucking music drifting into the air around us.

Our bodies slap together, pebbled with sweat. Our limbs entwine, connected in a way that was never intended, but one in which our bodies were destined to find. I wrap my arms around her, smothering her cries with my hungry mouth. She clenches, dragging me deeper, farther into her, and I suddenly…and blissfully…become her prisoner.

And I don't ever want to be released.

Though, I wouldn't be opposed to handcuffs…

I thrust hard into her carnal abyss…once, twice, three times, and as she whimpers against my lips, I let go…of everything.

What I'm supposed to do, what I'm instructed to control, what I'm responsible for managing…I let it all go.

In this second, I don't give a flying fuck about any of it.

I don't want to think.

I only want to feel.

So I let the blaze rage through me, incinerating all of the objections and the criticisms.

Sparks ignite deep within my groin and I explode inside of her with a loud roar that I don't bother to mask.

This is me, not giving a fuck about anything but the beauty writhing against my lust-soaked body.

My God, I'd wanted this so badly years ago.

And what I imagined doesn't even come close to the salacious reality.

I'll pay for it later, but right now?

I'm actually…good. Better than good.

I'm amazing, in a way I've never been before.

In a way I don't ever want to lose.

I let out a deep breath, settling myself against her flushed skin. "Damn…"

She flings an arm over me, her dark hair tickling my chest as she shifts herself closer. "Wow."

"Yeah." I can say other words but they're stuck in the back of my throat, along with all of the conflict.

Marchella rolls herself onto her elbow, her breaths short and sharp and her cheeks bright pink. I've never seen her look more beautiful, or alive, for that matter. "So, is this Stockholm Syndrome, but like, on steroids?"

I snicker. "I guess in some twisted way, it could be."

"How does one cure themselves of this syndrome?" she whispers, trailing a finger down the front of my chest. A shiver zips through me and she giggles. "You're ticklish?"

"Maybe…" I say, shuddering again as the tingles ripple across my skin.

That's all she needs to hear. Suddenly, those devious fingers are digging around into every possible crevice they can find and I wiggle and twist to get out of their path.

"S-stop!" I croak, clutching myself. This really isn't a good look for me, I know. But dammit, tickles are kind of my kryptonite.

Well, tickles and ego, if I'm being honest.

And I'd never willingly admit to either.

Marchella tilts her head back and chuckles, but she gives her hands…and me…a rest. "Wow, that's something I never expected you to admit."

"How can I lie? I can barely breathe," I grumble, still shielding myself because I don't fully trust that she won't try to wield her weapons over me again.

She lets out a sigh and leans back into the mattress. "You keep surprising me," she murmurs. "I don't know what to expect next."

"I like to keep people on their toes," I say, throwing caution to the wind and rolling onto my side. I'm exposed right now but hoping she will reserve her next attack. "In your case, on your back works well." I wink at her and she smiles up at me. I smooth a strand of her hair away from her face, her eyes now more blue than green. I've noticed that when she's happy, they tend to favor that sapphire hue.

I could watch them change color all day, every day.

I could allow myself to slip away into the pools of expressive color.

But I know my big, fat ego would just sling a line around my neck and pull me back out.

Because I have no business being with this girl. She shines brighter than a sky full of stars when she's content, and I'm the kind of guy who would only stomp out all of the sparkle.

I'm no knight in shining armor, and he's the kind of guy Marchella needs — someone she can trust, someone she can rely on, and someone she can respect.

I'm none of those things.

I wasn't ever those things.

Sure, I have my moments, but she shouldn't have to deal with all of the in-between bullshit. Sounds to me like her father was the same way, if I'm even the slightest bit like him.

She needs something more…something better.

Work is my life.

I don't have room for romance.

But even as my mind repeats the words, a nagging feeling deep in my gut reminds me about Bella, and I know I'm full of crap.

Not that I can do anything about it when I'm so close to dangling her brother over an open flame to get back what he stole.

That's not exactly white knight behavior.

That's the demon inside, the only role I can ever really play well.

So this thing between us?

This rush of electricity?

This all-consuming passion?

It can never be more than a blip on my radar.

No matter how much I want it…*us*…to be more.

And lying to myself about all the reasons why it can't happen will only make it harder to walk away.

Chapter Fourteen
MARCHELLA

It was a distraction. Plain and simple.

That's the story I'm selling.

Sleeping with Roman was just a way to keep me from letting my nightmares grab hold of me once more.

I needed a reprieve.

Period.

What I got, though?

Oh my God….

It was nothing short of the most sensuously blissful experience I've ever encountered.

I'm talking toe-curling, light my insides on fire, can't see anything but stars and glitter blissful.

When I used to daydream about his body pressed against me, he was just a boy. Now, he's all man — strong, sexy, and sensual.

And he just completely ruined me for any other guy who crosses my path in the future.

Well, if there is a future.

But like I said, it was just a distraction.

And the orgasms that rocketed my body into oblivion also damn-near melted my brain.

That will help when my head hits the pillow.

I don't think I can even conjure up the energy to dream after that.

It's like my brain short-circuited…in the best possible way.

But I can't stay here. I can't feed these insane feelings swirling through my insides. It's nuts! He's a criminal!

Assault!

Kidnapping!

And that's only what I've witnessed.

Lord only knows what else he's done.

I don't even want to try to imagine it because I'd really love for these body tingles to last a little longer. The aftershocks ripple over me like gentle waves, and I want to sing out with glee because he's made me feel lighter, brighter, and unexpectedly more peaceful than I have in months.

I can't stop smiling either.

And he definitely noticed that fact.

"You look…relaxed," he says, flipping onto his side and slinging an arm over me.

I think he might be doing that to make sure I don't launch a tickle attack on him.

But really, I'd much rather have his shredded muscles plastered against me.

I nod. "Yes. I feel kind of amazing, actually."

He grins. "That's good feedback. Thanks."

I reach around him, running my hand down the slope of his spine. He stiffens slightly because he doesn't know what I'm about to do next.

I can't blame him.

I swallow a chuckle.

Nice to have some of the power for once.

My mind flickers back to the nightmare that woke us both, the one that brought him to me, the one that led me to his bed.

And suddenly, the clouds of euphoria part and an icy hand clenches my heart.

I should have known the feelings of bliss would fizzle out sooner than later.

"You look like you wanna say something." His forehead creases.

Damn, he's perceptive.

When you look at him, you don't think he's going to be firing on all cylinders. He's just too gorgeous to have it all.

Another shocker.

His eyes blaze with longing, and while I want to flip him over and ride him until the sun comes up, he asked me something before and I need to give him an answer. I want him to know why what he did for me by bringing Bella here was so special.

I also need him to understand why she can't stay.

"When you came into my room before, you asked me if I was okay." I take a deep breath. "I'm not, for a lot of reasons. The past couple of days have turned me into a tangled mess of anxiety and panic and sadness. Oddly enough, even though you caused some of it, you did more than you know to relieve a lot of it."

He wraps his arm around me, obviously sensing that I need to be held.

Like I said, very perceptive.

I stare up into his face, a face that over the past couple of days I've wanted to both punch and kiss at varying intervals. He's gone from sexy to menacing to downright villainous. I get those transitions. It's who he is that drives them.

But maybe it's who he wants to be that morphs his expression into concern right now.

"It's a little weird for me to hear that I've helped more than I've hurt." A small smile tugs at his lips. "I don't get that often."

"Well, I guess there's a first time for everything."

"This is a first I never thought I'd experience."

Tears sting my eyes. "When I was younger, we had a dog. She was a Boston, just like Bella. Such a good dog," I muse.

"What happened?"

"Mama loved to visit me at school when I was at NYU. She'd take a car downtown and we'd walk in the park. Just the three of us. It was great. Those were the best days..." My voice trails off and an ache in my chest makes my voice quiver. "But then things got worse. The visits started to get more and more sporadic. Until the last time she came down to see me."

Roman just waits. He doesn't speak, just gives me a moment to breathe. It's like he can sense what I'm going to say next, and that it really needs no prompting at all.

"We went for a walk in the park, like always. Frankie came with her because she wasn't in great shape but desperately wanted to have one of our days. It was a beautiful one, too. The sky was clear, the air was crisp and fresh, the grass so green. But Mama was really tired and weak," I whisper. "And at one point, she collapsed onto a bench. I panicked and dropped the leash to help her. I blinked my eyes and she was gone, Roman. Forever."

He brushes his lips against my forehead as the tears roll down my cheeks. "I lost her. I lost my Princess."

"I'm sorry," he murmurs. "That's really horrible."

"The worst part is, we chipped her but something went wrong with the microchip registration. Her chip was registered to another family, who also had a Boston Terrier. It was a crazy mix-up, but we never were able to find her. And then not long afterward, Mom passed. I lost Princess, my mom, my dad…" I sniffle. "And now Frankie…" I shake my head as the tears slide down my cheeks, forcing a dry laugh. "Wow, talk about post-coital bliss, huh? I just wrecked that completely, didn't I?"

He shrugs. "Eh, bliss is overrated. I like to keep things real. They may suck and they may hurt but they make you stronger."

"I don't feel very strong right now," I whisper.

"You are. More than you know. You may have resisted being a mob enforcer's daughter, but that blood still flows through you. And you have that strength, Marchella. I can see it. I can feel it."

"Chella," I murmur.

He furrows his brow and I smile.

"Because we're friends."

He dips his head lower and takes my lower lip between his teeth, gently tugging it. "I think I like being friends with you."

"Same."

He brushes his fingertips down the side of my face, leaving a trail of kisses where the tears streamed down my cheeks. "Listen, I don't want you to worry about Frankie," he says. "I'm gonna take care of it, okay?"

I nod, another sob threatening to choke me. "Thank you."

I sit up, swiping my eyes and flashing him a watery smile. "I, um, guess I should go. I don't want Bella to wake up and get scared. She's been through enough." I grab the t-shirt that landed next to the bed and slide it on, running my hand through my sexed-up hair before I throw my legs over the side of the bed and stand up.

"You don't have to go back alone."

I can't see his face at this point because my back is to him. I did that on purpose because I knew he'd see it on my face and in my gaze…how much I want to stay.

How much I don't want to leave him.

I slowly turn in his direction, the irony of the situation not lost on me.

The guy who kidnapped me and stole my freedom now wants me to spend the night with him.

I tilt my head to the side. "Oh? And do you want to join me?"

His full lips lift and the dimple in his cheek appears.

Oh boy. The tingles are back in full force now.

"I do. Is that okay?"

I nod, a rush of heat flowing into my cheeks. "Yes," I whisper.

He gets up, pulls on his boxer briefs, and laces his fingers with mine, leading me back to me room.

This has got to be some kind of alternate reality because in what lifetime would I even consider doing all of that with a guy like Roman Villani? A man who holds a hell of a lot of power right now — over me, over my brother.

I needed a distraction.

Yes, Chella. Keep reminding yourself of that! See how far it gets you!

It may have started as a distraction, but it's quickly become more.

More.

But really, how much more can it possibly become?

This little fantasy bubble we're living in right now is just that! He's going to manipulate my brother to get what he wants and then he'll let me go. We'll both go our separate ways, in worlds which are galaxies apart. Neither one of us would have any clue how to exist in each other's lives now.

Still…

It feels so nice to have his muscular arms snaked around my front, my body spooning with his and Bella cuddled against my neck.

I haven't felt this safe or comforted in a long time.

Maybe ever.

When I drift off to sleep almost seconds after my head hits the pillow, one final thought floats into my mind.

The mafia thug actually brings me peace.

Who the hell would have ever guessed that?

Chapter Fifteen
ROMAN

I don't remember falling asleep. I only know I haven't woken up feeling this good in…fuck. Forever, maybe?

Feeling Chella's body tight against mine, her smooth skin brushing against my chest as she shifts closer with a sexy moan, like she's just been ravaged and is basking in the afterglow.

Oh, yeah.

That happened.

"What are we doing?" she murmurs with a deep sigh.

"I think it's called spooning, not that I've ever done it with anyone before."

Chella giggles. "Yes, it is called spooning and yes, that is what we're doing. I wasn't being that literal, though."

"I know."

"So?" she twists her head around to peer at me with heavy, sleepy eyes.

"I like how direct you are," I murmur.

She shrugs. "If you want an answer, the first step is to ask the question."

I bury my head in her wavy dark hair, breathing in her scent. Truth be told, I'd forgotten all about the big ass elephant in the room. "I didn't exactly plan for this to happen."

"Which part of 'this' do you mean? Just so we're on the same page."

"All of them." I stroke the back of her head. "This is wrong on every level. I never should have…*shit*. The whole thing was a big fucking mistake," I mutter.

Her eyes widen and she pulls away from me with a stricken look on her face and I let out a groan, realizing I actually spoke those words instead of thinking them.

"No, you're taking it the wrong way—"

She pulls the sheets around her, putting as much distance between us as she can without rolling off the bed. "I don't see another way of taking it, but I shouldn't be so surprised. I mean, I agreed to do things for you as part of my payment, so I guess this falls under my job responsibilities," she snips, pulling her hand away when I try to grab for it.

"Hey," I say, pulling her back to me. "Listen to me. Don't read anything into what I said. Just know this. You're the only bright spot in this fucking black hole of my life right now, Chella. That night at the restaurant…when I realized who you were, so many feelings came rushing back. I saw something in you, felt something I wanted to grasp onto, something I wasn't able to touch all those years ago. But I knew I couldn't. Not ever. You were too good, too high above me. I knew it the second you crashed into me at the bar."

She lifts an eyebrow. "If memory serves, *you* crashed into *me*."

"Eh, semantics," I say with a grin. "Maybe I did it on purpose because even though I knew you were out of reach, I still wanted to experience what it would feel like, being touched by that light of yours, even if it was for a split second. And I walked away feeling like I'd lost something huge that night. A second chance, maybe. Then my world got turned upside down and suddenly, the bright spot was within my reach again." I scrub a hand down the front of my face and fall onto the pillow, the usual heavy weight in my gut dissipating as the words tumble out of my mouth. "Just so you know, I don't ever talk like this. Hell, I don't think like this either. I don't give a damn about things like inner light and crap like that. I'm not a good guy, Chella. I do bad shit to people, and even if they deserve it, it still doesn't justify my actions." I let out a frustrated sigh. "I'm not making this any better, am I?"

"I didn't know you felt that way." She slowly creeps toward me, her eyes taking on a soft bluish-green tint, whereas only a minute ago, they were dark and heated, like flaming emeralds ready to impale my soul. "I didn't expect for this to happen either, but like I keep saying, you surprise me. Over and over."

"I hope that's not the only thing I'll get to do over and over," I murmur, grasping her ass and giving it a squeeze. She lets out a tiny squeal, jumping against me. Then I let out a groan and clap a hand to my forehead. "Christ! What the hell am I doing?"

"Is that supposed to be rhetorical?"

My hand drops to the side of the mattress. "Yeah. I really messed things up. And being with you is only gonna mess them up worse than I already have."

"Because you're a bad guy."

"Yes, because I'm a fucking bad guy!"

"You know what I think?" she asks, tracing a finger over my pecs. I have to grit my teeth to not let out a yelp because, you know, the tickle thing.

My jaw tightens and I shift my arm to knock off her hand.

She snickers. "I think you're more of a softy than you know."

"Why? Because I'm ticklish?"

She shakes her head. "No, because I think you have inner battles with yourself pretty often, the guy you really are fighting against is the guy you want the world to see. The push and pull. The constant surprises. If you were consistently a fuckhead, I'd say maybe you're right. Maybe you really are a bad guy. But you give glimpses of other things, deeper layers." She lifts an eyebrow. "Am I right?"

"Maybe."

"So why the constant battle?"

"Because people have certain expectations of me," I grumble. "I have to meet them or exceed them whenever I can."

"Or else?"

"Are you serious?"

She nods.

"Or else I get knocked down. Kicked away. Disregarded like I'm some punk ass kid who got his role because of his family name, not because he really deserves it. They'd think I was weak. I'd lose all credibility."

"Is it hard to live every day feeling like you have something to prove?"

"Yeah, but if I don't, someone will tear the rug out from under me. This is how I create my power."

She chuckles. "You sounded like some villainous super hero right then."

"Yeah, well, you're starting to look more and more like my kryptonite. In more ways than one," I say, taking her finger into my mouth and giving it a good suck.

"I'm just saying there's a lot more to you than meets the eye, and if you want people's respect, they should know everything you have to offer. You're a dick, yes. I mean, the other day…in the park, in your office," She shakes her head. "Total asshole. But then you went to find Bella and risked your car and your neck for her, you showed me a different side. And last night, when we were together…" Chella's voice trails off and her eyes take on a faraway look. "You were a completely different person. A guy I'd have never guessed was buried behind your thuggy façade. Stop warring against yourself. You want to lead? Then show people that your strength doesn't just come from your fists. You're more than that."

I drag my fingertip over the outline of her lips. "You're pretty perceptive."

She giggles. "Nah, I was just searching for some justification for me practically jumping you last night."

Suddenly, a high-pitched bark jolts me, and Bella climbs on top of us and positions herself right in front of Chella, going to town on her face like it's a lollipop.

Chella holds her, laughing and sputtering until tears spring to her eyes and I can't help but join in.

The laughing, not the licking.

I mean, I'd lick Chella like that too. She tastes sweeter than anything else I've ever had in my mouth.

I get Bella's obvious obsession with her flavor.

I'm kind of obsessed myself.

Like I need any more reasons for the battle to rage.

When Bella finally takes a breather and cuddles into her, Chella grazes my arm with her hand. But her expression in no way matches her incessant giggles from only seconds ago. That sober look makes my throat tighten and I can tell there's something she wants to say.

It's the 'what' that gives me pause.

"Roman," she murmurs, rubbing the top of Bella's head. "I need to tell you something."

"Anything," I reply.

"We can't keep Bella," she whispers, nuzzling the puppy's neck.

"What are you talking about?" I ask, sitting up. "Why not? I mean, she's already christened the place. I'll get you whatever you need—"

She shakes her head. "It's not that. Remember what I told you about Princess last night? She ran away and we never found her because she wasn't chipped. That was on us. But if Bella has some kind of identification, it's not right to keep her. Her owners must be worried sick about her. We should do the right thing."

Her voice quivers and even I feel a lump form in the back of my throat.

Some badass enforcer I am.

Guess I'm softer than I thought.

For fuck's sake!

But as much as I want to keep Bella and Chella…cute…I didn't catch that until just now…I know she's right.

"Are you sure that's what you want to do?"

She shakes her head. "It's not at all what I want to do. But it's the right thing to do. I'd be beside myself if I lost this beautiful little girl," she whispers against Bella's ear. A second later, she raises her distressed gaze up to me. "I don't want anyone to be missing her any longer than they already have been."

I watch her cuddle with Bella, sliding behind her once again, her shoulders quietly quaking.

After all this girl has been through, she's still worried about everyone else, even people she doesn't know.

What the hell am I doing to her?

What am I doing to myself?

A loud knock at the door alerts me that Dante is awake and probably pissed off that he won't be having any eggs for breakfast. I drop a kiss onto Chella's head and roll out of the bed. I grab my boxer briefs and pull them on before walking out into the hallway.

Dante is waiting for me, lounging against the wall with a smug smile on his face. "So. That's where you were shacked up last night, yeah?" He chuckles. "Rekindling old flames, yeah?"

I grab him by the wrist and pull him into my bedroom. "Shut the hell up," I grunt.

"Ooh, so sensitive." He nudges my shoulder. "Listen, Matteo is looking for you. He said he's been calling you for hours."

"My phone is charging," I say, nodding at my nightstand. "I wasn't really worried about whose calls I'd miss last night when I left it."

"Yep, I'm sure you had plenty of other things on your mind. And on your cock," he says.

I grab a pair of basketball shorts and tug them on. "When did he call?" I ask, ignoring his other comments. "And keep your damn voice down, will ya?"

"He just called now. Said he's been trying to get you for a while."

"Shit," I grumble. "I need to get back to him. Can you order some food for Marchella so I can take care of whatever he needs? We, ah, kind of made a little bit of a mess—"

"Yeah, yeah, yeah, I know all about it," Dante says with a wicked smile on his face. "There was a fucking egg puddle all over the floor and of course, I cleaned it up because you were too busy screwing your girl. Which, by the way, I had to listen to for hours, you sonofabitch. The screams and groans kept me up for fucking ever. How the hell did the dog sleep through all of that anyway?"

I snicker, running a hand through my hair. "I have no idea. Oh, and speaking of the dog, do me a favor and make sure she doesn't pee all over my sneakers again."

"I'll consider it," he says, strutting out the door and pulling it closed behind him.

I collapse onto my bed, pressing my fingertips to my temples. How much longer can I keep this whole thing going, this alternate reality I've created? The one where I keep ignoring the threats and the danger and play house with the girl I kidnapped?

She saw right through me like I was a pane of freshly washed glass.

She felt the inner turmoil.

She sensed the clash of wills deep inside of me.

When I pick up my laptop and stab Matteo's number into the keyboard, my gut twists because it's a sign that war will always rage on.

And I'll never be the victor.

When his face flashes on the screen, a pang assaults my chest. His eyes spit fire, his lips twisted into a grimace. "Roman, where the hell have you been?" he seethes. "I've been trying to call you for fucking hours!" But before I can speak, he holds up a hand. "No, you know what? I don't really give a shit. But do you know what I give a shit about?"

I rub the back of my neck. I'm sure there is a mile-long list, but I'll just humor him for now. "Right at this second? Um, breakfast?"

"You're a real fucking comedian, aren't you?" he shouts. "So let's try to find the joke in this one, Roman. You, getting taken for four fucking kilos of blow by fucking Frankie Amante! You, killing Salvatore Giaconne! And *you*, kidnapping Amante's sister! What is wrong with you? Is your head completely up your ass right now? Do you have any idea what you've done? And do you know what's worse? I spoke to you yesterday and you told me everything was fucking fine! *Fine!* You lied to me!"

"I didn't lie. At the exact time we spoke, everything was fine." I rub the back of my neck like that alone will relieve the growing stress knot at the base of my skull.

"You asshole!" he roars, and I swear I can see smoke coming out of his ears. "How the hell did you let this happen? All you had to do was keep an eye on things! What exactly were you doing at the club when they boosted that blow? Or maybe the better question is, *who* were you doing?" He slams his hand on the desk. "Frankie fucking Amante! I knew that slimeball bastard would be back to screw with us at some point! I can't believe you missed it!"

"Jesus Christ, do you always make the right decisions? Huh? Because I seem to remember one not too long ago where you put yourself and Heaven in the line of fire because of a bad fucking call!" My teeth grind together as I glare at my brother's face on the laptop screen.

"Don't talk to me like that!" he thunders, his face beet red. "I'm your fucking boss and you'd better remember that! I gave you that job and I can yank it away just as fast! Goddammit, Roman! Amante fucking robbed you blind! Do you know how that makes our family look? How we'll look to the syndicate?" Matteo slams his hand on the side of his desk. "I trusted you to keep things under control and you let that asshole ravage our business!"

"But I'm handling it, dammit! That's why I have Marchella. I needed a bargaining chip so he wouldn't bolt from the city before getting our drugs back!"

Matteo takes a second to breathe, and it's a good thing because I feel like his head is damn close to spinning off his shoulders, *Exorcist*-style.

"Roman," he says in a calmer voice. Not calm, calm*er*. "You really messed things up this time."

My shoulders sag as Matteo continues his verbal lashing, and I'm very happy he's on the other side of the country right now and not standing in front of me.

But once the immediate shock wears off and Matteo's tirade reverberates between my ears along with my thoughts, it dawns on me that someone ratted me out. He'd never get this kind of detailed information through the grapevine.

Someone told him what went down.

Someone who knows exactly what happened and who was involved.

Ray.

Motherfucker!

So much for him being my trusted sidekick.

"Well, I'm sure glad Ray alerted you about that one," I scoff sarcastically.

"At least someone believes in leveling with the boss." He sighs. "Roman, this is a bad fucking situation. You have no idea what Amante is planning or who he's planning it with. He came after us after all this time, now that his father is in jail…why? To save face, to make a quick buck, to get revenge since he's in a black hole and we're sitting on top of the food chain? All of the above? And you know what? It doesn't even matter. What matters is that he exposed a weakness. In you. And he's gonna come back to tear at it some more. He's always been a selfish prick and right now, I don't think he gives a damn about his sister. I think he's out for himself and he's got nothing to lose."

"Look, Matty. I know I didn't do things the way you would have, but I've got Amante's balls in a vise right now. I'm gonna handle it. He's gonna make us whole again. I will make sure he pays us for that blow."

"He's not gonna give you anything, Roman. No matter what he told you when you beat his ass. You let yourself get tangled up in the Amante net, and now there's an army out for blood…and money."

"What are you talking about? *Who* are you talking about? What goddamn army?"

Matteo lets out a deep sigh. "Frankie's dad got thrown in the clink for killing a couple of guys six months ago. You hear about that?"

"Yeah, I know. Left his family in shambles. So?"

"He's not the one who committed the actual murders, Roman. He took the blame for someone else…*his son*."

I furrow my brow. "What the hell are you talking about?"

Matteo's lips stretch into a tight line. "Frankie, as usual, pissed off some people. Badass Russian crew from Brooklyn. The Volkov Bratva. He stole one of their cars…one that had a shipment of uncut blow hidden in the trunk. When one of their guys found him, he panicked and killed him. His father tried to stop him because he knew what Volkov would do to the rest of his family in retaliation. He was too late, but Frankie escaped and his dad still took the fall for it when the cops showed up. They claimed it was second-degree murder because it was self-defense, but it's still a long fucking time to be put away for something you didn't do."

"Pretty noble of him," I mutter.

"Yeah, well, the Volkovs haven't forgotten about it. They want their drugs back. Sound familiar?"

"So you think he robbed us because he needed access to…*shit*," I mutter.

"He's not going to get you those drugs or the money," Matteo grunts. "It's all long fucking gone, don't you get it? Frankie's desperate, Roman. He's either gonna run to save his ass, or he's gonna hit you up again, but this time with his pals from the bratva on his heels because he knows he's dead if he doesn't pay them back every ounce of what he stole. You killed the wrong fucking guy, Roman. You should've killed Frankie because he's not finished with you. But you didn't. Instead, you took his sister, who is leverage not only for you, but for the Volkov Bratva. Do you know what that means?"

My spine stiffens and anger bubbles in my veins because the one thing I was trying so hard to prevent is the very thing that is coming back to bite me in the ass.

I took action to gain respect, to show leadership.

My most trusted guy fucking sold me out.

He decimated any shred of trust I may have had in him when he made that call.

I'm on my own now, neck-deep in the murk that is about to swallow me.

And yeah.

I know exactly what Matteo means.

Blood rushes between my ears and any sliver of control I may have had before slowly seeps out of me, dissipating into the air. My heart hammers against my chest, waiting for the words I know will come.

"Payback." Matteo's forehead creases. "It means they'll be coming for you, too. So you have a choice. Bend over and let them fuck you up the ass again, or show them what happens when they take what's ours. But make it fast, because you're almost out of time to stop them."

Chapter Sixteen
MARCHELLA

I sink onto the kitchen chair with Bella in my lap after she scarfs down an entire bowl of puppy kibble in what feels like seconds. Poor baby. I hate that she was wandering around on the streets of Inwood by herself, hungry and cold, for God only knows how long.

I pick at the bacon in front of me, unable to eat a single bite of the feast Dante ordered for breakfast. My heart clenches when I think about giving her up. I mean, it's been less than twelve hours that I've even known her, for Pete's sake.

Still, she represents a bittersweet memory, one that will be really hard to close the book on once we give her up to the police.

I release a shuddering sigh and slouch over in the chair.

It's the right thing to do, though.

I'm doing what's best for Bella.

And even though it really hurts now, I know I'll be making her owners really happy.

My eyes sting with tears and I force the images of that last day in the park to the dark corners of my mind. I can't think about that day and all of the trauma that came with it. I have to focus on what lies ahead and what's still in my control.

Admittedly, with Roman in the picture, what's in my control for the foreseeable future is a bit fuzzy, especially after last night.

I wrap my arms around Bella as she curls up in my lap, her little body warm against my bare legs. A loud snore breaks the silence and I giggle, despite the tear sliding down my cheek.

A shiver slides down my back and I bite down hard on my lower lip remembering his hands stroking my prickled skin, his hungry mouth devouring me like I was his last meal, his muscles rippling beneath my hands.

And his eyes…blazing with a heat so intense, it could singe my insides from a mile away.

"How twisted am I, Bella?" I whisper. "How can I feel these things? How can I get swept away like this, knowing that he's still a—"

"Hey!" A booming voice silences my next words and I look up in a panic at Dante strutting into the kitchen. "How's the food?" He pulls on a baseball cap and slides his arms into a sweatshirt.

"Good," I say even though I haven't been able to stomach a single bite. "Are you heading out?"

"Yeah, I'm going for a run. Give you a chance to, ah, bond some more with Romo," he says with a wink.

My face flushes with heat and I manage a weak smile. "I'll let Roman know."

Dante chuckles, shaking his head. "Oh, so you're his assistant now, too?"

I shrug. "I think it's written somewhere in the employment contract I signed."

"Nice. Don't ever lose that sense of humor, Marchella," Dante quips. "Especially if you're gonna be hanging around my brother. Trust me, you'll need it."

"Thanks for the tip," I murmur, the hot flush now flooding my insides as he turns to open the front door.

I stare at the door as it slams closed behind him, almost in a trance until reality smacks me in the face.

All good things come to an end.

No matter what I think or feel or want.

Mama, Papa, my career, Princess, Bella…Jesus, it's a depressing list.

And I'm only twenty-four!

I lean my head back, expelling a loud sigh. "I'm so tired of losing, Bella," I whisper. "When the hell is it going to end?"

Roman clears his throat behind me and I gasp, twisting around at the intruding sound. "You scared me," I yelp.

He runs a hand through his hair, avoiding my eyes. He obviously heard what I said, although he chooses to ignore it as he grabs a bottle of water from the fridge.

Maybe he thinks it was a rhetorical question.

I guess it was, but only because I don't have a freaking answer myself.

I stare at his back as he guzzles it down before tossing the empty into a recycling container under the sink.

"Everything okay?" I ask.

He shrugs, still unable…or unwilling…to look at me. "Yeah."

A stab of rejection slices into my heart. "Is there any reason why you insist on keeping your back turned?"

His spine stiffens and he slowly rotates so I can see the hardened expression on his face. The gaze that melted away my inhibitions such a short time ago is now sharp and cold.

Completely void of emotion.

"Did something happen with your brother?" I ask, gathering Bella into my arms and hugging her tight against me as if she's the only thing that can shield me from the apparent stranger in front of me.

"Yeah," he rasps, narrowing his eyes at me. "Something happened."

I pull my lips into a tight line, trying desperately to calm my galloping heart. "What's going on here, Roman?" I ask. "You left me and everything was fine. Now you're looking at me like you want me dead." I swallow hard. "What changed?"

His lips twist into a grimace. "Nothing!" he bellows, stalking past me toward the living room. Then he stops short and spins around, glowering at me. "No, you know what? There is something. See, all the bullshit you fed me about seeing something deeper inside of me, someone who's good and soft and all that crap?" He stomps back toward the kitchen table. "That's not who I really am," he says in a choked voice. "It may be what you want to believe, but it's not who you really see. It can't be! Because I'm not any of that!"

I recoil as he shouts those last words, turning around and fisting his hair as he stalks past the coffee table. "I'm the guy who needs to be in control, Chella! I'm the guy who gets things done, no matter what the cost!" He gets right in my face, his teeth clenched, his forehead pinched. "I'm the one who people have to count on," he growls, jabbing himself in the chest with his thumb. "Me! And that guy doesn't have the luxury of being good! If I snooze on my work, if I don't do what's expected of me, I fucking fail and everything crumbles. Do you understand that?"

My mouth drops open because whomever this guy is, he's most definitely not the guy I spent the night with...the guy I thought I might actually be falling for by some bizarre twist of fate. It takes me a second to process his words, just enough time for my stomach to knot like a giant pretzel. I watch him collapse onto the couch cushion, his head dropping into his hands, and I'm still shocked into silence.

Bella wiggles around in my arms until I finally lean down and let her leap out of them. She trots right over to where Roman is sitting and hops up onto the couch next to him, resting her head on his leg. My eyes widen. The guy is like a ticking time bomb right now. I don't know if it's such a great idea for Bella to be in the line of fire—

That's when he reaches over to stroke the top of her head with the same gentleness he displayed when we were together.

And suddenly, the guy I know who's inside of him, the one he's so bent on rejecting, claws his way through that vicious exterior.

He's not the monster he is so desperate to put on display.

With a deep, shuddering sigh, he leans back against the cushion, his eyes closed. He hasn't moved his hand, though, and he's still nuzzling Bella's ears. Pretty soon, her body begins to quake and she's snoring.

Because she's comfortable.

And because she sees exactly what I do, the real Roman Villani.

Not the nefarious alter ago he insists on showing the world.

"I'm the youngest of all my brothers," he murmurs, his tired voice shattering the still, tense air. "I always got away with everything because of it. My dad tried to shield me from the family businesses because he knew how dangerous things could get if I got involved too early without knowing how to handle things. But I was a rebel. I didn't care about consequences, and it always pissed me off that they'd hold me back. I couldn't learn if they didn't trust me to do the work." He runs a hand through his hair, tugging at the ends. "So a couple of years after your family left Sicily, I tagged along on a job that Dante did. He didn't know it until I showed up, and to say he was angry is a huge understatement. I didn't know what was about to go down and me being there, in the center of something really dangerous, knocked him off his game. He was doing a hit and I was in the way. I distracted him from his targets. One guy got away, the other one came after us. Shot Dante in the chest. I didn't realize he'd been wearing a Kevlar vest, but thank fuck, he was."

I bite down on my lower lip. "What did you do?"

He sits up and looks at me, his expression grave. "I killed him," he says, his voice hoarse. "First guy I ever popped."

I inch toward him. "So you saved Dante."

"That time, yeah. But when the other guy got away, he came after my family. Opened us up to attacks from all directions. All the bottom-dwelling scumbags who were trying to claim a piece of what we had came after us because I made a mess of everything. The hit was supposed to be clean and untraceable. I fucked all of that up and it put us all in a bad place for a long time afterward." He drops his gaze to Bella. "It's something I know they all think about and even now, years later, I still feel like a liability, like I have to prove to them that I'm not that fucked-up kid anymore, that I can make good decisions, that they can trust me."

Gingerly, I lower myself to the couch. "And that call with your brother?"

"It just brought everything back," he grumbles. "Because I feel like every time they give me an inch of rope, I end up hanging myself with it. I lose sight of what's important and shit goes sideways. I try to recover but keep sinking deeper into the mess I've created."

I nibble at my fingernail. "I think you need to stop getting sucked into the past. You're battling against it so hard that you can't move forward. Things happen. You've made up for them and your brother clearly trusts you or he wouldn't have left you in charge."

Roman's eyes rake over me, the icy glare melting to reveal a mix of emotions that are even more startling.

Regret, remorse, and guilt.

Color me completely confused about now.

"You can't move forward if you keep making the same mistakes," he murmurs. "Making the wrong choices, not seeing the writing on the wall, being so intent to follow a certain path even though I'd have known it would lead to a dead-end if I spent the time thinking about it instead of bulldozing my way toward it." His hand creeps over to me, grazing the top of my leg. "Deciding how the hell I'm supposed to deliver on the one thing that can save our livelihood," he rasps, his blue eyes darkening with each word spoken.

I smile at him, lacing my fingers with his. "Nobody ever said being the boss was easy," I whisper, stroking the side of his face.

"Neither is giving up something you want more than anything," he says.

"This life is all about choices, Roman. I learned that the hard way when my dad made his," I say.

"Chella…" he whispers, moving closer still, careful not to disturb Bella.

"Yeah?"

"I need to tell you something."

Chapter Seventeen
ROMAN

"Don't make the mistake of cutting off ties with your father," I say. "I've learned the hard way that people have reasons for doing things. They may be good reasons, may be bad ones. But before you decide to turn your back on him forever, you should listen to his."

God only knows, my own father could have shut me out plenty of times but didn't.

Family needs to stick together, no matter how bad things get.

And even though he caused my own family a hell of a lot of headaches and is a piece of garbage, he's still her father. He's still her blood.

She furrows her brow. "Why should I listen now when he had plenty of opportunities to tell me his reasons before? I mean, he spent my whole life doing things 'his way', and he never gave a damn about what I thought before. If he cared about me, he'd have tried to talk to me when he wasn't behind bulletproof Plexiglas," she huffs, folding her arms over her chest. Bright pink spots appear in her cheeks and I know she's angry.

I also know she'd never forgive herself if she knew the truth and didn't do anything to fix the splintered relationship. This girl, the one I've gotten to know pretty well over the past couple of days, is so good at seeing things in others, but she really can't see past her own nose.

"Look, all I'm saying is that there might be more to it than the story you know. Trust me, I spent a long damn time being pissed off about the way my brother Matteo handled things that involved me before I realized that he was doing them for the good of the family and the organization." I push back my hair. "Hell, I still get pissed off," I grumble. "But sometimes that's what you need to spark the conversation, you know? I'd do anything for my brothers, even though I'd like to kick the shit outta them more often than not. Family fights. It's the way things go. You get knocked down and then you jump back up only to get kicked in the teeth again."

Chella lifts an eyebrow. "I think you have somewhat of a different dynamic with your family than I do with mine."

"The point is, you don't ever want to be in a place where you can't make things right."

"You don't know the whole—"

I shake my head. "I don't give a shit about the whole story. I only give a shit about *you*."

Oh, Christ. I said that?

Her eyes pop open wide, more blue than I've ever seen them, glittering like diamonds. "You…um, *me?*"

I give her a long, hard look, my gaze tracing over the perfect arch of her eyebrows, the dark lashes framing her eyes, the perfect pink lips that taste like fucking heaven.

Yeah, I mean her.

I reach toward her, my thumb and forefinger stroking the side of her smooth cheek. Her skin is bright pink, the color deepening as the intensity of my stare increases. "Something happened that I didn't expect," I croak. "A lot of things, actually, but this whole thing…with you…and me…" I reach my hand around the back of her head, pulling her toward me. "I don't know what this is, Chella," I whisper. "Or what to call it. But I know how I feel when you're near me. I know how I feel when you look at me, when you see into my soul. I'd cut anyone who came too close to seeing right through me because it's a dangerous fucking thing to be exposed like that. But when you do it…" I shake my head. "I feel hopeful. Relieved that you don't see the same monster that everyone else does. Because you're right. I'm not that guy."

She smiles at me, lacing her fingers with mine. "I know that."

I nod. "I've never been able to show anyone who I really am. That shit can get you killed."

"So you're not threatened by me?" she asks in a coy voice.

"Not threatened," I murmur. "Just in awe of you and what you've done to me."

"I feel the same way. And I know that's insane because of the situation." She looks away for a split second. "I have to tell you something, too."

"Yeah…"

"Before we slept together…" Chella clears her throat. "I, ah, I'd thought about seducing you, so that maybe you'd be more agreeable and let me check on Frankie."

"I didn't let you call him, though."

"I still slept with you, though."

I snake my arm tighter around her. "And did you have an ulterior motive last night when we were sitting in a puddle of egg yolks?"

"No. I just…I wanted to be close to you. I wanted to be with you." So open. So honest. So fucking perfect.

Our foreheads touch, our lips practically grazing each other.

"I wanted that, too."

"I think I might be losing my mind. Is it absolutely crazy to be falling for your kidnapper?" Chella whispers.

My lips curl into a grin. "When your kidnapper is hung like an ox? Nah. I think it's perfectly normal."

She giggles and gives my arm a swat. "You're a real dick."

"Yeah, I've heard that plenty." I capture her hand and bring it to my lips. "I'm falling for you, too, Chella. And it scares the shit out of me."

"I know exactly what you mean."

But…she really doesn't.

And since I can't explain the reasons why, I do the next best thing and smother her mouth with the deep-seated passion that's been rippling through me since she barreled into my life.

I grasp the sides of her face, plunging my tongue into her eager mouth. She lets out a low moan as our tongues tangle together, the coiling heat blasting through my insides. Bella, thankfully, senses she's about to get edged out and she jumps to the other side of the couch.

She's damn perceptive for a puppy.

I lean Chella backward against the cushion, straddling her as I lift the t-shirt over her head. I bury my head in her neck, teasing the sensitive area behind her ear with my tongue. Her body arches, her lush tits pressed against my chest.

"Roman," she murmurs, her eyes fluttering open.

My lips curl upward as I wrap my arms around her, holding her close enough to feel her heartbeat hammering against me. My cock jumps as she slides my shorts to my ankles, freeing me from the fabric. With trembling fingers, I do the same to her, pulling off the shorts I'd given her before breakfast. I slide my hands down the sides of her slim torso, her skin pebbled with goosebumps as I run the pads of my fingers over her curves. The head of my dick is swollen, aching, and ready to explode into her. I dip my head lower, capturing her lips with my tongue and teeth as I press into her slick opening. Her wet heat blankets me, her body drawing me farther inside of her. I thrust into her with long, slow strokes, the kind that made her body quiver and quake last night and earlier this morning.

I know what she likes.

I know what she needs.

I slide in and out, dragging the top of my shaft against her clit with every push and pull. Her legs tighten around me as I drive deeper. She meets every one of my thrusts, rotating her hips against mine and making my balls ache for release.

Her nails dig into my back, lancing the flesh as I fuck her sweet pussy. She screams out, clawing and pinching and wailing as I hit her spot, over and over and over until her body tenses up, her quivering lips clamping around my dick as tremors rocket through her.

And only a few thrusts later, I finally let the explosion erupt. I clench my teeth, roaring as the orgasm tears through me, practically splitting me in two with its force.

I have nothing left.

And yet, I have it all.

I collapse on top of Chella, letting my head fall onto her shoulder. She runs her hands through my hair and I shiver at her touch. "Your fingers feel a lot nicer now than they did a few minutes ago. You were like fucking Freddy Krueger with those nails slicing and dicing my back."

"Sorry not sorry," she whispers. "Besides, I thought you liked it rough?"

"Did I ever tell you that?"

"Well, after last night and this morning, I just kind of assumed…"

I chuckle. "I think you like it the same way."

Her eyes glimmer in the overhead light. "Only with you," she says softly.

I trace the outline of her lips with my forefinger before covering them with my own. It's like a magnet to steel — the pull is too strong and I have no desire to escape.

I open her lips with my tongue, my pulse throbbing against my neck as my cock jerks.

Jesus, just kissing her has me hard again.

This hunger, this ache…only she can satisfy it.

And that's when the nagging reminder about my terse call with Matteo flashes across my mind.

Bad fucking timing.

My brother's angry face is enough to make my dick go limp in a hot second, and there go my plans for round four. I pull slightly away, expelling a sharp breath.

"What's wrong?" she asks. "I just lost you."

"No, it's nothing, I just...*ahh!*" I jump as something cold and wet assaults the bottom of my foot.

Chella giggles because she can see that it's Bella attacking my foot like it's a piece of filet mignon. "Aww, she loves you. Dogs kiss you like that to show affection."

I wiggle my toes, not that it stops her. It's cute, albeit a little gross. I give up when it only seems to egg her on. It's hard not to smile at her bouncing on the opposite end of the couch like a happy puppy who's finally found her place. A quick look at Chella confirms that she's thinking the same thing. The sadness in her expression makes my throat tight. "Hey," I murmur, tilting her chin toward me. "I was thinking. Why don't we just keep her for a little longer? A few more days? We can still bring her back, but I, ah, I think you need this right now. And...I don't know. Maybe I do, too."

Chella's brow furrows. "But think of her real family and what she's missing."

"You don't know the circumstances," I say. "Look at her. She's happy." Something deep inside of me is connected to this dog. I can't explain it since I've never even had one before, but when she came and tried to comfort me when I had that fucking meltdown, I just knew she was supposed to be here for that.

She has to stay.

I need to hang on to this feeling of being whole for as long as I can because my next moves are definitely going to blow my world to bits, leaving me empty and shattered beyond repair.

Sure, I'll still have my work, but over the past couple of days, I've come to realize that it's not enough. Respect and loyalty *is* what I want…but I want it from the one person who is currently under me.

Literally.

I desperately want what I can't have.

So I'm trying to hang onto it for as long as I can.

"I'd be so sad if she was my dog—"

"Chell," I say. "In a couple of days, we'll take her to the police station. I promise. I just…I think she needs to stay with us right now."

"That doesn't sound like something a badass mafia thug would say."

I shrug. "You keep telling me I'm not that guy."

"You aren't," she says. "Are you finally accepting it?"

I flash a small smile. It doesn't really matter whether or not I accept it.

What matters is that I can never embrace it.

Chella bites down on her lower lip. "Okay, a few more days." Her expression darkens. "It might be over by then, anyway…"

Yeah. If Matteo has anything to say, it definitely will.

Fuck!

"I'm going to take care of everything," I croak. "I promise I'll figure this out and make sure Frankie stays out of danger."

"Is that what you were talking to your brother about?"

"Yes," I lie. "I told him I have Frankie getting our drugs back and he was good with that."

A hopeful smile lifts her lips and she hugs me tighter, making me feel like a bigger piece of shit than I already know I am for lying to her.

There's that goddamn conflict again, tugging so hard around my neck I can barely breathe.

"Thank you," she says, her lips nuzzling my ear. "I know he'll take care of it for you. He'd never do anything to hurt me."

My gut twists at that.

If only she knew the truth.

"Hey, did Dante say where he was going?" If I'm going to fix this my way instead of Matteo's way, I'm going to need help.

"He said something about going for a run." Chella grins. "We should probably take this behind closed doors, just in case he comes back early."

I force a smile, rolling off the couch and pulling on my shorts. "Oh hey, we need to find you a dress for that event tonight."

Her eyes immediately brighten and she sits up. "I'd love that. But... do you think I can call Frankie? Please, just let me make sure he's okay."

I grind my teeth together but give a swift nod. Let her talk to him now. Who the fuck knows how much longer he has to speak before someone yanks that tongue out of his double-crossing, lying fucking mouth? I reach onto the coffee table and hand her my phone, walking into the kitchen while she dials.

A minute passes and she lets out an impatient huff before speaking into the phone.

"Frankie, it's me. I just wanted to make sure you're okay. I'm fine, so don't worry about me." She pauses for a second before speaking again. "Just please do what he needs, Frankie. Help him fix things and get him his stuff back so that nobody else gets hurt. Please. I…I love you."

I can hear the sigh of frustration as she stabs the End button.

She joins me in the kitchen and hands me my phone. Panic settles into her features as she raises her gaze toward me. "No answer," she mumbles, nibbling on her thumbnail.

"It's, ah, kinda early," I offer. "Maybe he's still passed out?"

"Maybe," she says, bending down to ruffle Bella's fur.

I sink down next to her and place my hands on her shoulders. "Hey, don't worry. I told you I'd handle it, didn't I?"

She nods. "Yes."

"So, you have to trust me."

Those words don't taste fabulous on my lips, I'll tell ya that.

"Okay." She takes a deep breath. "I do."

The ache in my chest is tearing me apart right now, but this is the only way I can fix things.

And Frankie is the problem, not the solution.

"So go get dressed. I left a sweatshirt and pair of sweatpants on the bed in your room. Once we're out, I'll get you something that actually fits."

Chella snickers and runs into her room to change. She turns to peek over her shoulder before disappearing down the hallway, flashing a teasing grin at me. "Wait, so you're letting me go to a place where you know I'm about to strip down and you're not going to follow me?"

I hold up my phone. "I've got fires to fight. And I don't mind tearing off your clothes. Makes the prize even more worth the effort."

Her giggles travel down the hallway with her, and once I hear the door close, I dial Bobby's number, hissing into the phone as soon as he answers.

"Listen, I need you to find Frankie Amante for me as soon as possible."

"Sure, boss. What do you want me to do with him once I find him?"

"Bring him to the place where we took care of Salvatore. I wanna talk to him."

"Okay. I'll take care of it."

"And whatever you do, leave Ray out of it. He knows nothing, you got that? Don't tell anyone where you're going or why."

"Yeah. No problem, boss."

I end the call and quickly get myself together. Then I pop a few Advil because the throbbing between my temples makes me want to collapse on the couch and smother my face with a pillow.

I need a fucking plan!

I am exposed, like an open wound, and if I don't figure out a way to plug it, I'm gonna bleed out.

Literally *and* figuratively.

I sink onto the couch, fisting my hair.

Frankie won't stop unless someone cuts him off at the knees. He's brought a cash cow to the Volkovs in Brooklyn, and now that they know they have an in to keep milking it, they will drain us of everything, just like Matteo said they would.

I don't have a lot of time to fix this. The Volkovs aren't the type to sit back on their asses and wait for a windfall. They're the types to make the windfall happen in the first place.

They'll use Frankie to get inside again since he knows too fucking much about our operations.

And then they'll kill the whole Amante family because that's just the kind of vengeful fuckers they are.

Returning what he stole isn't enough to keep Frankie alive.

Matteo thinks that killing Frankie will solve our problem and show strength.

I hate to admit it…but he's right.

Chapter Eighteen
MARCHELLA

I feel amazing as I do a half-twirl in front of the full-length mirror in the exclusive boutique that Roman picked out on Fifth Avenue. The soft folds of the fabric cling to my body like the dress was made especially for me. I haven't worn something this luxurious in a long time, and for a minute, I just want to enjoy it. I want to feel wanted and beautiful and…happy.

I can feel Roman's eyes rake over me as I catch his heated stare in the mirror. He shifts on the leather couch as Bella yips and yaps, snuggled in his lap. He's been distracted ever since we left his building, and I only asked once what was wrong. He dismissed his behavior, saying he was preoccupied with the event, but I'm not stupid.

I know there's more at play than what he's letting on. I know something happened when he was on the phone with his brother, Matteo. The 'what' is what's evading me right now. A shiver zips through me, almost immediately followed by an impending sense of dread that I can no longer squelch with memories of his body plastered on top of mine, driving me into a euphoric bliss over and over and over…

I take a deep breath, letting it take hold after ignoring the gnawing feeling in my gut.

Frankie is still MIA.

I have no business traipsing around in this dress, planning for an evening where I will be playing the part of princess while my brother could very well be lying in a ditch somewhere.

It's insane to be putting so much trust in someone I barely know.

I'm relying on his power to save my brother.

But what if he can't deliver?

What if—?

Roman's phone rings, his forehead pinched as he grunts into the phone. I can see his body tense as he mumbles to whomever is on the line. I pretend not to pay attention while desperately straining my ears to hear something…anything…that can explain his sudden change in mood.

I didn't expect his meltdown earlier, and something tells me it won't be the last one I witness.

When he finally hangs up the phone, his jaw tightens and he stares out the window behind him. The sales associate walks over with a tray of champagne flutes, offering one to each of us. I take one and he waves the other one away. I take a few tentative steps toward him before dropping to one knee.

"Hey," I say softly. "Want to come into the fitting room? I can use some help unzipping this dress…"

He barely acknowledges me, though. He's obviously far away and his indifference is like a slap in the face. I grit my teeth and slowly rise to a standing position. "Okay, then, I'll just take care of it myself."

I turn toward the back room and he grasps my wrist, pulling me back to him. "Chella," he says in a gruff voice. "You look gorgeous."

"Thanks," I say.

I stand there, staring at him and then at his hand. "Roman, listen, I know—"

He shakes his head. "No, you don't."

"Then tell me so I do."

"I can't. You just have to tru—"

"Right, trust you. I get it." I roll my eyes. "But here's the thing. I'm putting a lot of blind faith in you and you're not giving me anything in return."

"I don't owe you anything, Chella," he says, rising up from the couch. He draws himself up to his full height, staring down at me with those stormy irises.

"And everything you said before? It was all bullshit? Were you working me?"

"Just because I have feelings for you doesn't mean I can choose you over my work. I have responsibilities, Marchella, responsibilities I take very seriously."

"You're trying so hard to battle this, Roman—"

"Stop trying to psychoanalyze me," he hisses. "You're not my fucking therapist."

I gasp, recoiling. "You asshole," I seethe. I yank my wrist out of his grip and storm toward the fitting room.

But I don't get very far.

He closes the distance between us, fisting my hair and backing me against the mirror, pushing his tongue between my lips. I dig my fingers into the back of his head like the twisted addict I am for his affection. I drink him in, all of his angst, rage, and lust flooding my body with unresolved emotion.

I hold on tight to the one lifeline I still have left.

I've been floundering for so long, trying to keep my eye on the future, desperate to stay positive and hopeful that things will change for the better, that I'll be able to fix the damage done to my life.

So I cling to Roman, the most unlikely bright spot in my otherwise murky existence.

"I'm sorry," he murmurs against my lips when we're both breathless and sated…at least, temporarily. "I'm sorry for everything."

The voice in my head begs me to ask why he's sorry, but the heaviness in my gut already suspects the answer.

He pays for the dress, shoes, and earrings I'd been admiring, as well as some other clothes I picked out for every day, and we head back to his car, driving home with the same ominous cloud of silence hanging over us. It's thick enough to choke me, and I want to scream to shatter it. Once we pull into the garage, I get out of the car with Bella in my arms as Roman grabs the dress bag from the backseat. He holds open the door to the basement for me and I cringe as I pass the elevator and head for the stairs.

"You gonna tell me what that's all about?" he asks.

I square my shoulders. He had an emotional breakdown before. I guess it's only fair to share my abhorrence of elevators.

"The last time I was in an elevator, it was at Memorial Sloane Kettering, on the day my mother died," I say, tears stinging my eyes at the memory. It stings like I just pulled the scab off of a deep and painful wound.

His hand grazes my arm, tugging me closer even though I just want to get away from the elevator door. I don't want to hear the door open, the creaking sound still haunts me to this day.

I turn to look at him. "We were going up to her room to see her," I whisper. "She'd had a good couple of days and I'd left the night before feeling that we might actually have more time. She'd been awake and alert and aware. They were all good signs. And I just felt hopeful, you know? It was like she wasn't ready to go yet." My gaze drops to the floor. "But something happened overnight. I'd left because the doctors said I should get some rest, that she would be fine. But I guess they had it all wrong."

Roman stares at me, silently waiting for me to finish.

My God, every time I think about it, it feels like my heart is literally being impaled with a hot poker and shredded.

I blink fast to hold back the tears, taking one last shuddering breath before I continue. "Frankie and I went back in the morning. I remember getting onto the elevator with him, talking and laughing and feeling positive for the first time in a while. Then the elevator doors creaked open on her floor and my dad was waiting for us. He'd stayed…he was there with her when she… when she…"

And then the hot tears spill over, streaming down my face.

I just can't say the words.

It's probably the closest I'd ever felt to my father. In those horrific moments, we were bonded, sharing in the grief and the loss. We were connected, all three of us.

And when he left, when he made the decision that cost him his life, I guess I felt like he deserted me...us. He made a conscious decision to break our connection, to tear apart those bonds, to leave us on our own to battle the heartache and life on our own.

Roman pulls me into his arms, stroking the back of my head as my body quakes with sobs.

I'm still fighting that battle.

And yet it's a war I will never win.

Chapter Nineteen
ROMAN

I stand there, holding her as she weeps like her heart is breaking.

And here I am, getting ready to break it all over again.

"I lost my mother, too," I murmur, stroking the back of her head. "I know it hurts, and I'm sorry."

Her tears soak through the thin fabric of my t-shirt, grief quaking her whole body. We stand there, silent save for her soft sobs. I can't fix this for her, much as I want to take away her pain and sadness.

I can only make it worse.

That's what I'm good for.

When she finally pulls away, I sweep my finger under her eyes, wiping away her tears. "Chella, I know you feel like you're isolated and alone right now. But don't miss a chance to fix things with your father. If you've never listened to his side, maybe you should hear him out. He lost a lot, too, you know?"

She raises her tear-filled eyes up at me. They're greener now, because she's upset. It's a realization that makes my chest tighten, and one I can't really do much about since telling her the truth will open up a can of worms that needs to stay sealed for the time being. I can't tell her how I know the truth. I can only urge her to find it out for herself.

"Why do you even care? I mean, he hurt your family way back when. And it's because of him that Frankie screwed you over." She sniffles.

I capture her chin in my hand. "I care because of you. Your father made mistakes, yeah. But it's hard for me to hold a grudge when my family has been so successful. He definitely deserves to be punished for his scumbag ways, but trust me, he is. Rikers is a fucking hellhole, Chella. He's paying big time."

Jesus, if my brothers and father heard me talking like this, they'd go crazy. Me, being all forgiving and shit. Me, being so affected by a woman. Me, being…I don't know…human, I guess.

She furrows her brow. "Are you saying all this so that I make amends before he loses something else?"

I shake my head. "No, I'm telling you this as a friend. Don't waste any more time. Fix things while you have the chance."

She backs away, wiping her eyes. "Is this because of what you're going to do to Frankie if he doesn't come through? If he fails you? You want me to let my father know he still has at least one kid left?"

I grasp her wrist and pull her back toward me. "Stop being so suspicious," I say. "This doesn't have anything to do with Frankie. This is about you and your pop. Period."

Chella nods slowly. "It's just weird that Frankie hasn't called back and you're here telling me to make amends with my dad."

"Don't read into it, Chella. I told you, I'm gonna take care of things."

"Okay," she whispers. "And I'll think about the other stuff." Bella yaps, winding her leash around our ankles as we walk up the five flights of stairs. I'm out of breath once we get upstairs, again. I really need to get some more cardio in.

I can think of a very carnal set of exercises to add into my day, too.

I open the door and grab my phone out of my pocket when it vibrates against my leg. A text from Bobby flashes on the screen.

I've got him.

I take a deep breath. "Chella, I need you to hang out here for a little while, okay? I have something to handle for work before the event tonight."

She flashes a small smile. "So you trust me enough not to bolt once you're gone?"

I wrap my arms around her and gather her close. "I'm pretty confident that you'll stay put, especially if you know what's gonna happen after the event tonight."

"Are you going to leave me in suspense?"

"Let's just say dessert won't be served to you at the event. It'll be served to you right here. By me."

"Sounds delicious," she murmurs.

I give her ass a squeeze and she lets out a tiny squeal. Of course, Bella joins in, jumping in between us for her turn to play. She nips at my ankles and Chella giggles. "You sure you have to go? Your girls want to play."

"Later," I murmur, dropping a kiss onto her lips. "Be ready."

I walk out of the apartment and close the door behind me, leaning my back against it for a second. I hate like hell that I'm lying to her. If what Matteo told me is true, the Volkovs are edging closer. And they won't wait. They'll just plunder the shit out of our organization.

And God only knows what they'll do to Marchella if they find her.

I need to do this.

I need to handle Frankie.

I need to show the Volkovs that they can't fuck with our business.

I take the elevator down to the basement and jump into my car, the tires squealing as I pull the car out of the private parking garage. Twenty minutes later, I'm hurrying into the same deserted warehouse where I handled Dario less than twenty-four hours ago.

I'd really hoped I wouldn't have to see the inside of this place again so soon.

The air is dank and damp, and a chill seeps into my bones as I near the single light shining toward the back of the building.

The interrogation room.

Or the maiming room.

Depending on the nature of the business being conducted.

I walk into the room to find Frankie sitting in a chair with Bobby holding a gun to the back of his head. His wrists are bound with duct tape, but he's not tied to the chair. At least he's smart enough not to make any moves to leave.

"Why am I here?" he yells. "And where the fuck is my sister, you bastard?"

I glare at him, my fingers itching to punch a hole into his jaw. But I stand down. I need him conscious to get my information.

There will be plenty of time later to knock him into next year if he doesn't learn to keep his goddamn mouth shut.

"I know everything, Frankie," I seethe, grabbing his hair and yanking his head back. "I know you have access to the drugs. I know you fucked with the Volkovs. And I know it was you who made that hit, not your father."

He narrows his still-swollen eyes at me. "You don't know anything," he spits out. "I don't have access to anything!"

"Bullshit!" I yell, pulling his hair harder. "You fucking banded together with Salvatore to set us up. Was it all about revenge, Frankie? Huh? You figured you'd screw us and walk away with a wad of our product at the same time? Enough to pay off the Volkovs and then some for yourself? Was that it? You're looking to make a name for yourself, Frankie, since nobody in this fucking town will take you seriously because of who and what you are?"

"No!"

I let go of his hair and grab him by the neck. "Then tell me what I don't know!"

"They were gonna kill my dad and Chella!" he chokes out, his voice raspy as he struggles for air. "Unless I got them the drugs! I can't get what you asked for!"

"Goddammit!" I scream, shoving him against the back of the chair.

"But I can tell you one thing," he says, clutching his throat as he gasps for breath. "They want more. And they're planning another hit."

"Why are you telling me this?" I hiss.

"Because you have my sister. And I'm afraid they'll come for her, too. I need you to be ready for them or else you're gonna lose a fuck ton more than you already have."

"And I'm supposed to believe you…why? You're a two-faced scumbag, just like your father. Why would I trust you?"

"Because of Marchella," he says. "I know you don't want her to get hurt. Hell, I knew it years ago when we were kids. I saw the way you'd look at her. You haven't forgotten about that, have you? You won't put her in danger, Roman."

"I don't fucking believe you," I seethe, clenching my fists at my side.

"If you don't listen to me, the Volkovs will crush you! They smell blood and they're gonna attack, don't you get it?"

"Okay, fine," I say. "Say I do believe you? How the fuck am I supposed to stop them?"

"They're planning to hit you again tonight. You need to be ready for them. You need to move your shit before they show up. Get things outta that storage room as soon as possible."

"And why the hell are you telling me? They'll kill you if they find out."

Frankie lets out a dry laugh. "I'm dead either way. Nobody will work with me because of my dad. I'm no use to the Volkovs now that I've already delivered for them. I should be the one rotting in jail," he mutters.

"So I hear," I say.

He looks up at me, his breathing labored. His eyes are heavy, riddled with anger and dejection. They used to be full of fire, but now they're just filled with defeat. "You don't know what it was like, Roman. To be yanked out of a life you loved and thrown into a new one. A fucking horrible one where you constantly have to look over your shoulder because you never knew when someone might jump out and slit your throat. All because of shit your father did." He takes a deep, shuddering breath. "Do you know how many times I needed to run into the fire because of some shit he pulled? I bailed him out so many times because if I didn't, I knew my mother and Chella would get hurt. Or worse. I know Chella thinks I'm just like him, but the reality is, I needed to be, so I could stay a step ahead of him."

"What the hell happened with the Volkovs, then? Why'd you do it?"

"I was desperate," he mumbles. "We had no money, shit was being repossessed left and right. We'd just lost Mama. I just snapped, I guess. I was tired of always being the one to bail out Papa and I figured this could be an easy way to make some quick cash. I had buyers lined up." He shrugs. "The car was supposed to be empty. It wasn't. The soldier manning the stash saw my face so I knew if I didn't kill him, the Volkovs would come back for us. Papa got there just in time to save my ass from the cops. He took the fall, I don't know, I guess because he thought my life was worth more than his on the outside." He lifts an eyebrow. "Guess not, huh?"

I kneel down in front of him, looking at the beaten, broken down man who used to be my best friend so many years ago.

I give a swift nod. "I'll be ready."

"You can't be there," he says, his forehead pinched.

"What the hell are you talking about?"

"If you're there, they'll know I told you about it. And they'll come after Marchella and my dad and kill us all. You need to stay with her. I know you can protect her."

"Why should I give a damn what happens to you or your father?" I growl.

"You shouldn't. But you won't hurt Chella like that," he says. "You won't let her lose the rest of her family. I know you, Roman."

"Not anymore you don't." I hover over him. "You're a piece of shit, Frankie. And I don't owe you a goddamn thing. But Chella doesn't deserve any of this."

"You have the power to keep her safe and to keep her from getting hurt again," Frankie mutters. "Don't let the Volkovs win. I told you what you need to know. Get your guys on it and watch over my sister."

I stare at him for a long minute, my arms folded over my chest before meeting Bobby's gaze. "Make the call," I grunt. He nods and pulls out his phone to give the order as he walks out of the room.

The corners of Frankie's lips curl slightly upward. "What are you out to prove this time, Roman?" he says. "That baby bro can actually deliver for the family? That he's just as much of a badass as the rest of the Villani men? That he can keep the empire protected?"

"What the fuck are you talking about?" I growl.

"You were always looking for your time to shine. You fucked around a lot because you knew you could get away with it. But then when you wanted to be taken seriously, nobody believed you'd amount to anything." He lets out a menacing laugh. "I remember it all. You rebelling and then trying to find your place in a family that thought you were a useless fucking peon."

"Fuck you!" I bellow, pulling him up from the chair and grabbing him by the shirt collar.

"You're as weak and stupid now as you were back then," he snarls, clearly not giving a damn that I've got a gun and he can't protect himself at all.

I turn and throw him against the cement wall, letting out a loud roar that reverberates in the space.

And the sonofabitch just laughs.

At me.

The one thing I've been trying for so long to overcome is the one insecurity he just tore open like a wound that's been scabbed over for over a decade.

"You really think I'd help you, Roman? Huh? After you fucked me over and kicked me to the curb back in Sicily? Little fucking prince. You knew who was gonna butter your bread and you weren't gonna do anything to screw up your place!"

I launch my fist backward, ready to let it fly against his already bruised and swollen jaw.

Then I remember his wrists are taped together.

And I want him ready to fight!

I pull out a knife and cut the tape off his wrists. Then I toss the knife onto the concrete, edging close to him. He sways left and right, trying to get his bearings.

I catch Bobby's incredulous stare as he walks back in but I don't give a damn.

I want Frankie free right now.

I want to pummel him into the ground knowing that it's because I'm stronger and more powerful.

I don't want to pussy out and beat the shit out of him while he can't protect himself.

That's pathetic and weak.

And I'm not that guy!

Not any fucking more!

"Come on, you bastard!" I yell, holding up my fists. "You're free! So fucking take the shot!"

He swings at me and I duck backward before landing a solid punch to his gut. He lets out a loud moan and hunches over.

"That's all you've got, Frankie? That's the best you can do?" I launch my fist out again once he lifts his head. It explodes against his jaw and he stumbles backward against the concrete. Blood oozes from the corner of his mouth and he glares at me. "It's about time you learned how to throw a goddamn punch," he hisses, launching himself at me. We crash into the chair, landing on the cold ground with a loud thud. I swing like my life depends on it, smashing my fists into his midsection, since I know that's his weakness.

At least, since yesterday when my guys kicked the crap out of him before dragging him to my office.

I slam my fists into his face, his throat, his temple, all while my vision is blanketed in a deep red haze.

Fury floods my insides until my fingers can't take any more and I collapse on the ground next to Frankie. His lip is split, his jaw bloody and even more bruised than before.

He rolls away from me, groaning as he lands on his side. "You can't stop it," he hisses. "I led the Volkovs to you to save my ass, Roman. I more than made up for what I took from them. I gave them the keys to your kingdom, and now they're gonna plunder it until there's nothing left! Because that's what you deserve! You took for so long, now someone else is gonna take from you!" He struggles to get up and turns to look at me. "How's that for karma, bitch?"

With all the force I can muster, I land one final punch and Frankie goes down like a bag of cement, his head cracking on the floor.

I stagger to my feet, raking a hand through my hair. "That asshole is working with the Volkov Bratva," I mutter. "Did you lock down the drugs?"

Bobby nods. "I had more security put on the new location since we moved them after the first robbery. The Volkovs won't find anything if they show up again at Risk."

I nod. "Good. Now help me get this piece of shit into my trunk. I'm not letting him out of my sight."

"But what about the bratva? Frankie said they're coming."

"Make sure security is prepped at the club." But a nagging feeling tells me the club isn't the target. "I've gotta get back to my place now."

Except, I don't really know what the hell to do once I get back there.

I don't have any bad blood with the Volkovs.

They run their territories and we run ours. Why the hell would they come into Manhattan to mess with our businesses, especially knowing we're connected to the Severinov Bratva, our

Russian counterparts in Las Vegas?

The Severinovs would decimate them.

They know that.

It doesn't make sense.

I rub the back of my neck once Frankie is locked in my trunk, and I drive back to my building with crazed thoughts flying through my mind.

I feel like I'm missing something and I fucking hate it!

I dropped the ball once by not calling Matteo.

He needs to hear this firsthand.

I've been so focused on making a name for myself that I forgot the whole reason why I'm in this position in the first place.

I need to do what's right for the family, not for myself.

Every time I lose sight of that, something else crumbles.

My chest tightens as I think of Chella back at my place, wondering where the hell I am.

What would she say if she knew I had her beloved brother laid out in my trunk?

I scrub a hand down the front of my face.

I can't think about that now.

I need to focus!

I pull my car into the garage and dart up the stairs, bypassing the elevator completely.

Somehow, it feels wrong to take it.

Especially now.

I throw open the door to the apartment to find Dante lounging on the couch, flipping through Netflix shows. "Where's Chella?" I say in a low voice.

He nods toward the bathroom. "Getting ready for that charity thing. She's been in there for over an hour."

"Good," I say. "Come into my office. We need to call Matteo."

Dante narrows his eyes at me. "Where the hell have you been? And whose blood is all over your shirt and hands?"

"Frankie's."

"Fuuuuck," he breathes. "This should be a fun call."

I close the door behind us and open the lid of my laptop. Then I pull up Matteo's number and make the call. His face flashes on the screen a minute later and he looks hella tense. I brace myself for another lashing because there's no way I'll escape his wrath right now.

"Did you take care of it?" he asks, not even bothering with a quick greeting.

"Not exactly," I say. I recount the whole story for my brothers, including Frankie's whole sob story and then one-hundred-and-eighty-degree about-face that confirmed his revenge plot against me.

Us.

It doesn't really matter.

He fucking crossed the line.

"I hammered him pretty bad then threw him in my trunk," I say, folding my arms over my chest.

"What the hell are you gonna do with him in your trunk?" Matteo shouts.

"I was trying to come up with a different plan," I say through gritted teeth. "I didn't want to have to kill anyone else, don't you get that? I wanted to solve this without any more blood!"

"But you couldn't do that, could you?" Matteo sneers. "And now we're going to war with the fucking Volkovs? How in the hell did you let this happen, Roman?"

"Look, I made a mistake! A lot of them! But I'm trying to fix it all!"

"And why did you think meeting with Frankie was gonna solve anything? The guy is a goddamn weasel! He's never gonna change! And he wants to take us down. Him, his father. They were just waiting for the right time…" Matteo narrows his eyes. "For the little prince to step in so they could cut him off at the knees!"

Dante looks at me and gives me a little shrug. "We've gotta find out if this whole thing with the Volkovs is a real threat or if it's Frankie fucking with your head."

"So, what, you wanna go to Brooklyn and meet them for fucking borscht and vodka to talk it all out?" I snip.

Matteo holds up his hands. "Okay, just relax, dammit. I'll talk to Alek. He'll make a call."

"No," I say. "This is my mess to clean up. I don't need the Severinovs to run interference for me. I'll figure it out!"

"Did you ever think Frankie might be baiting you?" Dante asks. "He and Sal pulled the first job. The Volkovs weren't involved. We have no dealings with them."

"Yeah, so?" The stress knot at the base of my skull is growing with alarming speed.

"Maybe he's trying to distract you again. Have you looking out for the Volkovs when the threat is right under your nose. He wants to take us down, to make sure we suffer like his family did. Him, not the Volkovs."

"Dante is right," Matteo says. "Save yourself the aggravation and kill the fucking prick! Kill Frankie before he—"

My blood boils, rushing between my ears with such force that I don't even hear the door slam open.

"Kill Frankie?" A high-pitched female voice cuts through the tension in the room as Marchella storms into the room, looking like a goddess in the floor-length gown I bought her earlier today. Her high heels click angrily on the hardwood floor, her face twisted with rage. She walks right over to me, not even bothering to acknowledge the computer screen, and she shoves her hands against my chest. "You fucking liar!" she screams. "You promised me you'd take care of everything, that you wouldn't hurt him!" Her eyes spit emerald fire as she pushes against me again. "You told me to trust you, that we'd be safe! And you're planning to kill him!" She reaches out and slaps me across the face with a force that sends a stinging sensation exploding across my jaw. "I hate you!"

I capture her wrist in my hand before she can land another smack, hissing at her. "I did what had to be done. I wasn't about to let him hurt my family!"

"What about what you promised me? I guess that doesn't count, right? Because I'm not one of your brothers? I don't rate?"

"I have a responsibility to my family, Marchella," I growl. "It's my job to keep our organization protected."

"Well, I guess that 'job' will have to be what keeps you warm at night, Roman." She flips her wrist, pulling it from my grip. "Because I'm done playing your fucking games!" Marchella twists around and stalks out of the room.

I run after her, yanking her back toward me. "Your brother is the liar," I mutter. "He doesn't give a damn about anything other than revenge. He wants to see my family crumble!"

"Can you blame him, after everything that happened?"

I fist my hair. "This is all on your father! Why is that little detail something you and Frankie keep on forgetting? And for the record, he's lucky my father didn't have him killed after what he did to us back in Sicily!"

"You are an insufferable asshole!" she yells, twisting around to grab a bottle of red wine from the counter in the kitchen. She hurls it toward my head and I duck in time for it to shatter against the wall…a wall that had been stark white only seconds earlier. Now, it looks like a murder scene with splotches of red wine soaking into the sheetrock.

I run after her, reaching an arm around her midsection, but she swings her shoulder into my chest. She tries to punch me again but I capture her fist before she has the chance to crack it against my jaw. "Ahh!" she screams, stomping on my foot with the skinny heel of her shoe, and then driving her knee right into my balls.

I release her, crumbling onto the floor, doubled over from the hit, and she grabs my car keys from the kitchen island before darting out of the apartment.

The girl literally brought me to my goddamn knees.

I struggle to my feet, gasping for breath and clutching myself as Dante comes out of the office a minute later.

"Damn, Romo. Your girl is fucking brutal. Listen, Matteo is pissed as hell and he wants us to—"

"Forget…Matteo. She has…my keys…" I rasp. "Frankie is…in trunk."

"Christ," he mutters, sliding on his sneakers and running out the door. I pull myself to a half-standing position and go after him, taking the steps as fast as I can, which isn't saying much since I'm still partially incapacitated.

I'm almost at the bottom floor when Dante disappears through the door into the garage. "Jesus Christ!" he yells. I run-walk to the door, grasping the handle and pulling it open to find Frankie scrambling out of my trunk and Chella firing me a death glare from across the space. The driver's side door is open. I guess she got sidetracked when she heard her idiot brother thrashing around in the trunk.

"You fucking asshole!" she screams, shaking her fists in the air. "How could you do this to him? He was about to suffocate in there!"

Frankie doesn't waste a second before he lunges for me, throwing his body into me with such force, we land against the glass wall with a loud thud. I roll him over and pound his face with my fist, forgetting about the trauma recently done to my manhood.

"You forget how this ended the first time?" I grunt as he smashes his fists into my covered midsection. "Did you forget how you ended up in the goddamn trunk? Huh?"

I stagger to my feet, spitting blood from where he landed his one good hook against my jaw. He drags himself up to a half-standing position, breathing heavily as Dante rolls his eyes at me.

"You think you're getting the last word, huh, Roman?" Frankie hisses, inching toward me. "Well, guess what? You're wrong. So fucking wrong and I can't wait until I can see it on your face! The look that says *I'm about to be fucked by Frankie Amante again and there's nothing I can do about it except bend over!*"

Dante groans. "Oh, for fuck's sake, that's not an image I want burned into my memory."

Frankie dives for my ankles, tackling me to the ground. My head narrowly misses the car door before I hit the cement. He rolls on top of me, his knee digging into my throat, and then something distracts him and he jumps off of me and into the driver's seat of my already beaten-up Bentley.

I clutch my throat, sputtering for breath as I hear a piercing scream followed by one single gunshot to the ceiling.

"Frankie, no!" Chella yells.

My fucking gun!

Goddammit, why the hell did I leave it on the front seat?

Another shot fires just as I duck around the front of the car to shield myself, the rogue bullet wedging itself into the bullet-proof glass wall behind me.

"Stop shooting!" Chella grabs Frankie's shirt and points a finger at me. "And you! You deceitful sack of shit! You did this to him! You beat the hell out of him and stuffed him in your trunk! How could you do that, you fucking animal? If I hadn't heard him banging, he'd have died!"

Frankie lets out a dry chuckle. "Lucky for me, my sister saw through your bullshit in enough time to get me out so I could take care of you myself!"

"Put the gun down, Frankie!" Dante roars from his spot behind a column. "You won't get out of here alive if you don't!"

"Fuck you, Dante!" Frankie yells back, pointing my gun at us. "I'm done with any Villani dictating my fucking next moves!"

"Should I parrot Matteo right now and say you shoulda popped a cap in that idiot's skull a long time ago?" Dante shouts to me.

I push back my hair, letting out a loud groan. "Sure, if you want me to kick your fucking ass!"

"Later," Dante snips, pointing his gun at Frankie as the asshole smashes the one window of my car that was still intact with the barrel of the gun he's holding. "But hopefully before he completely destroys your ride." He fires off a warning shot, missing Frankie by a mile but jolting him enough to remember we're still here.

Frankie lets out a primal scream and fires off a few more shots at the side of my car, bullets peppering the metal. Chella shrieks, grabbing him by the back of the shirt.

"Stop it, you fucking psychopath!"

He turns and unleashes years of pent-up rage on her, and I use that as my chance to escape my own gun, darting over to where Dante stands. "This is happening because of *him*! The Villani family destroyed us and he is one of them! He deserves everything coming to him! But you never could see who he really was, could you? Huh? Because you were too busy finger-fucking yourself over him, right? Tell the truth, Chell!"

"That's not true!" she shrieks. "I hated him just as much as you did!"

"Hated? Past tense?" He sneers at me. "So ya brainwashed her, Roman? Is that how you were able to get her into bed?" He looks back at Chella, a grimace shadowing his already-bruised skin. "You loved playing house with him. Admit it! I mean, look at yourself in that dress! You were just living the fucking life, weren't you?"

Chella smacks him across the face. "You are the one who destroyed us! You and Papa! Have you forgotten that? You're always ready to blame others for shit that's gone wrong in your life! How dare you insinuate that I was okay with being kidnapped because of something you did because you're a bitter, selfish prick?"

Frankie lets out a low, menacing laugh. "Yeah, well, I'm gonna be the one to make us whole again, too." He swings around, a look of confusion on his face because I'm no longer cowering in front of my car. He narrows his eyes at me where I now stand and points the gun at me. Another shot explodes into the air and I grab Dante's wrist just as he's about to take a retaliatory shot.

"Don't. He's standing too close to Chella," I hiss. "Too dangerous."

"Are we supposed to wait until he hits one or both of us?" Dante grumbles. "I'm a fucking assassin. This is what I do for a living, Romo! Have a little goddamn faith!"

"See, this is what happens when you leave your gun on the front seat in your car, dumbass," Frankie yells. "Now I'm gonna blow off your fucking head! You were never gonna escape, Roman! Never!"

"I'm not taking any chances with her. Besides, he's gonna find out very soon that he's out of options," I whisper to Dante. "Once that clip is empty, it's over. And judging by the number of shots he just took, we're clear."

"Frankie, what the hell are you talking about? Escape what?" Chella screams. "And stop shooting that gun!"

"Your brother is a lying sack of shit, Chella!" I yell. "You were so pissed off, thinking I went behind your back to kill him, which I fucking should have, by the way. But you didn't let me get to the part where he screwed my family over again and partnered with the Volkov Bratva to rob me for the second time!"

"The Volkov Bratva?" Chella furrows her brow. "Why the hell would you work with them after everything that happened?" She shoves Frankie. "Are you fucking insane? After what happened to Papa?"

"Yeah, why don't you tell her the truth about that, Frankie?" I stand up and Dante grabs me to pull me back. I shake my head. "Let me go, Dante," I say through clenched teeth. "I'm fucking tired of this guy and it's time to shut him the hell up!" I stalk over to Frankie as his eyes widen. He waves the gun in my face and I just smirk. "Fuck you, Frankie. Why don't you tell her the truth?" I thunder, launching my fist at his jaw. He doubles over, as expected, and I hover over him. "That's for messing with my car!"

"Your car was fucked to begin with!" Frankie lets out a roar and shoves me backward hard enough that I stumble into another column and he storms over to me, holding the gun in his outstretched hand. "I hate you, you sonofabitch! And now you're gonna pay for everything your family has done to us! I hope you rot in hell!"

He pulls the trigger, but the only sound to follow is a clicking sound.

I smirk at him. "You mighta wanted to check the clip before you emptied it into the wall and my car."

Chella punches Frankie as her screeches pierce the air. "What is wrong with you? Haven't we lost enough?"

The approaching sound of squealing tires on the cobblestone driveway outside makes my spine stiffen. From where Dante and I are standing, it's too dark to make out much on the outside of the garage. The walls are all bulletproof glass, but all of the trees lining the perimeter of the building make it hard to see much.

Great for ambiance, bad for reconnaissance.

And something tells me we're about to come face to face with something damn ominous very soon.

"Who the hell is that?" Dante groans, raking a hand through his hair.

Frankie snickers, staring at the Apple watch on his wrist. He looks at me. "Perfect timing," he snarls.

That motherfucker. I should have put a bullet in his brain when I had the chance.

Approaching footsteps get louder until I can make out three faint shapes in the courtyard. Three guys.

Correction.

When they come into view, I swallow hard.

Three massive, hulking guys — tall, with shaved heads and inked necks.

And they each have a star tattooed on their necks.

Bratva.

You have got to be kidding me right now...

Most times, I love that this building is secluded from the rest of the city. I like my privacy ninety-nine percent of the time.

But that nagging one percent comes back to haunt me on occasion.

Case in point, *now*.

"Boris," Frankie says, holding up a hand. "Listen, I told you this was the place where you could collect the rest of the drugs. This guy right here will lead you to them. So now we're even, okay?" He glares at me. "But once you have your money, I wanna finish this cocksucker off myself."

"Frankie!" Chella yells. "You aren't finishing anyone, do you understand? Jesus Christ, haven't you learned? And who the hell are these guys?"

The one I guess named Boris steps forward. "We work for the Volkovs," he grunts in a deep, gravelly voice.

Chella gasps. "The Volkovs? You mean, the—"

Boris nods. "The ones your brother stole from."

"Yeah, yeah, but I got some of them back for you and the rest you can get from—" Frankie stammers.

"Shut up!" Boris yells, narrowing his eyes at Frankie. "Drugs weren't all you stole that night, were they?" He steps farther into the space, his voice echoing as he moves closer. "That's right, Amante. We know the truth about what really happened that night. So that means we're nowhere close to even."

Frankie's fingers close on the handle of the gun at the same time that he remembers the clip is empty.

And he realizes in that moment that he's screwed.

"What is he talking about?" Chella says, her voice quivering. "What else did you take, dammit?"

Chella's panicked gaze locks with mine and I step forward, my hands in the air when Boris points his gun toward me.

"Roman Villani," he says, narrowing his blue eyes. He holds a shotgun in one hand and his big, heavy black boots thump along the concrete floor as he approaches.

Dante points his own gun at Boris but I hold up a hand. "Listen, Boris, we have no interest in starting a war with you. For years, we've run our own territories without a problem. Let's not create one now, yeah?"

Boris's lips twist into a grimace as he closes the space between us. "I didn't come here to start a war," he grumbles. "And I have no interest in your money." He holds out the shotgun and twists in Frankie's direction. "We came for him."

Frankie staggers backward, still clutching the gun. "Boris, what the hell are you…we had a deal! I delivered Villani, just like I said I would. I led you straight over here so you collect the rest!"

"The deal was that *you* pay a debt to us," Boris yells.

"B-boris," Frankie stammers. "I told you I'd get you all of the goods and then some. What fucking more do you want from me? You can't seriously be pissed off about that guy I popped! I mean, he was a fucking low-level peon, for fuck's sake! They're a dime a dozen!"

Boris swings the shotgun at Frankie's jaw. "He was my nephew, you piece of shit! And you don't get to negotiate the life of family, do you understand?"

"What the hell is going on?" Chella screams. "He didn't kill anyone that night! My father did!"

Boris levels her with a cold stare before scowling at Frankie. "Is that what you told her?"

Frankie's jaw tightens, his Adam's apple bobbing in his throat as Boris's gun settles between his eyes.

Chella's hands fly up to her mouth when Frankie doesn't answer. Fucking pussy doesn't even own up to what he did. "No! All of this time, you've made me believe that Papa was the reason...and I turned my back on him for it!" She slams her hands against his chest, shoving him hard. "Oh my God, tell me that's not true! Tell me you haven't been lying to me all of this time!"

And still, he doesn't acknowledge that the story he fed her is complete bullshit. Fury rages through me and the urge to put him through a wall overwhelms me. Frankie shakes uncontrollably as Boris' shotgun slides down the side of his smashed-up face. "Boris, please, I'm so sorry. There has to be something else I can do to make up for it. I didn't think anyone was gonna be in that car! Please, just tell me what will let me off the hook—"

Chella reaches out a hand to Boris. "Please don't hurt him," she says, her voice choked with sobs. "Please, he'll make it up to you. Please don't take him. *Roman!*" she shrieks as Boris raises the gun to the side of Frankie's head.

"Oh, Jesus Christ," Dante mutters.

"Boris," I say. "Let's talk about this, okay? I know you lost someone close to you—"

"The fuck we'll talk!" Boris yells. "Don't tell me how to conduct business, Villani, or I'll make sure you're next!"

"Hey!" I shout. "A little fucking respect, please. This is my goddamn place, do you understand? Let me handle the

Amantes. He put a hit on me, let *me* take care of the shithead instead!"

"I have my orders," he seethes.

"Yeah, well, you're in my fucking area," I grunt. "And in my territory, I handle my own business!"

He raises the gun at me. "Don't fuck with me. I have no problem with your family...yet. But that can change very quickly if you get in my way!" His nostrils flare and his jaw tightens as he growls his next words at me. "This is revenge, plain and simple. And I'm not leaving until I get it!"

As Boris takes his attention off of Frankie, the chicken shit shoves Chella away and makes a run for it and darts out of the garage. Boris fires his gun at Frankie's back, the glass absorbing the impact of the shots. The panes crack but don't shatter, a fact that clearly pisses him off and hampers his efforts to stop Frankie. With a demonic glare in my direction, Boris takes off like a shot after Frankie, both of them disappearing through the trees and into the private courtyard. The other two Russians run after them with Chella on their heels.

I don't stop to think about the fact that I don't have a weapon. I just run into the darkness without a lifeline.

I paid a lot of money for my secluded building...the privacy, the exclusivity. It's nice to have your own space, away from the rest of the somewhat civilized world.

They say luxury comes with a price.

And it's fucking steep.

"Boris! Don't fucking do it!" I shout, squinting in the darkness since the dim lighting isn't enough to make out much of anything. "I will take care—"

Crack! Pop! Bang!

I can hear Chella's thick sobs shattering the silence as I weave in and out of bushes to find her. She collapses next to where Frankie's limp body is sprawled over the bricks. A large red puddle has spread under him and she grabs his hands, holding them tight to her chest. "No, Frankie! Don't you leave me! Please don't leave me!"

Boris stands still for a second, watching her before he yanks her by the arm and drags her away from Frankie.

He spits on Frankie, nodding at me as I approach, panting. "This ends right here, right now, Villani. It's over. If you don't wanna end up like Amante here, you'll leave it the fuck alone."

He puts his gun to Chella's temple and pulls her down the driveway toward his car. The two Russians are already inside and seconds later, Dante rushes up to me. I grab his gun and take off after the car where Chella struggles against Boris in the backseat.

My legs cramp up with each step I take, my muscles tensing up as they near the corner. I can't get close enough to take a shot, even to blow out a fucking tire!

If they make it to that corner, it'll be over.

I'll never see Chella again…

Screeching tires round the corner from the opposite direction, going the wrong way down my one-way street. The Russians' car veers off the side of the road, coming to a screeching stop, skidding across the cobblestones and into a lamppost to avoid hitting the other car.

"Chella!" I roar.

My lungs feel like they're about to explode as my feet pound against the ground to get to her. Her side of the car took the full impact, and all I can see is her head rolling against the backseat where only seconds earlier she'd been clawing at Boris's face.

I pull open the backdoor, pressing my gun against Boris's head and yanking him out of the car as Dante runs up to us.

He holds out his hand to Boris and Boris shoves his gun into it, muttering some shit in Russian to his guys.

I climb into the backseat, kneeling next to Chella. I run my fingers down the left side of her face, my fingertips soaked with her blood.

"Chell," I say in a choked whisper. The door is smashed in but it looks like the back quarter panel took the biggest hit. She must have slammed her head against the window. I run my fingers down the column of her neck and her eyes flutter open.

"Roman," she moans.

"I'm here, babe." I lace my fingers with hers. "You're gonna be okay."

"Frankie…" she whispers, her eyes shining with tears.

I'm ready to tell her it will be fine when I snap my lips closed.

I can't lie to her again.

And right now, I don't have the truth for her, anyway.

Not about Frankie.

I only have my own truth, and that is to promise that I will do everything in my power to keep her safe.

"Can you move?" I ask.

She nods and I snake an arm around her, sliding her out of the car.

Dante has Boris backed against the car along with the other two guys, and I look up for a split second before I scoop Chella into my arms, my voice a deep growl. "You're not taking her. You came here for Frankie and you did what you were ordered to do. Now get the fuck out of—"

Another set of footsteps behind Boris stops me mid-thought, and I look past Boris to see a familiar face stagger over to us.

Ray.

He's the one who ran his car into the Russians, and now he has his gun out and pointed at Boris' sidekicks. "I got this, boss."

I give him a quick nod and return my attention to Boris. "You're outnumbered, Boris. Leave before you start something you will never win. And just remember that you're completely fucked if you decide to pull another stunt like this in my territory. Always remember that."

Boris's lips curl upward into a nasty smirk. "I guess I'll just have to wait until your family passes through *my* territory, then."

"Don't hold your breath," I seethe.

"Well then, it looks like our business has come to a close," he says in an exaggerated Russian accent.

"And it looks like you need to call an Uber." I nod at Dante and Ray. "These guys will make sure you don't get diverted." I wrap my arm around Chella, guiding her away from the Russians, away from the smoldering metal, away from the man who took the last thing in her life that she'd been trying to protect.

It's not that far of a walk back to where we left Frankie but good God, I wish it was miles away.

But I can see the reality lying there on the cobblestones, motionless, bloody, and void of any indication of life. Chella's legs buckle as we approach, a strangled cry piercing the otherwise still night air.

"Frankie," she whimpers, slowly lowering herself down to the ground. She presses her head against his chest, reaching around him to hug him tight.

My jaw tightens as I look down at him, contempt flooding me at the person he'd become.

Maybe it was the person he'd always been and I just didn't see it until it was too late.

Chella's body quakes as she weeps for him.

I know how she feels, how helpless you feel when shit goes sideways and you can't stop the inevitable from happening.

And death for Frankie?

It was always inevitable.

Surprising that he evaded it for as long as he did.

Chella turns her tear-stained face up toward me. "Is he really gone?" she asks, her voice a tormented whisper.

I kneel down next to her and press my ear against Frankie's chest, noting that his skin is already pasty. I can't hear a goddamn thing. I press my fingertips against his throat, holding my face right over his mouth but there's nothing.

No thump of a heart.

No thrum of a pulse.

No wisp of a breath.

Nothing.

No sign of life at all.

I pull Chella into my arms. "I'm so sorry," I murmur.

And she bawls as the realization grabs hold that yet another piece of her heart and soul has been taken away forever.

A few minutes later, we stagger into the apartment and Chella sinks onto the couch, her head in her hands.

Bella runs into the living room, yapping and doing her play bow until she sees the tears and stops short, like she senses Marchella's pain. Her barks turn to soft whimpers and she hops up onto the sofa and lays her head in Chella's lap, just like she did to me earlier.

A lump swells in my throat as I watch Chella pick up Bella and hug her tight against her chest. The dog doesn't even try to squirm or lick her tears. She just stays still, as if she knows it's exactly what Chella needs at this moment.

Ray and Dante come into the apartment a little while later and I nod toward the office to give Chella some privacy. Ray pauses as Dante goes down the hallway. He looks at me, scrubbing a hand down the front of his face.

"Boss, look, I wanna apol—" he starts, but I hold up a hand.

"Stop," I say. "You don't need to apologize. I respect what you did and why you did it."

"I shouldn't have gone over your head like that. I didn't trust Frankie and I was afraid shit was gonna come down on you."

"Which it did," I mutter. "My fault."

"You, Matteo, Dante — I'd do anything for your family. You've always taken care of me."

"And by going to Matteo, you took care of me," I say, clapping him on the shoulder. "You showed up when I needed you, Ray. That's what matters to me." I lean closer, lowering my voice. "But here's the thing about second chances. If you fuck around again, I'll kill ya."

His eyes widen and he recoils slightly and I let out a chuckle at the stricken look on his face.

He relaxes his shoulders and smiles.

I wink at him. "So long as we're on the same page."

I shove him toward the office and close the door once we're all inside.

Dante is already on the phone with the cleaners. The benefit to my space is that it's secluded, so having Frankie's body handled won't raise eyebrows because there aren't any around to raise. He hangs up a minute later and folds his arms over his chest.

"Are the Russians gone?" I ask.

They look at each other and nod.

"For now," Dante grumbles with a shake of his head. "They aren't happy that you kept a trophy."

"Well, they're gonna have to deal with it," I growl. "Unless they want us to bring hell to their doorstep in the armpit of Brooklyn."

"Nobody is looking for a battle, not over Frankie Amante. But the first chance they get to retaliate, you know they'll take it. They left things alone tonight, but they wanna be made whole, too. Boris is pissed as hell that you cut him down in front of his guys, and that I sent him packing with his dick between his legs. He's gonna be back, Romo."

"Yeah," I say, rubbing the back of my neck. "Well, it looks like we need to do a better job of building up our alliances here in the city."

"Or," Dante says. "You know, maybe you stop fucking shit up and creating new enemies. Just a thought."

I give him a punch. "Maybe you need to go back to whatever far-off land you came from and wait for your next hit."

Dante snickers. "Might be you. Just saying. There's gotta be a decent bounty on your ass in some country, Romo."

"Millions," I say with a wink. "Don't do it for anything less."

Chapter Twenty
MARCHELLA

I open my eyes a crack early the next morning. Roman's arms are wrapped securely around me and they tighten when I shift on the mattress. Bella is still snuggled into me, her body warm and calm against mine.

My sleep was fitful at best, splintered with nightmares and haunting words and images that made me cry out more than once.

But Roman never moved from my side. He held me as I wept for my brother, for my father, for fucking everything I've lost.

It feels like my heart was shredded, stomped on, and then shoved back into my chest.

Images that I will never forget will likely torment me until the day I die.

But what's worse are the unresolved emotions flooding my mind and soul.

The deceit, the anger, the betrayal…

My God, it feels like I didn't even know my brother.

All of this time, I've been working my ass off to save us and he'd only been working to save himself.

My gut twists.

As much as I despise him for what he did to us and how I let his lies dictate my actions, I miss him…so much.

I choke back a sob and Roman nuzzles my neck. "Why did he have to do all of that?" I whisper. "Why the hell did he have to ruin everything?"

"Hey," Roman whispers. "You'll never understand what went through his head, Chell. People grieve in different ways."

"How can you be so matter-of-fact?" I ask, twisting my head to look at him. "After everything he did to you and your family? To those guys he killed? He didn't give a damn about anyone but himself. He let my dad take the fall for him. I mean, because of his stupid ass choices, I was kidnapped!"

"And did that turn out so badly for you?" he asks, a smile tugging at his lips.

I sniffle. "No, but that's not the point."

"I know. And you have a lot of rage inside of you right now. I get it. I'd feel the same way. But you need to figure out a way to move past it. He went off the deep end, yeah, but you shouldn't remember that part. You need to hold onto everything else, otherwise you'll be poisoning yourself every time you think of him." He drops a kiss onto my forehead. "Besides, now you're going to make things right with your dad. That's a good thing."

"Great. One good thing," I mumble.

"You have me, too," he says. "And Bella."

I shake my head. "No, we need to take her to the police. I can't keep her in good conscience. She needs to be with her rightful owners. I've lost too much to deny someone else the happiness she can bring. We've already kept her for too long."

Roman's brow furrows. "Are you sure?"

I nod. "Yes." My heart is already breaking. Why not say goodbye to one more thing?

"We'll stop on our way to see your dad." His lips stretch into a tight line. "If it's what you really want."

"It is," I say, swiping at my eyes. "I'm going to take a quick shower and then we can get going."

He nods. "Okay. Do you want anything to eat? Coffee?"

"I can't even think about it," I murmur. "And then later…we need to talk about what we're…what happens with…" I take a deep breath. "What we do with the…body."

I gently lay Bella next to Roman and slide out of the bed, grabbing some of the clothes he bought me the day before during our shopping spree.

My temples throb as I brush my teeth and turn on the hot shower spray. The water scalds my skin, making it tingle. It mixes with the tears running down my face as the events from the last twenty-four hours replay in my mind.

I don't know how much time passes while I stand there. Could be minutes. Could be hours. But instead of making me feel better, more refreshed, the shower only fuels my fury.

I wasted so much time, so much energy, so much of everything to make a better life for someone who didn't even think enough about me to do the same.

We were strangers, and that realization makes the tears fall faster and harder.

I finally step out of the shower, moving around like a zombie.

Roman takes a quick shower once I am finished and I spend a few minutes playing with Bella before my heart takes its final, I hope, beating of the day.

One of Roman's guys drops off a car for us to drive since the Bentley is in desperate need of body work. We climb into the BMW 7 series and I hold Bella tight in my lap as he drives uptown toward the police station in Inwood.

A fleeting thought occurs to me when I remember the rent on our apartment is overdue.

Our apartment.

A gaggle of tears forms in my throat as Roman makes a turn down Shipwell Avenue and pulls up to the curb. He turns off the ignition and looks at me. "You sure you want to do this?" he asks.

I take a deep breath. "Yes, at least someone should be happy today."

He snakes an arm around me as we walk inside with Bella. We stop in front of a one-way mirror and pick up the phone to let them know the reason for our visit. A few minutes later, a tall officer with kind eyes walks out and motions for us to follow him. He introduces himself as Officer Johnson.

He asks some questions about Bella — where we found her, if we'd seen her before that day, if she'd had on a collar.

She clings to me like she knows something is about to change for the worse, and I hold her tight because I know she's right.

Officer Johnson brings us into a room and takes a device out of one of the drawers of the desk. "This is a chip reader," he explains. "So it'll tell us all of the information we need to locate her owners."

I nod, and what feels like a watermelon-sized lump forms in my throat. I can't even squeak out a response.

Officer Johnson holds the reader out to the top of her neck and presses a button. His brows furrow and he holds it over each of her hind legs.

Beep.

Beep.

Beep.

He keeps clicking the damn thing.

How many chips are there, for Christ's sake?

"That's strange," he murmurs, trying the underside of her belly.

"What?" I rasp, clearing my throat.

"Well, the reader isn't registering anything," he says. "I've checked her out from head to toe and I can't find a chip anywhere."

My heart hammers in my chest. "Wait…so what does that mean?" I ask.

He shrugs. "It means I can't locate her owner. There's one other thing I can look at, though," he says, his fingers flying over the keyboard sitting on top of the desk. He frowns at the screen, scrolling through whatever appears in front of him.

The silence is deafening and finally, I have to ask. "Is there anything in the system?"

Roman squeezes my shoulder and my heart damn near stops beating as we wait for his answer.

He finally looks away from the screen and throws his hands in the air. "I can't find a single thing about this dog."

My eyes widen. "So, wait, what happens to her, then?"

Officer Johnson grins at me. "Well, are you volunteering to adopt her?"

I almost jump out of my chair. "Are you serious?" I squeak, tears pooling in my eyes yet again.

"I certainly am. You'll have to fill out some paperwork, but since we don't have any record of her, she can be yours if you want her."

I squeeze her tight, burying my head in her glossy fur. "Did you hear that, baby? You're coming home with us."

Bella's big eyes open even wider as she goes to town, attacking me with her tongue. I giggle-sniffle as she laps up my tears.

The first happy ones I've cried today.

A chill shuttles through me as I walk down a long hallway of white cinderblocks. My sneakers squeak on the shiny tile floor, the sound reverberating between the walls in the stark space. The guard leading me toward the prison visiting room unlocks the steel gate at the end of the corridor, pulling it open. He points toward a doorway.

"Take a seat at the glass and pick up the phone to talk," he says in a no-nonsense tone that makes the hairs on the back of my neck stand on end.

I nod and take a few tentative steps into the room. A few others are there, chatting in hushed tones to the inmates whom they are visiting. I walk toward the stool at the far end of the row and sink onto the cold plastic stool as I wait for Papa to appear. I stick my thumbnail into my mouth and nibble it, my eyes darting left and right. There are multiple guards standing around the perimeter of the visitor room and even more guarding the prisoners on the other side of the glass.

Finally, Papa is led over to me by a guard who unlocks his handcuffs so he can pick up the phone. His appearance makes my heart ache. His eyes are heavy with dark circles underneath them. His skin is ashen and worn with deep wrinkles covering areas where only a few small lines took up residence before. His hair is graying, his body so much thinner.

I clap a hand over my mouth to prevent the whimper from escaping my lips.

I need to get a hold of myself, for fuck's sake.

I know how much I've missed but I'm here now.

That's what counts.

Papa's lips lift into a smile as he speaks into the phone. His deep, raspy voice is so familiar and I've missed it…a lot more than I would have ever imagined.

"*Bellisima*," he says. "I am so happy to see you."

I try to return the smile, but I can't. My lips quiver, my shoulders quake. "Papa, I'm so sorry…so sorry for turning my back on you. I didn't know what happened that night. I didn't know the truth. And even if it was true, I never should have ignored you that way and left you here by yourself."

He shakes his head. "Don't cry, *mi amore*. I always knew Frankie would get you to come for a visit."

"I-I shouldn't have waited," I sputter. "I should have come on my own."

"I am just so happy to see you," he whispers, a tear in his eye. "I don't care why you didn't come before." He peers behind me. "Did you come alone? Is Frankie with you?"

"No, Papa." I wipe my eyes with the back of my hand, my voice cracking as I deliver the news that no parent ever wants to hear. "Something happened. Something bad, and he...he..." I shake my head, knowing I need to speak the words, but also fearing what the reality will do to my father who's already lost so much.

But Papa doesn't need me to say a thing. He can see it in my eyes and on my face, and big tears slide down his sunken cheeks as we grieve over our loss.

I long to reach out and grab him, to pull him close and to bury my head in his neck like I did when I was a little girl who needed the comfort of her papa. Back then, I always believed he'd protect me and keep me safe.

I know he'd do the same right now if he could.

Except now he's behind bars serving a life sentence for a crime he didn't commit.

And the Plexiglas prevents me from giving him comfort when he needs it most.

I'll never be able to hold him, to hug him, to feel his warmth.

I'll never be able to cry on his shoulder.

I'll never be able to hold his hand.

And I'll never be able to kiss him goodbye.

There are so many things I'll never be able to do…things I took for granted before because I didn't accept him or the life he lived.

But now I understand his truth and the price he is paying for his own sins.

He may not have killed the Russian soldier, but he battled with others and took plenty from them.

His penance is living with the harsh realization that almost everything good in his life is no longer.

Almost everything.

Because he still has me.

And I still have him.

I hate that I wasted so much time, but at least, I have the rest of his life to make up for it.

That is, if he doesn't disown me for falling in love with the son of his enemy.

But if it's one thing I've learned in the past twenty-four hours, it's that the lives we lead are a direct result of the choices we make…good, bad, or otherwise.

I think we've both made enough bad ones to last us a lifetime.

It's time to start making some good ones.

Starting right now.

Judging by the way Papa is looking at me, I know he would agree.

EPILOGUE

PART ONE: ROMAN

I clutch Marchella's hand as we run through the revolving glass doors of Sunrise Hospital and Medical Center in Las Vegas. We're greeted by a whoosh of cold air as we hurry toward the reception desk.

I scrub a hand down the front of my face, my mind still processing Matteo's words. The whole thing still just seems so…surreal.

The middle-of-the-night call, the urgency and concern in Matteo's voice, the screaming sounds in the background, the crashing of something glass against a wall…

I should have been more prepared.

I mean, I know what date it is.

I guess I just still can't wrap my head around the fact that my brother is gonna be a dad.

Is a dad…

God help that kid with those fiery Irish and stubborn Italian genes battling for victory.

It'll be a brutal one, for sure.

Chella's hand is cold and a little bit clammy, and it makes sense that she's nervous even though I've told her everything will be fine with my family.

Her memory of my brothers isn't fabulous, and even though she's made a fan out of Dante, Matteo and Sergio are definitely the toughest out of the three.

But she has nothing to worry about.

My brothers are rowdy and menacing, but they are loyal to a fault.

And they always look out for their own.

Family comes first…always.

And Marchella is now a part of that.

Well, not exactly yet, but it's all part of my plan.

I sign our names and grab her hand, tugging her past the elevator to the stairwell next to it. The maternity wing is on the third floor, but Matteo has Heaven and the baby tucked away in a private wing, away from the craziness of the rest of the floor.

When you live our lives, you can never be too careful.

I can't stop smiling as we run down corridors toward the exclusive suite where my family is congregated. I guess it's good we're clear of the rest of the floor since there are so many of us. I can hear talking and laughter as we take a final right turn.

"Sounds crowded," Chella mutters as we get closer to the room. "I really feel a little bit weird...I mean, it's your family. Isn't it odd for me to be meeting them all for the first time at the hospital like this?"

But before I can assure her that the Villanis don't do anything in a conventional way, my brother Sergio pops his head out of the doorway, a big smile on his face. "Romo!" he bellows, walking over to give me a hug. His fiancée, Jaelyn, rushes out behind him and throws her arms around me and then around Marchella. I haven't been out here since Sergio got engaged, so this is the first time we're "officially" meeting.

"FaceTime doesn't do you justice," I say to Jaelyn and she lets out a hearty chuckle before she gives Marchella a big hug.

"I'm so glad you're both here in the flesh!" she exclaims. "We're going to have such a fun time together!" Jaelyn turns back to me. "Where's Dante?"

"He had a few things to take care of back at the hotel. He'll be here in a little while." I nod toward the room. "Who else is here? Did Heaven's family make it?"

Jaelyn rolls her eyes. "Patrick and her Aunt Maura are here, but none of the others. Fucking Conor threatened them with their lives if they made the trip."

"Asshole," I mutter. Heaven had a pretty major falling out with her family after her father promoted her dickhead brother, Conor, over her months ago. She'd just married Matteo at her father's request, and he shoved her aside, giving the reins to his oldest son, a complete shit heel who tried to kill her while high as a goddamn kite. He's been running that organization deep into the core of the Earth since she cut ties with them, and in my opinion, it serves them right for fucking her over like that.

Marchella furrows her brow. "None of them? Not even her father?"

Sergio shakes his head, his jaw tight. "And she's upset. Of course, she won't admit to it, but you can see it. Matty is ready to flip his shit right now."

"At least the two people she's closest to are here," I say as Matteo comes up behind me, a grimace on his face.

"Those assholes don't deserve this kind of air time, not when there is someone very important you need to meet."

"Well, before I meet that very important person, I'd like you to meet my important person. *In* person."

A smile spreads over Matteo's face and he pulls Marchella in for a bear hug. He's not a huggy type of guy, so he must really be feeling the love today. Her face glows, her smile stretching from ear to ear.

"I'm so happy to be here," she says, her face buried in his massive chest. "And so happy for you both. Congratulations!"

A minute later, Matteo leads us into the suite, every available space filled with flowers of every shape and size and bunches of helium balloons. There's barely any room for visitors.

I leave Marchella with Jaelyn and Sergio and walk right up to the bed where Heaven is sitting up with a tiny pink bundle in her arms. She grins at me, looking every bit as gorgeous as she usually does, despite the fact that she just gave birth.

"That motherly glow is a good look for you," I say, giving her a kiss.

"Roman, meet your niece, Aisling Lucia," Heaven murmurs, gazing down at her daughter.

"After Mama," I whisper, grazing the tip of her nose with the pad of my finger. Her skin is smooth and pink, her lips shaped like a perfect heart.

"She looks just like you," I say. "Beautiful. I love her already."

Heaven giggles softly. "You're going to have to make some more trips out here."

I furrow my brow, leaning back slightly. "You mean, you guys are staying?"

Matteo joins me and smiles at Heaven. "We've tossed the idea around. There's a lot to do out here and farther west in California. Maybe it's time for a change of pace." He lifts an eyebrow. "You think you can handle things in the city?"

"Well, you haven't fired my ass yet, so I'm thinking you already know the answer to that question."

"You narrowly escaped my firing squad," he says with a pointed look.

"Escaped is the key word there," I say.

Matteo snickers. "Lucky is another word. Just saying."

"Admit it. Baby bro has the skills he needs."

Matteo lifts an eyebrow at me. "Baby bro needs to keep a closer eye on shit in the future or I'm gonna poke them both out."

"Noted," I say as Heaven chuckles.

"Matty, can you just get back to being the big ol' pile of mush? Save the badass stuff for another day. Today is a special one. It's your daughter's birthday and we're celebrating, not making thinly veiled threats about gouging out eyeballs."

"My favorite sister-in-law," I say.

"Hey!" Jaelyn says, walking over with her hands on her hips. "Maybe now she is, but pretty soon, she's gonna be sharing that title!"

Heaven gives an exaggerated eye roll. "My God, you are so competitive. Just like your fiancé."

"There's no reason to be competitive when you know you're the best," Sergio calls out from his spot against the wall.

I catch Marcella's eye and wink. "What can I say? Love it or leave it, but this is us."

About an hour later, Marchella and I wander away from the now-overcrowded suite, our arms snaked around each other's waists. She lets out a little sigh and leans her head on my shoulder. "Aisling is so gorgeous," she breathes. "I can't believe how tiny she is!"

"Yeah, she's cute." I say.

"I can't wait to have kids," she says. "I adore them."

"You'd be a really great mom," I murmur.

"Thanks." She sighs. "I really miss the kids I used to teach. I always had so much fun going to work, you know, before everything happened with my dad. I mean, I love volunteering at the animal shelter now, especially since I can bring Bella with me. And I'm so glad I'm still able to visit the kids at the old community center and read to them. But I need something more, you know? I have a pretty expensive bilingual teaching degree, now I'm going for my masters. I want to use my credentials. I want a career. Purpose. Fulfillment. All of it."

"I think we might be able to do something about that," I say. "I can call in a few favors, get you set up at one of the private schools in the city."

"Oh my God, like that wouldn't be worse than dealing with the public school parents! How would private school parents react to having an Amante teach their kids? I mean, with the tuition they must pay?" She looks over at me like I've grown another two heads.

"Trust me, I can take care of everything. You're smart, gorgeous, and accomplished. They will love you." I smirk. "Now, can we get back to the baby conversation?"

"Oh, are you ready for fatherhood?"

"Nah," I say with a chuckle. "But I'll tell ya, I suddenly have the urge to do a test run." I stop suddenly in front of a door, backing her against it. "What do you say? Wanna fake make a baby with me?

The corners of her lips lift. "Oh, *yes*."

I jiggle the lock and the door opens into a huge restroom. Oh, fuck yeah, this is how we roll in the VIP maternity wing.

I shut the door behind us, locking it before I turn toward Marchella. She eyes me with that come-hither look that always makes my cock tingle and slides her hand up her thigh, revealing a lacy pink thong under her skirt. With a quick, sexy wiggle, she manages to get the panties off before sashaying toward me, a seductive grin tugging at her lips. She grabs my belt buckle and yanks my shorts open. My dick springs to attention, precum glistening at the tip the second she starts stroking my hard length. I lift her into my arms and swing around so her back is against the wall.

She lets out a yelp. "Oh my God, cold tile!"

I snicker. "Don't worry. I'm gonna warm you up nice." I rub the swollen head of my cock against her wet slit. "You're dripping for me, you dirty girl. You wanted me to fuck you against a wall in a bathroom, didn't you?"

"Oh yeah," she says in a breathy voice. "It's the fantasy I've always wanted to live out with you."

I cover my mouth with hers and she fists my hair, gasping against my lips as I slide my cock into her tight pussy. I thrust hard and fast as soon as I sink into her heat, unable to control myself.

Maybe it's the baby stuff.

Maybe it's the family stuff.

Or maybe it's just because for the first time in my life, I'm really and truly happy.

All I know is that I need to be connected to her in every possible way.

And I couldn't wait another second for it.

She digs her fingers into my back as I glide in and out, dragging my cock against her clit with each push and pull. Her walls clench around me, soft whimpers slipping from her mouth as she meets my every thrust. Her legs are locked around my waist, her body beckoning me, driving me deeper and deeper until I don't know where I end and where she begins.

Her head falls back against the wall, her eyes the brightest blue as they glitter with deep-seated desire. She squeezes my cock, her juices flowing over me. Her body trembles, her pussy quivering as I drive into her with long, hard strokes. "Oh...my...God," she moans. "So...good!"

I squeeze my eyes shut, sparks igniting into flames that rage through me as the orgasm explodes, sizzling every cell in my body. My body spasms against her as the euphoric sensations consume me like a tidal wave.

We collapse against each other, breathless, sated, and smiling.

I tangle my fingers in her long hair, dropping my head into her sweet-smelling neck. "I fucking love you," I rasp.

"I fucking love you, too," she whispers, her tongue poking out to tickle the area behind my ear.

I pull away slightly, staring into her eyes. "I mean it, Chell. You're it for me. Forever. I wanna marry you."

She cocks her head to the side. "So…are you…proposing?"

"Maybe," I say.

"You didn't ask me a question," she whispers.

"Well, I wasn't exactly planning this. I mean, I was, but not here."

"In Vegas?"

"In a bathroom," I say with a chuckle. "I was gonna do it tonight, with the ring and everything. But I got caught up. I didn't want to wait. I love you, and I want you to be my wife. Will you marry me?"

Bright pink spots color her cheeks. "Yes," she says, tears glistening in her eyes. "Of course I will. But…"

I lift an eyebrow. "Yeah…"

"Can we wait to tell everyone? I'd really like to be able to paint a different picture for your family when they ask, other than the one where you nail me against a wall in a hospital bathroom because you just couldn't wait."

I laugh, hugging her tight. "You've got it. I'll give you a different picture. It's gonna be damn colorful, too, so get ready."

"I'm always ready," she says with a sly smile on her flushed face. "For anything with you."

PART TWO: DANTE

I trudge down the hallway with my hands shoved deep into the pockets of my jeans, my mind spinning with explicit details about my latest target.

My client expected me to land in Dubai last night, and judging by the scathing tone in his voice when he called, he sure as hell isn't happy about my little detour.

But fuck him.

I'm an uncle now, for Christ's sake.

And an assassin.

In that order.

Let the motherfucker live a day longer so I can meet our girl.

In my periphery, I see the nurses pointing and whispering softly as I pass. I flash them my signature smirk and one of them turns beet red when she catches my eye. "The VIP maternity wing?" I ask.

She clears her throat and points in the direction I'm walking. "Right through those doors."

I wink at her. "Thanks. Big day."

"Congratulations!" they all say with bright smiles.

"Come back later and we can celebrate," one of them quips when she thinks I'm just out of earshot. The rest of them giggle, and I swallow my own chuckle as I push open the doors. I walk right up to Matteo where he's standing with Sergio and give him a big hug. "Congratulations, Matty."

He claps me on the back. "Thanks, bro. It's really good to see you." His expression sobers slightly and my eyebrows furrow.

"Something wrong? I thought you'd be on top of the stratosphere today." I chuckle. "You know, because the Stratosphere… is right out there…" I say, nodding toward the window where the hotel stands tall and proud across the street.

"Yeah, well, I am, but…" He rubs the back of his head and looks past me down the hall. "I need to talk to you about something."

"Sure, what's up?"

Matteo gives Sergio a look and he backs away, his hands held up. "Private shit. Got it. I'm just gonna go back inside and fight Jae to hold the baby again."

"Good luck with that," Jaelyn calls from inside the room.

Once Sergio disappears, Matteo turns back to me. "I need you to be here, Dante."

"I am here," I say. "See? Trust me, I ain't no mirage." Then I let out another laugh. "Because, you know…"

"The Mirage. Yeah, I get it." He rolls his eyes. "Jesus, when did you become such a comedian?"

"I don't know. Maybe it's the uncle thing. I'm like a new man or something. You know, the fun uncle…the funcle."

"Or maybe it's the job," Matteo says.

"Maybe. Contract killers don't get a lot of on-the-job laughs, so we look for 'em when we're off the clock."

"I'm sure." His eyebrows knit together and a chill shuttles down my spine. He's being more evasive than usual, and his expression isn't the usual stoic one he sports.

He's nervous.

Matteo never gets nervous.

That makes me more than a little curious to hear the reason.

"What's happening, Matty?" I ask in a low voice. "What the hell do I need to know?"

Hs blue eyes darken as he leans in closer, his voice a choked whisper. "It's what you already *do* know that's the problem."

THE END

MEET KRISTEN

Kristen Luciani is a *USA Today* bestselling romance author and coach with a penchant for stilettos, kickboxing, and grapefruit martinis. As a deep-rooted romantic who loves steamy, sexy, and suspense-filled stories, she tried her hand at creating a world of enchantment, sensuality, and intrigue, finally uncovering her true passion. Pun intended…

Follow for Giveaways
Facebook Kristen Luciani

Private Reader Group
The Stiletto Click

Complete Works On Amazon
Follow My Amazon Author Page

VIP Newsletter
Click Here To Join My VIP Newsletter

Feedback Or Suggestions For New Books?
Email Me! kristen@kristenluciani.com

Want To Join My ARC Team?
Join My Amazing ARC Team!

Want A FREE Book?
Click Here To Download!

Instagram
@kristen_luciani

BookBub
Follow Me on BookBub

facebook.com/kristenlucianiauthor
twitter.com/kristen_luciani
instagram.com/kristen_luciani